The Blue Fetal Touch

Sylvie Poudrette

The Blue Fetal Touch

Publisher: Sylvie Poudrette
First Edition
Published: April 2013

ISBN: 978-0-9879902-3-5

Sales and distribution: Lulu.com
Printed by Lulu.com

To the memory of
Claire Godbout

THE BLUE FETAL TOUCH

Sylvie Poudrette

CONTENTS

PROLOGUE 9

CHAPTER ONE..12

    CHILHOOD 12
    THE MIRROR IN THE BATHROOM 12

CHAPTER TWO..28

    THE SURREAL NIGHT 28

CHAPTER THREE 41

    THE OLD DANISH LADY 41

CHAPTER FOUR...57

    A NEW BEGINNING 57

CHAPTER FIVE...70

    THE MAN WITH THE PLAN 70

CHAPTER SIX..91

    VOYAGE OF DISCOVERY 91

CHAPTER SEVEN 120

    THE RED FOREST 120

CHAPTER EIGHT 131

    THE BLUE BOOK 131

CHAPTER NINE..155

    BETWEEN THE LINES 155

CHAPTER TEN 166

    ROCKY ROAD 166

CHAPTER ELEVEN..197

    IN DOUBT..197

CHAPTER TWELVE..**233**

    BLUE WATERS...233

CHAPTER THIRTEEN **288**

    THE BIG HEADS 288

EPILOGUE **316**

PROLOGUE

Sitting on a big rock, a glass of white wine in her hand, Kara Lewis was contemplating the ocean. Very slowly, her thoughts turned inward. Thinking about her life, she knew she had little time left on earth to map out for the last time the itinerary of the journey and retrace the past. When and where had it started were the questions she would search deeply inside? The end was not important, still in the air and fresh like the one coming from the sea.

She took a deep breath and prepared herself for the inner voyage.

Kara recalled having been very interested at an early age about the past and how they knew what they knew. She had promised herself that she would study the prehistoric period and antiquity because she could not figure out why so many women were not interested by the power of governing or any kind of power at all. Years later, she succeeded to fulfill her promise and obtained a BA in archeology and another in social work.

While studying prehistory and antiquity, she noticed with awe in her readings that few women in the history of humanity had made tools or created objects of art or monuments. In fact, she realized that women had not played an important part in the making of big decisions concerning their lives or others in the long, long story of human being.

Perhaps, they had done it at the beginning but that was so deeply buried in the recesses of the earth, it would take forever to dig it out for proves to materialize in real terrestrial time.

After graduating, Kara could not find work in archeology—therefore, she became a community worker. She enjoyed it very much for years—however, as time passed by, she began thinking about working for herself.

Not knowing what she really wanted to do with her life, Kara ended up as a photographer more by chance than by choice. One day, she bought a camera and started taking pictures of anything she liked. After that, she remembered choosing mainly quick snapshots of people faces, hoping to catch the truth behind the mask through their light or darkness. To her, variations of shades and colors on their faces never lied while following the mood of the moment.

Then the miracle happened, the more she practiced photographing, the more she began to like it.

Kara felt different as soon as she took that new direction in life. The little voice inside that had been silent for so many years reappeared and became more insistent. She could not stop it anymore. The questions coming out were always the same: "Why don't you want more out of life?" "Why did you lose your interest for the Cause of Women?"

Sipping her wine, Kara looked around—nobody was there but her. She sat on the sand and leaned back on the rock. The place was so peaceful. She stayed there gazing at the limitless blue sky. Through the gentle breeze, she started to breathe deeply and made her body relax completely.

She began reminding herself that nature in its unpredictable ways of creating sunny days or disasters had never betrayed or deceived her. Witnessing first hand, droughts, earthquakes and volcano eruptions in her life, she never thought that those sudden changes had been unfair to people. Instead, she felt that the earth simply wanted to renew itself while moving its celestial body through space and thus, altering its cosmic dance.

Kara burst out laughing about the history of the word unfair in her life and the implications brought with it. She smiled at the ocean and closed her eyes.

Her past started unfolding before her.

CHAPTER ONE

CHILHOOD
THE MIRROR IN THE BATHROOM

Kara always wondered why the grown-ups when looking at their faces, particularly in the bathroom, seemed to see something she could not. After having watched her parents carefully, she had observed that some days they gave the impression to be happy and other days, sad or discouraged. "What makes it so repelling or attracting?" She asked herself. Perplexed over the question, she decided to check it out.

She went to get a stool and pull it along the bathroom. After climbing it, she said, "This mirror must be different from others." She looked at her little face. She waited. Nothing. So she smiled at herself. A few seconds later, a vague sensation came up and began invading her body. Suddenly, she became conscious of her existence and the connection with life. She was life itself looking at its reflection. Seized by what she experienced, she felt and knew without a doubt that at four years old—she was not only alive but a whole entity by herself, a part of life, as life was part of her. She would never forget that powerful moment of consciousness.

Life went on. With the years, Kara developed a strong personality. She had sometimes a hard time to deal with reality. The day she understood that her parents and people in general made a huge difference between girls and boys, it broke her heart—she was eight years old, and had never considered it a threat before. She knew that her body was different from her only good friend Bruce, the boy next door but never thought of him to be wiser, stronger or more powerful than her. She just liked him for who he was. They had a lot of fun together—innocent and lovely to watch. But one day, their two mothers caught them kissing each other. From that day on, they were not allowed to be alone together anymore. Her mother told her to hang out with girls instead. Kara did not feel guilty about kissing Bruce but preferred not to argue with her mother.

At school, she tried to become friendlier with girls at the recess. It paid off—one of them invited her the following week at her home. The mother's little girl welcomed Kara at the door and took her to the playroom where her daughter and three other girls from school were busy playing the grown-ups. First, the view of dolls everywhere overwhelmed Kara. Then, she saw in the middle of the room a small table set up with funny little flatware plates and a set of tea and cakes. She liked eating the cakes but felt so awkward playing the grown-up that it led up to broken dishes on the floor. Kara was simply not used to play that game with the delicate manner that her new friends seemed to possess naturally.

When returning home that late afternoon, she immediately informed her mother that these girls let her know she was a wild child. And with a smile on her face, she added, "I took it as a compliment because I don't like their games and rules. So...going back there is out of question. I tried my best and it didn't work."

She patiently waited in the hope that her mother would say, "Fine! After all, you gave it your best shot." But instead, her mother stayed silent. Kara thought the story was over and the matter closed. But at the minute, she opened the kitchen door to go playing outside—her mother strongly suggested that she should try again and again just in case she would like it someday. Kara sighed and went out.

Through the kitchen window over the sink, her mother observed Kara climbing a tree. She could not figure out why she was so different from others. Something else bothered her—Kara had become very moody lately. "What are we going to do with her?"

#

Leaning on the school wall with a book in her hand, Kara stopped reading and began observing girls and boys playing in the yard. She noticed that boys seemed to have more fun with each other, more relaxed and powerful than girls did. "Why is that?" She wondered.

When she came back home that day, she made up her mind for good about the world—she convinced herself that boys acted that way because they had a better place in the world than girls. She envied them but resented it forcefully. To her, no matter how hard she tried to be good at home—helping her mother in the garden or father in his workshop—her two brothers were always more encouraged than her to perform or succeed. Kara would be left with the words—not bad for a girl—it sounded cheap in her ears. Week after week, resentment and anger started taking shape in her mind. At home, she would burst out into tears of rage more and more often while screaming at her family, "It is unfair." That word would be as part of her as she would be part of the world.

After such crisis, her parents would send Kara in her room. She was not allowed to come out until she apologized to everyone in the room. Then one day, her father let her know for good that he would not tolerate that bad behavior anymore. She would have to reflect on it as long as necessary. Kara spent a lot of time alone in her room in those days but it gave her a chance to think more deeply about the word <u>unfair</u>.

Confronted with that big issue, she often asked herself, "There must be a better way to be fair—without hurting the other one?"

For a year, Kara tested the two camps at school and once again ended up disappointed. She liked talking and sharing ideas with girls but could perceive that she scared them. They did not always appreciate her wit and kind of toughness. On the other side, boys accepted her at the condition of not sounding smarter than them. It bothered her a lot but she survived.

#

The school had just finished. In the park, Kara and her four so-called friends were relaxing under the sun. After talking about how they would spend their vacations, one of the boys asked if they had watched on TV the night before the documentary on the mysteries of the origins of human beings. Kara and two other boys acknowledged that they did. As they loved to think that they were the "little intello" of their class, they began talking on the subject just for the fun of it. One boy came up with an amazing theory. After a short silence, Paul the more articulate, nodded at him and then asked the group, "Who made it happen?"

"What do you mean?" Kara replied.

He candidly went on, "I mean the civilization. At the beginning of time, men and women must have signed a kind of contract on whatever they used at that period to communicate between them."

Kara still listening to him, said, "And..."

"Well, we must accept that boys, men or males, whatever, were and will always be more accepted than girls when they succeed..."

"What has that to do with the origins of human beings?" Kara asked.

Paul looked at her, "You're a pain in the neck sometimes." He stopped then laughed. "I cannot tell you how it has started but if they survive, it's because of men."

Another boy continued, "I think you're right Paul. After all, men have created the world, the society, the culture although different from one another. They fought and still fight for the freedom of people, the rights of everyone for a better quality of life."

Another one added, "Men went to wars, conquered and also defended their countries against the invaders."

Each of the boys went on and on and finally, Paul said to Kara, "No matter how badly girls want to be our equals, it won't happen because from the beginning of time, men are running the show and women follow. They didn't do too much to build the world, did they?"

Kara looked upset. Paul quickly added, "Of course, they helped a lot to shape the world the way we know it; however their jobs were to take care of the ones who made it happen. Hey! Somebody had to do it. Men ruled and made laws, they discovered new world and— they were the first ones in whatever subject you may pick, take medicine for instance, and even fashion and cooking and the list can go on and on."

Kara argued with them that there had been great women too as Cleopatra, Joan of Arc, Marie-Curie and Indira Gandhi but she knew they were so few that they looked like sardines in the big ocean.

"Anyway, women must have agreed with it otherwise they wouldn't be in this position today, in 1962," one of the boys concluded.

He had a good point. After observing girls at school, she had to admit that most of them behaved in a way that confirmed their theory—the big contract made between male and female. However, Kara could hear a voice inside screaming that it was pure bullshit because they and she didn't know better. Another voice was telling her, "Face it, Kara. The facts are there—the law of the strongest ones dominates. They built, they ruled, they won and gained more and more power and be sure, they won't give it away." Before losing it, she left the boys and went home.

In her room, she lay down on the bed thinking about that. The week before, she had heard a conversation in the kitchen between her mother and two aunts talking about the situation of women. They were saying that men wouldn't let women having more power because sharing with women was still too dangerous for them even if the pressure was there.

Kara let her imagination fly. It took her to the idea that women were getting too smart around the planet and men were afraid to lose the power they had secretly created in one of those caves, may be somewhere in Europe.

With her twelve year old eyes, she tried visualizing what the scene would look like and then, concocted her own little story: she saw women taking care of children, preparing food and making sure the fire wouldn't go out. Being so busy all day, they wouldn't have time to attend the secret meetings. Of course, they were big gatherings where were discussed the tasks to be shared, the meals to be prepared, the stories to be told and so on. Occasionally, some women fed up with picking up berries and taking care of children wanted to participate in the hunting and fishing. Men would agree with them, smiling at each other—knowing that their lack of experience of hunting big animals would discourage them. If not, then they would come back home with a body tore into pieces, a real dead body that would prove to other women that that one did not make it. They would tell them that she was not strong enough for the fight. Of course, they wouldn't mention that they didn't help her when the mammoths charged toward her.

Using the documentary seen on TV, she continued her story. She imagined that the point men wanted to make for the last time was the fact that they not only brought meat home, they also exercised their bodies more than women did by hunting and chasing their prey. Therefore, by being stronger, they were most likely the ones to survive and if they did, women too. After all, that was the survival of the fittest. However, physical strength being the special power meant also to women that men could get rid of them at any time if they felt like it.

She remembered having read a book at the library about the caves paintings of Lascaux. According to the experts, the Palaeolithic Man had already developed his imagination and art skills at that period—he could paint bison and hunting scenes on a cave wall. After that last thought, Kara's imagination began running wild. She could see clearly in her mind when and where the big contract never written had been signed in blood somewhere in Europe probably around fifteen thousand years ago. Then everything started to make sense in her little head. It was probably around that period too that women shut up, she thought. Even if the language was not very elaborate, they did not take part in the making of big decisions for the survival of the group.

And then, something very unusual happened—in a split second, Kara flipped in another time frame. She could actually see and hear in her head what those women were saying to each other. "They will kill us if we don't agree with them and all we want is just to be alive. That's the only thing that counts now. We're going to keep in our hearts what remains, our silent anger. That's all we have left since the rest has been taken away from us. However, we will stay on friendly terms with the enemy lover. Life is too sacred."

Then, she shifted to another dimension. Standing alone on the top of a mountain with stars as friends, Kara heard a strong voice. "From that on, staying alive would be the only soul song these women would hear from the resonance of their choices." Right after that, a softer voice replaced it, "You think that these women made a very poor choice but understand that they began liking the torturer as in the tortured victim's syndrome. They would even say that the treatment of inflicting severe pains and agony year after year had not been so bad after all because that had made them stronger to survive anything."

Kara could not actually comprehend what those voices were talking about. She began feeling numb and then fell over a precipice. When she opened her eyes, she was back in her room. My God, what a trip, she thought. She shook herself up whispering, "My imagination played tricks on me." But then, all those women's voices started buzzing at the same time in her head again. She didn't know what to say to them; she got upset. She put both hands on each side of her head and shouted, "Please stop—sorry, I cannot help you...I'm just a little girl. I don't know what you want..." She started crying. After wiping her eyes, she ran to the bathroom and washed her face under the tap. When looking closely at her in the mirror, a warm sensation came up. She recognized it—she had the same when she was four. She didn't like it at all; it scared her to death. She slammed the door and ran outside, picked up her bicycle and rode as fast as she could in the street.

That evening, her sister Morgan was trying a new makeup on when Kara walked in the room. She sat on a little stool next to Morgan and watched with interest what her big sister was attempting to do. Morgan would choose a colour and put it on her eyelids, looked at it in the mirror, and then wiped it off with a white tissue and tried again with a different shade. After doing it for a while, she stopped. She finally seemed satisfied with the result. And then, looking as if she was a big movie star, she asked Kara, "What did you do today?"

"I spent the afternoon in the park with my friends." Then, Kara told her about the conversation she had with them.

Morgan listened quietly. When Kara stopped, she said, "Do you want to know what I think about that?"

Kara nodded enthusiastically.

Morgan quickly pointed out, "First of all, all the boys and you have a very wild and vivid imagination of the past. It's interesting though...However, I think that you have a lack of knowledge of the evolution of Homo sapiens." Still looking at her mirror image, she smiled and added, "May be like...hum...you need to read more on the subject of the history of humanity before making up your mind, and I must tell you that it will take longer than you think before that happens." She laughed then asked, "Where did you get this idea of contract anyway? And why are you coming up with this weird theory or whatever it is...about women got stuck since that time unaware that...fifteen thousand years ago, hunters and gatherers had already decided their fate?"

She did not let Kara answer and continued, "I agree with you that many women had been treated very badly in the past. The violence done to them was still horrible even at the beginning of the century. However, you now have to admit that for the past twenty years, a lot of good things happened to women. There's a new wind of fresh ideas in the air and things are changing faster than before. More women find and mark their places in the world these days. Nevertheless, there's a lot of work to be done." She paused and then added, "So roll up your sleeves, sister and start working on it! I think this is a big step for women. We never have seen it before so spectacularly if you compare with the past century."

Kara gave her a quick nod. She might be right, she thought. First, Morgan was six years older than her and second, she was studying philosophy at the university that year. Kara believed that it helped Morgan sharpen her thinking. However, after a quick look at her sister's candy pink room, she doubted that that philosophy bubble helped her get smarter in everything. She got up and checked the books on the bed.

Morgan turned her head. She asked for the second time, "Don't you agree, Kara?"

"Oh! Yes, I do,"

At that moment, Morgan thought that it was time to tell her. "Since you're here, I want to talk about something that affects the whole family right now and it's about..." She stopped for a few seconds. "Well, it's about your disturbing behaviour. You know that I've been looking for an apartment—so I won't be here anymore...and mom...well! She doesn't feel very well since Christmas." Then looking directly at Kara, she continued. "Dad, Dave and Steve and I are fed up of your bursts of anger in which you blame us or others about anything you find unacceptable in this world. Personally, I find it very annoying. You know what I mean!"

With a wide-open mouth, Kara turned red. She couldn't believe what her sister was saying to her. When Morgan paused, she shouted out, "Go ahead, shoot!"

And Morgan went on. "Don't you see that we all have a hard time with you at home? Mom doesn't know how to approach you anymore, and the way you react doesn't help either. I know you won't like the rest of what I'm going to say but just for once listen till the end."

Her face became pale that time. Kara repeated, "Shoot, Morgan."

"First, you never listen to what people say to you. It can be good or bad; you couldn't care less—you always want the final word. Can you give them a chance? They have the same right than you to be heard. Seeing you screaming, shouting or crying—it's not fair—it's very exasperating. You usually do it when it doesn't go your way and to me, it's pure madness. We are from the same family, so why are we so different you and I? You always want to compete with boys even if you say that you hate competition. Don't you see yourself, Kara? The way you act annoys me greatly and I don't know why you are so rebel either. Three years ago, remember we had so much fun together. Tell me Kara, what's going on with you? Is it something that somebody said or did to you? Please, tell me."

Stupefied, Kara couldn't talk for a while. Humiliated, she was. After a short while, she tried to redeem herself. "Oh! Boy, I didn't see myself that way. I know that I go too far sometimes but it's always for a good reason." Her eyes started focusing on the floor for a few seconds; she was thinking.

Then, she bounced back. She looked up at Morgan and said, "You have the right to see me the way you want. I listened to everything you said and now it's my turn to let you know what I think about you."

On a nasty tone, she continued. "Morgan, do you know what your problem is? You're too nice, naive and romantic." She opened her mouth and put a finger in it as if she would throw up. "Of course, you are in love. And you see everything through your pink glasses. Just look at your room! And...I'm afraid that studying philosophy will not help you get smarter. You always obey mom and dad because they keep telling you that the older one has to give the good example and you always comply. You think it's the right thing to do because you don't know any better. You're so pathetic!"

Kara knew she was just plainly mean but she was still so angry, she went on. "And the fact that you are in love with this guy, so pretentious by the way, made you see the world through little pink heart-lens. So, it's difficult for me too to see you when you're upset trying to control yourself and yet sulking for three days on the row, not talking to anyone and suffering in silence. Amen."

Kara got up and walked to the door. Before closing the door behind her, she maliciously articulated, "By the way, I think sulkiness sucks and love stinks."

Back to her room, she crashed on the bed and hit the pillows for a while. She felt low about not wanting to lose face. Deep inside, she knew that her sister was damn right about her bad temper. She was even sure that Morgan said it for her own good and therefore, couldn't really hate her. She then focused all her attention on her mother. She was aware that she had been looking very tired lately. Suddenly, she felt guilty and started crying. Wiping her eyes, she swore she would improve herself and become a better human being. Five days later, her mom died of a heart attack.

Kara felt responsible for her death because in her little mind, she couldn't see any other reasons. Her mother had always eaten right; she had taken good care of her body and had never drunk or smoked. Moreover, she had never sworn or gossiped about people; so to Kara, it was not fair. Her mother was too young to die.

#

Four years later, things had changed radically for everyone in the family. Her father still young went out more frequently. Her two brothers Dave and Steve, two and three years older than her were never home—they attended university by day and spent their evenings with friends. Her sister Morgan, then married, lived in LA. She rarely visited the family. As for Kara, she attended school all day and spent the evenings all by herself. She didn't mind—she liked spending her time at night in a kind of dreamy state. On weekends, she would go to the library and read books on life after death. She literally devoured those books.

That afternoon, she was glad to be home. Sitting on the large windowsill in the living room, she watched the rain changing into hail. The kitten Mitsou jumped on her lap and got off, and then ran after a cat toy on the floor. Kara adored that playful, foolish and loveable fur ball that just arrived in her life. It had made such a nice change. The cat was always happy to see her coming home—each time, welcoming Kara with a new performance, a new pirouette.

Mitsou, a yellow soft fur coat with white paws was very cute. Her big green eyes responded to anything moving in the house—always ready to defend her territory.

That little life helped her go through the days. Before her, time had been filled with guilt, remorse and grief. Kara was still depressed but knew that only time could heal the sadness. However, understanding and living it were two things. Life and its contradictions would mess up with her on a regular basis to make sure she got it right.

#

A year after, her father met a woman he liked and announced to the family that he would marry her in a short while. He looked better and a way happier than before. Dave and Steve were still attending some courses at the university—they were both working part-time. But they were not anymore living home. They were both living with their girlfriends.

When she heard the news, Morgan came for the occasion. It was the Easter long weekend. All together for the first time, they met their father's future wife and celebrated his new life. That was a joyous reunion.

A month before the wedding, Kara had a serious talk with her father. She let him know that his girlfriend was a very nice person but confessed she was not sure she would manage to live under the same roof. "Seeing you kissing and enjoying each other in the same house I used to see you with mom would be too painful for me to watch," she added. Then she reminded him. "I still picture mom and you as eternal lovers who were never afraid to show it before us. And...another woman in the house would hurt my feelings—I'm not ready to live it."

Kara felt good about it. By then, she was able to communicate more easily with her father. They spent all night talking and reached a kind of compromise.

"You're almost seventeen years old and you're going to college next year. So why don't you stay another year at home?" he asked.

Kara stayed silent. He smiled. "It's time to let you know what Jody and I have decided to do." He got up and went to get a magazine. It was about RV motor homes. He sat next to Kara on the couch and showed her the one he would buy. "Jody and I want to go on the road for our honey moon. We expect to travel for a year before setting down for good. Tonight while we were talking, I came up with the idea that you could take care of the house when we would be away. Of course, your brothers would visit you often and help you with any problem you might encounter. Your uncles and aunts are all around, so they could often drop by; take care of the lawn and any outside work. You could also go to their places if you feel too lonely." He stopped and then said "Kara, you would have the whole house by yourself. Tell me what you think about that idea."

At first, Kara thought it was scary and exciting at the same time. Everything was going fast in her mind—it would give her time to go through her mother's belongings still in the basement. That was something she wanted to do alone. And she would be free to do whatever she liked. The more she thought about it, the better it sounded. She said enthusiastically, "That's a great idea! Dad."

"I knew you would like that," her father said. "However, even if I know that you are very responsible, you're still very young. And...the only thing that I don't want you to do is having parties in the house."

"But Dad."

"I know...I know...You can bring some friends home if you like to but I want them out by eleven o'clock. I assure you that you will have many spies like neighbours, uncles, brothers that will watch over you and if I hear...that a boy has slept overnight...I'll come back home immediately and the whole story will be over. Understood!"

With a big smile on her face, Kara nodded. He then made her swear and sign a symbolic agreement written by both parts. She didn't mind. She knew that she would move the year after. To her, this agreement was acceptable—her freedom not jeopardized by anything and anyway, she didn't have too many friends—Kara was a loner.

She shook her father's hand and said, "It's a done deal, dad."

CHAPTER TWO

THE SURREAL NIGHT

At the beginning, she found it difficult to get used to the silence of the house during the night. However, days after days, she became more relaxed—happy to have that big house for her alone. She spent hours daydreaming and musing on her future.

On that Saturday morning, she got up earlier to check the newspaper for part-time jobs. She picked it up at the door and put it on the kitchen table. When she came back with an orange juice, her eyes froze on the front page. She sat down and just stared at the title—the rapist is still at large...The cat came in the kitchen. She got up and fed her. After it, she read the article. It said that a man had raped two women in the past week.

It was not too far away from her area, she thought. One of the women had died shortly after arriving at the hospital and the other one was in a coma. She stopped reading. To change her mind, she went to wash the dishes. Then, she looked back at the paper on the table and for a few seconds, she felt uncomfortable. She was not afraid, just a little anxious—she threw away the paper in the garbage can and that was it.

In the evening, her aunt Laura phoned. She was concerned that the man had not been arrested by then. So she asked Kara to spend the night at her home. She explained that it would give her uncle and her peace of mind if they knew where she was. Kara agreed reluctantly. She didn't want to upset her aunt. They made arrangements just in case the police could not find the man in the following weeks. So one week, she would sleep over at her uncle Danny and aunt Laura's house and the other one, at her uncle Jack and aunt Barbara's. As soon as she hung up the phone, she swore loudly. She put some clothes in her backpack, locked everything and walked out.

Weeks after, Kara was still shuttling between houses. She had enough. She said to her uncle Danny that night, "The school is almost over. I hope they will catch him...I just want to return home." She had planned many projects for the summer.

Her uncle nodded. He gave her a tap on the back. "They will, Kara. They will."

The morning after, she went home to feed the cat and had breakfast. She got the books she needed for the day and went to school. After school, she returned home and played with Mitsou. Then, she ate and studied for a while. Just as she was about to leave the house, her dad called. He asked her if everything was all right.

"Well, it's okay. I had to change my plans but..." she said. She explained briefly what it was. Feeling her dad's worry, she assured him right away that she would take extra care. Then, she tried to change the subject but her father came right back to the issue. "Dad, everybody is on high alert in the area and I feel very safe. Everyone is taking care of me. You have no reason to be bothered by the situation," she added.

"I am very concerned, and you bet young lady that I will call your uncles every night to make sure everything is okay," he replied firmly.

They talked for another ten minutes and then, she left the house.

#

Summer arrived but nothing new under the sun. When waking up that morning Kara thought she was pretty fed up of moving around. The media had not reported anything yet and the police had not said much about the case. They only stated that they were still investigating the cases and checking clues. However, the community in the area was getting anxious with the time. Therefore, the police finally said in order to ease the public pressure that they had some suspects and were close to apprehending the perpetrator.

Kara was pleased to hear it. However, the whole damned thing was not going fast enough for her. Her uncle Danny had four children from three to ten. He owned a very small house and privacy was hard to find over there. Although her uncle and aunt were very nice to her, she knew that they had enough to do on their own without trying to entertain her when she arrived at their home around nine o'clock in the evening.

And with the weeks, Kara became more and more impatient with her limited freedom. She had not done anything during the summertime except babysitting her nephews and nieces and then it was time to go back to school. Every day, she read the newspapers and watched the news on television in the hope they had arrested him but nothing happened. At school, it was almost the only subject of conversation. Day after day, her neighbours waited for her outside their houses after school to make sure she was all right. Even her brothers wanted to have dinner in turn with her.

To her, that situation stank. In her head, thoughts coming up were, "First, it upsets everyone in the community. They think their quiet neighbourhood is not safe anymore. Second, the bastard out there has managed to disturb people and frighten them enough to change their habits and take away their freedom."

That evening, her brother Steve left right after dinner. After washing the dishes, Kara didn't know what to do with herself and began walking around the couch in the living room thinking, thinking. She checked the time and decided to watch the latest news before going to her uncle's house. As she turned on the TV, a police spokesperson was saying, "We have reason to believe..." He reported they had a new case of attack and recommended strongly to all women living alone to take extra care about their security at home and if they had to go out, to be very vigilant.

Before leaving home, Kara put the cat in the basement, double-checked all doors and windows and went out.

In the street, she checked over her shoulder from time to time. Then, she shook her head—completely disgusted by that newfound fear. Deep inside, she felt terribly angry about not having control over the circumstances.

The next morning, she went home again and checked everywhere from the top floor to the basement. After it, she petted the cat for a while, had breakfast, then picked up her books and headed for school. "I hate Monday," she said with a sigh.

Coming back from school, her brother Dave welcomed her outside. He was trying to fix the garage door, which had not properly worked since her father had left. An hour later, he finally got it work. While washing his hands in the kitchen sink, he told Kara he couldn't stay for dinner. He had first an appointment with his teacher at the university and after it, had to meet his girlfriend at the theatre. Kara didn't mind, she had to prepare for school exams. She was determined to pass them no matter what. After studying till eight thirty, she grabbed her backpack and left home.

Her aunt Barbara opened the door and invited Kara to join her in the kitchen. She was her father's youngest sister. Kara liked her a lot. She was not only beautiful but also adorable, easygoing and warm. Sitting at the kitchen counter, her aunt asked, "Would you like to drink something before going to sleep?"

"An herbal tea would be perfect. Thanks."

Her cousin Marleen came in and chatted for a while with them. She was just twelve years old but looked older than her age. She was beautiful as her mother and had her father's wonderful sense of humour. She made them laugh a lot until her mother checking the time told her that it was bedtime.

Marleen argued with her mother for a few minutes. Then, she came up with an idea. "Mom, I want to sleep in the living room tonight." Looking at her cousin, she added, "I insist that Kara sleeps in my bedroom for the rest of the week. Please, mom, say yes..."

"I don't think so, my sweet heart," Kara replied. "I have no intention of sleeping in your bed and changing the family's world because of me. Please Marleen; don't change your habits for me."

But Marleen did not give up so easily and kept asking her mother.

Embarrassed, Kara shook again her head. Then, Marleen's eyes besought her mother for an approval. They all knew that she had in mind to watch TV late at night.

Her mother looked at Kara and finally said, "Well, you must be tired of sleeping on a couch, my dear. Why not make a change this week. All right Marleen, you got what you want but don't think you're going to stay up all night. I'll be watching you. You get that."

"Okay mom," she answered victoriously. She looked at Kara. "Is it all right with you?"

"All right then." Kara said.

Kara got up, washed her cup and said, "Good night." She went up to Marleen's bedroom and threw her stuff on the bed.

On her way back from the bathroom, she heard her uncle snoring like crazy. She smiled. Then, she heard her aunt saying to her daughter downstairs, "You have to get up early tomorrow. So just forget about watching TV tonight." She turned off the television set and said good night.

Kara had difficulties to fall asleep. She forced herself to relax but her mind and body were restless. Finally, she found the right position. She had a last look at the alarm clock. It was already two o'clock in the morning and she had to wake up at six. She closed her eyes hoping she would be able to get up on her own. On that last thought, she dozed off.

A scream coming from the first floor woke her up quickly. She checked the time—it was five forty-five a.m. She jumped out of bed and ran down the stairs. Entering the living room, she saw her aunt crying and her uncle yelling at some invisible entities. Kara looked down the floor. The scene horrified her. Marleen was lying there, naked and covered by blood; her pyjamas torn to pieces on her right side. The view of it was too awful to watch for Kara. She turned around and ran to the washroom to vomit. Coming back, she tried to regain some control and asked them if they had called the police.

"We just woke up five minutes ago. I'm losing my mind! Kara, go call the police right away!" her uncle shouted. Then he ran upstairs, yelling, "I'm gone to check the house. I'm gone to find you and I'm gone to kill you bastard!"

In a nervous and confused state of mind, Kara tried to explain on the phone what had happened. She was crying and screaming at the same time. At the end, she understood that the police was on its way. While waiting for them, she watched her uncle. He was talking alone running up and down the stairs with a baseball bat in his hand. Like a zombie, she went back to the living room. Her aunt sitting on the floor beside her daughter was howling at the top of her voice, "You killed my daughter, son of a bitch. I will kill you myself with my two hands."

Ten minutes later, four police cars and an ambulance arrived on the premises. Five police officers and two paramedics came in. The other officers were checking around the house outside. The officer in charge asked her aunt very gently not to touch the body. Then, seeing her husband and Kara so petrified, he told them to calm down. He helped Marleen's mother to get up and led them to the entrance. They sat there while they were searching for evidence and clues in all rooms.

After the kitchen had been thoroughly inspected, he told them to go sit there adding that stepping out of the way would help them a lot. Then he let them know that the detectives were on their way. The coroner first arrived and confirmed officially Marleen's death. Minutes later, the chef inspector and his assistant entered the house.

Kara went to the washroom again and tried to drink a glass of water. Her hand was shaking too much, she gave up and left the glass half full on the counter. On her way to the kitchen, she stopped at the living room entry and heard what the doctor was saying to the two officers dressed in dark suits. He was telling them that Marleen had been dead for at least two hours. Then, he asked them to have a close look at the neck marks. The coroner added that she probably died by strangulation, and then the perpetrator ended up cutting her body with a knife. On that, Kara went right back to the kitchen.

The police photographer took pictures of the body from different angles and some more from other rooms of the house. Later on, a third investigator came in. The coroner showed him his report. As soon as he finished reading, he checked Marleen's body carefully from the top to the bottom—he had a long last look around the neck.

Before giving permission to remove the body, he went to see Marleen's parents. The two investigators were already in the kitchen talking to them. With a paper form in his hands, he sat at the table. "Your daughter will be sent to the morgue. A forensic examination will be performed on her body. Would you please sign it?" he said.

The situation was so surreal that Kara lost notion of time. Police officers were still walking everywhere in and around the house, checking for prints—anything and everything they could find—all working silently, seriously and diligently.

After the body had been removed, the chef inspector, his assistant and the investigator in charge of the case went back to the kitchen. They sat at the table with them. The first question the investigator asked them was if they heard anything suspicious during the night. Marleen's parents and Kara answered negatively. Kara appeared so nervous that they all turned their attention on her. The chef inspector asked Kara if she wanted to say something that could help them to understand what happened.

Kara did not dare looking at her aunt and uncle while telling the investigators that it was all her fault if Marleen died; it should have been her instead. With a trembling voice, she explained to them what happened the night before. They asked her to be more explicit and she restated it. "Marleen wanted me to sleep in her bedroom instead of the living room. She asked her mother if she could sleep on the couch for the whole week. Her mother agreed and I accepted..." Kara looked at her aunt and uncle with tears in her eyes. "I'm so sorry—she died because of me..."

Kara kept repeating that until one of the officers stood up and put his hand on her shoulder. "It's okay, Kara. Try to come down. It's not your fault."

She just wanted her relatives to know how guilty she felt but they were so absorbed by their own pain, they didn't even look at her.

The investigator asked her what she was doing there anyway. Right after saying the reasons she was there, she began to lose control. In a kind of delirium, she got up and started to kick the kitchen door screaming, "I was here because of him, because of him—and now Marleen is dead because of him..."

Kara remembered nothing of what went on after it. She didn't know where she was anymore. She felt terribly confused until her two brothers Steve and Dave touched her on each shoulder. They talked to the detectives for a while and gave them their names and addresses. A short while after, their uncle Danny and aunt Laura arrived. They asked Marleen's parents to go to their place for as long as it would be needed.

Back home, Kara went directly to her room, closed the door and started crying desperately. Meanwhile, Dave succeeded to reach his father on the phone and let him know about the terrible event. His father immediately told him he would be there the day after late in the afternoon. He then asked Dave to make sure that Kara would not be left alone.

Lying on the bed, Kara felt anxious, sad and pretty out of space. She got up, opened the door and listened. She could hear her brothers downstairs talking softly to their girlfriends, and then it became just murmurs to her ears. She knew she had to make a move.

After washing her face with cold water, she went downstairs. When she entered the living room, they all stopped talking. She could feel their compassion as well as their sorrow. She tried to respond to them with a little smile but her face was too swollen by the tears of the day. Michelle and Nancy got up and hugged her. She let them know that she was not yet ready to talk about what happened. She demanded to just let her be—listening to them would be enough for her. With a blank look, she sat on the couch and began stroking the cat. Mitsou let her do it for a few minutes. Then, she jumped on the floor and went after a cat toy.

After a while, still sitting on the couch Kara felt like having an "out of body's experience", but somehow the pain was so deep—the body fought to bring her back. She began being dizzy and then she started sweating. The cat felt it and jumped on her lap. It gave her a little sense of sanity for a short time. However, reality was too far gone to be reached at that moment.

Steve observed her. He knew something was not right. He went sitting beside Kara and put his arm around her. "Everything is okay. Nobody will hurt you. We are here with you," he said. Shortly after, he added, "We expect Morgan to be here tonight and dad is on his way..."

Morgan took the first flight available. She felt terribly sad about Marleen's death and was anxious to be with her family.

Steve's girlfriend Michelle came to sit on the other side of the couch. She asked Kara if she wanted to drink or eat something. Kara shook her head and Michelle told her gently, "May be later, just let me know."

Dave and Nancy joined them. They sat at Kara's feet not saying anything, just touching her knees. They were waiting for Morgan.

At midnight, Morgan showed up at the door. Like a hurricane, she entered the living room and walked directly to Kara, still sitting on the couch. She took her in her arms and started crying. Wiping her tears with her hands, she said, "What a tragedy. It's awful!" Then she put Kara's hands in hers. "What happened there?" she asked.

Traumatized by the arrival of Morgan and her questions, Kara froze there. I must find the strength to get up, Kara thought. Slowly, she removed her hands. "I'm not feeling well," she said. She excused herself and went up directly to her room.

Dave hugged Morgan and invited her to sit down. "I think she cannot take anything anymore for tonight. We will tell you what we know instead. Okay, the police told us..."

In her room, Kara sat at her desk and started breathing deeply. The feeling of being hopeless and powerless over that situation had overwhelmed her so intensely since the morning that she was now thinking of taking her own life in order to be done with it. She kept breathing and not long after, she began experiencing a deep sadness going through her whole body. The more she allowed herself to feel it with all her body cells, the better she saw why she had been in that catatonic state of mind all day. She kept breathing and out of the blue, the feeling of grief gave place to anger and rage. While experiencing these last sensations, she began being aware of what was going on inside. All these emotions, sensations and feelings seemed to float there on the surface of her soul. She pictured a boat on a tormented sea. I will wreck if I do nothing, she thought.

Kara closed her eyes. In the dark, she could see a little light approaching her and then, it changed. She saw herself before her smiling at her. I'm losing it, she thought. She opened her eyes and closed them again. The image was still there. Then, the feeling of anger disappeared completely as if someone else took it away from her mind. She touched herself carefully in case she died without knowing that. Her whole body responded to her touch. It vibrated back, "I'm alive and I've the intention to stay this way until you decide that is time to go."

As soon as the image disappeared, she heard a voice. "Just think about the solution. You know what to do."

Kara looked around her—nobody was in the room but the cat. The first thought was, I'm really crackpot. I'm gone. That became even worse when she repeated it aloud. Then right in front of her, she began experiencing visions of violent scenes and hearing different voices of women all talking at the same time. "Not that again!" she said. "What's going on here, I'm out of my mind or what!" she screamed. She put her hand on her mouth and had a quick look at Mitsou. She seemed to see something too. Then the audio-visual apparitions vanished as fast as they came—the cat was now staring at her.

She got up, shook her head. "Enough is enough," she mumbled. Suddenly, without forcing her mind, she visualized clearly the face of the man who had killed Marleen. She didn't know him at all but knew undoubtedly that he was the killer. Then, the vision faded away.

Kara didn't know what to think or to do—she walked back and forth in her room trying to make sense of the whole thing. Finally, she convinced herself that she had read too many of those stupid books, so after such a terrible event as that one, she had simply a spiritual overdose. It was time to come down before losing the little reality left. In a low voice, she said, "There is just here and now..." She repeated it over and over on her way to the bathroom. She had a hot bath. It relieved the pain a little. When back in her room, she fell asleep almost immediately at Mitsou's purrs.

Kara woke up in the morning at ten. She felt surprisingly calm and lucid. She got dressed and went downstairs. Her sister and brothers were already in the kitchen having breakfast, she joined them.

Dave got up and gave her a cup of coffee. He checked the time and put the radio on. "Stop talking and listen!" he said. He turned the volume on. They heard that the police had arrested a suspect early in the morning.

The police officer giving the short interview said, "We are now waiting for blood results to confirm if it is the same blood left on the late victim. However, we cannot say anymore than that for the moment..."

Dave contacted immediately the police department. The detective in charge informed him that they were quite sure he was the right man. However, he did not want to release too many details. As Dave insisted, he mentioned quickly that they had found the man under his kitchen table in a foetus position sucking his thumb, and on that, he hung up.

CHAPTER THREE

THE OLD DANISH LADY

Late in the evening, Kara was watching TV. Lying on the couch, she thought, I have to buy another couch; this one is so uncomfortable. After zapping the channels for a while, she got bored and turned the TV off. She stayed in the dark trying to convince herself to go to bed. It did not work—something was bothering her. So she opted to pamper herself.

After preparing a bubble bath, she lit candles all around the tub. The hot water soothed her aching muscles. She let her body relax while listening to the sound of divine music playing in the background. She reached a glass of red wine and said, "It feels so good!"

That little ritual always helped her whenever she had an important decision to make. She thought about her work. Five years in the social field as a counsellor is enough. It's time to take a new direction. She immersed her head in the water. When coming up, she asked herself, "Now, what am I going to do with my life?"

She focused on that last question for a while. Then, she reviewed her past twelve years. She could describe her university years as great—she made good friends, had a good time and felt very alive. She loved that world of free thinking. Moving to the big city had been a huge and beneficial change for her—the island was too far away from the world and Victoria, a too small town for her dreams. And being far away from the family helped her become more autonomous, find her place and forget from time to time the painful past left behind.

Even after all those years, she still felt like something died within her. Although she worked very hard to recreate herself, something was missing. In the river of mistrust, she had lost forever her sense of innocence; then hope for a joyful future seemed farfetched. She took a sip of wine and closed her eyes. That brought her back to what happened after her father returned home. She accepted quickly Steve's offer to move with him and his girlfriend Michelle, a French girl from Paris. To her, staying close to her aunt and uncle was impossible, and living with her dad and his new wife was also out of question.

Months after, her aunt Barbara made a deep depression—she could not cope with the loss of her only daughter. In despair, her uncle Jack decided that it would be best for them to live in a new place where people did not know them. They moved to Toronto. Kara had not heard from them since.

It was all right at Steve's place. However, Michelle wanted Kara to see a psychologist. She told her that it would help her go through that rocky time.

Therefore, Kara had seen one for a year just to make Michelle happy—she knew she had to go through that rotten period on her knees or upright. She had nothing against the shrink—she did a good job—finding ways to cope with that awful event. However, the shrink really annoyed her in the last session when she told her that the time had come to forgive the man for what he had done. Kara was not sure about that one. She remembered listening to the shrink and thinking about him at the same time.

The man had been put in a mental institution. He was still in the same twisted position. His story was strange. At first look, the man appeared clean—he had a steady job and no criminal record. His neighbours and the ones who knew him at work were so surprised by the whole story that they came forward and told the police that they got the wrong man. All of them believed that the man was mentally well, down to earth and friendly. To them, it was almost impossible he could have committed such a crime. However, the police denied strongly those facts. After searching carefully his apartment, they found enough evidence to prove his guilt. His fingerprints and the blood test added to it convinced the detectives that in each murder case, he was the right man. They also discovered on the premises a hidden room behind a closet wall. On the floor, they found different strings, piles and piles of porn tapes, guns, knives and women underwear. Those last ones were from women he had raped in the past five years but because these women did not report it or came forward to—the police could not make a profile of the culprit until they got him. The way they had him was pure luck.

On that day, the man did not show up for work and he did not call. His boss found it unusual. After calling many times at his home, he became worried and sent one of his co-workers to have a check on the man.

After knocking at the door, the man found it unlocked and entered. He walked through the apartment calling his name. He finally discovered the man under the kitchen table in an awkward position. After examining his scratched face and shirt covered of bloodstains, he had a last look around and called the police thinking the man had been assaulted. What an irony! He would say after he got the facts. The police found in his apartment a journal where he recorded very accurately and precisely how he chose his victims, what he did to them and why.

He reported in it that killing was a new thing to do for him. He approached it like practicing a new sport and found it very exhilarating. He also wrote that all the violent porn tapes he had, gave him a virtual ecstasy for many years; however, it could not fill up his urge for the real thing anymore. He wrote that women were filthy, ignorant, sneaky and dangerous for men, and deserved that punishment. His job was to make sure he did it right. When the police released his picture in the media, several women recognized him and came forward. They agreed to talk about what happened to them to the investigators and later on to the press.

The silence was finally broken. The media were then ready to expose the little dirty secrets in the most intimate fashion to the thirsty readers in order to make money once again on the back of the victims. Horrible sex stories always sold well. Media love to say that it was done in the name of Justice and good information. Kara disagreed with the sensationalism. However, she knew that by talking about that, these women would start the process of healing.

Finally, her mind came back to the shrink. She was asking Kara for the third time if she was still with her. With an icy look, Kara nodded. To her, forgiving him for what he had done to Marleen and other women was out of question for the moment. In fact, she was glad he was still in a mental institution instead of being on death row. Without having an explanation for it, she knew that the man, at that very moment, was capable of thinking clearly. He was aware of his condition and yet, reduced to show off in that fetal position for the rest of his miserable life on earth. Kara could hear the therapist talking at the same time she was telling the murderer in her head. That's what you got bastard when you stay too long in your anal phase. Life stinks after that.

Then she turned her attention to what the psychologist was trying to make her understand for the last hour. Still on the subject of forgiveness, the shrink said, "Say something. Silence is not a good friend."

"All that is psycho-pop bla-bla-bla, I'm done with it," Kara replied. She got up and put her coat on. "How can you forgive the unforgivable?" she asked.

"You know that this man is very sick, deeply mentally ill. Therefore, he is not completely conscious of his behaviour—forgiveness is easier to do when you know in what state of mind he was when he committed those crimes."

The shrink asked Kara to sit back which she reluctantly did.

"What about those men who are not mentally ill and still do those atrocities to humankind, women, children and animals?" Kara asked.

"We are not talking about that—"

Kara cut her. "They got away with it." She continued, "Okay...the man became physically handicapped but what tells you he's mentally ill."

"I have read all the reports and believe me this man is..."

Kara did not say anything. In her head, she knew without a doubt that the man knew exactly what he was doing, and as far as she was concerned, he would stay in that condition until he died. After his death, she would have nothing to do with it anymore.

The shrink looked at her watch. "Well, I guess it's the last time I'll be seeing you. However, if you feel you need more help; don't hesitate and call me. All right."

Kara nodded. They both got up and shook hands.

On her way to the door, Kara turned back and said, "You know, life has a way to get even."

After that last session, she moved on. She never told anyone what happened that night when she saw the killer face and the morning after. For a long time, she denied it because she could not believe it either. To her, the only way to make sense of it was to assume that the combination of mixed feelings and high level of stress with those bad circumstances had to get out of her psyche in one way or another. If not, it would have driven her directly to suicide. The whole affair was just a coincidence. So she tried to conciliate the two parts that were still arguing in her consciousness by concluding that her imagination had taken control of the situation that night. She made up her mind about not tolerating that inner dialogue anymore. You better listen to what I said, I mean real business here. After declaring that, Kara recalled that the voices vanished without a trace, well at least for a while. That is all she asked for—a break from herself.

While adding some more bubble bath and hot water to the tub, her job came back to mind. She worked with people in difficulties. Those five years of social work made her realize that some people had a harder time sometimes to deal with what she called the cancer of life. They could come from all walks of life—if they got it—these people could be stuck with it for a long long time. Getting rid of it was not an easy thing to do. To her, depression was like an unwelcome so-called friend. He didn't knock before entering. He just showed up at the door and got you right in the middle of your guts while insisting that he needed a place to stay for the night.

In her case, dealing with what life presented to her was difficult at the beginning but as soon as she understood for good that she had no power over the situation, she began to change her thinking. And she knew that entertaining these negative thoughts would destroy her—the man would win in the end and she could not let it happen. In her work, Kara also understood that everyone being different, one had to find in oneself his own solution, magic potion or the right shrink if she or he wanted to survive. Nevertheless, when the source of depression came from a deliberate violent act, it appeared different in the heart and needed a different frame of mind to comprehend it.

As a counsellor for different clienteles—seniors, children and battered women, she witnessed a lot of distress, hurt and pain out there but also remembered having laughed as hard as them when they had good times. However, with the time, she felt that it was not the right path for her to follow anymore. She needed to do something lighter—it was becoming a burden to show up for work every day.

Kara held an extremely high respect for those who believed in the cause of relieving the human misery. That was not an easy task to do. They were almost missionaries spending their lifetime doing it with grace and courage—they were the real angels of life.

One of the candles went out and the water was getting cold in the bathtub. On that, she concluded that she didn't receive the call. She thought that it was time to do something else for a living.

While putting her nightgown on, she looked at the cat sitting on the toilet lid. "What am I going to do with myself, Mitsou?" The cat looked back at her and she imagined her say, "Take it easy, Kara—don't be impatient. It will come to you." Kara smiled and thanked Mitsou for the good advice.

The moonlight Sonata of Beethoven was playing. Indulging her solitary mood, she lay down on the bed and tuned in. She would have the whole weekend to find out what would be the right move to do.

The following week on a Wednesday morning, she gave a two-week notice and then quit her job. She began breathing more easily right after that.

That morning, she woke up in a very good mood. She looked at herself in the big bedroom mirror and said, "Okay, yesterday was my last day of work and tomorrow well, I didn't plan anything but that's the fun of it—I'll find something to do, I'll improvise. Wow! I am starting to enjoy myself. What a treat! Unknown, here I am!" She laughed thinking she was not enough serious about her future. Her colleagues at work couldn't understand why she didn't look for other opportunities before quitting her job. She couldn't answer it either but for the moment that was all right. One thing was sure—she had all her life to find it even if it didn't make sense to others.

With a cup of coffee, she sat down on the bed and picked up the TV remote control. Each time, she zapped the channels, she got advertising. She smiled. The big message from the outside world was still resonating in her head. <u>You must make up your mind fast about what you are going to do next because if you don't, you'll be swallowing up by the sea of winners.</u>

<u>The quest for a better quality of life is a must but it is also good to take a break from it,</u> she thought. In fact, Kara hated competition with a passion. Winning to her was getting what she wanted without fighting stupidly for it—she stuck to that principle all her life, certain of its efficiency.

She tasted every minute of that new day. When she went to bed that night, she felt very relaxed and comfortable. She closed her eyes and basked in that state of well-being. <u>It would be nice to experience it all the time no matter where you are, whatever you do. Succeeding more often at doing it would be the biggest achievement of my life,</u> she mused. She fell asleep with

Mitsou on her side. They both dreamed—Kara, about flying in the sky without wings and the cat, about visualizing 'with intention' the big catch she would make in the morning.

Around nine o'clock, Mitsou woke up Kara by walking all over her body. She finally got up and stretched slowly. In the kitchen, she made some coffee and fed the cat. She looked through the window—a sunny day was on the menu. "Summer has arrived," she said to the cat. With a cup of coffee in her hand, she sat at the table—she looked around—she was pleased to live in that small apartment. She had found it the year before and fell immediately in love with it. At the back was a little terrace with a small table and two chairs—next to it, was a shelf filled with plants and flowers. She got up and opened the fridge. "I'll have breakfast outside this morning," she said to herself.

Kara lived on the first floor and the owners of the house occupied the second. They were retired and travelled a lot. However each year, they came back in the middle of spring and took care of a huge garden surrounded by roses.

The morning air was still fresh when she sat at the table outside. She liked it—she could smell more acutely the fragrance of all flowers at the same time. It was delightful. She savoured slowly her breakfast.

In the afternoon, she wandered in the downtown area and began checking all the pawnshops. I could find some forgotten treasure, she thought. At one of them, she saw in the window an old camera that appeared to be in good shape. She went in to check the price. The owner was very friendly. Kara learned that the camera had belonged to a famous photographer who happened to be broke more than once because of a bad habit.

The store owner went to the front window and while getting it, let Kara know, "He had died recently—so

there's no reason anymore for me to keep it aside."
Coming back to the counter, she continued, "I'm
Danish and so he was. I tried to help him when he was
in need of money but...anyway, this camera now needs
a new owner who's going to take care of it and use it."
She looked at Kara with her intense blue eyes and
smiled.

Kara smiled back. "This place looks more like a
museum than a pawnshop," she said. "If you don't
mind, I'm going first to have a look at what you got
around here."

With a wave of her hand, the old lady said, "Please,
feel free to do so," still looking right in Kara's eyes.

Kara was the only client in the store. She pleasurably
took her time to see all the wonderful things that place
held—touching carefully objects coming from the
seventeen and eighteen centuries. Later on, she checked
the time and noticed that nobody came in during the
whole hour. She continued to look around. However,
she started feeling uneasy. The owner is keeping an eye
on me. I can feel it on my back. She might be afraid
that I would steal something or whatever, she thought.
She turned back quickly. The woman looked at her with
a big smile on her face. At that moment, Kara was sure
that something was not right. She tried to relax;
however, discomfort came back.

The old lady went to the end of the counter and put
on some beautiful music, unknown to Kara. While
walking between alleys, she thought that this
experimental music seemed to put her in a kind of
trance. She didn't like the feeling at all.

She slowly returned to the counter with an old lamp,
a wooden bowl and a woven basket. All she could think
of was, time to go; time to go. She had already made up
her mind that she would forget about the camera. Kara
put the items on the counter, took the wallet out of her

backpack and rapidly said, "Sorry, I decided not to take the camera. How much for these things, please?"

The Danish lady ignored it. "Do you know how to operate a camera like this one?" she asked Kara.

She answered negatively. And then, added, "I already decided not to buy it and..."

"There's no problem. I'll show you the basis if you like," the old lady replied. "It's not difficult once you know how to use all the buttons and the zoom. Now let me tell you that you'll be amazed of its performance as soon as you see the given results."

She paused and then continued, "You see, that man came often here and he taught me a lot about the subject of photography. Now, it's time to pass on what I know while I can still remember." She laughed. "I'll give you a good price too. What do you think about that?" Again she didn't give time to Kara to answer. "Let's get over with it."

Kara wanted to say no but instead babbled nervously an excuse to the woman.

With her intense blue eyes, she looked at Kara and reminded her, "It was the first reason you came in for...Why not give it a try."

Kara thought about that. The price was affordable and she had enough cash on her to buy it. So two minutes after, she said, "Okay, I'll take it." In attempt to relieve the tension between them, she jokingly asked, "Have you hypnotized me without my knowledge? If so, you have done a good job."

The Danish lady laughed but didn't add anything to it.

She showed Kara the multiple functions of the camera, and then stopped talking. Her face changed suddenly. She touched quickly Kara's hand. "I knew you would come today and buy this camera," she said.

"Well, well, well..." Kara replied.

"Don't get me wrong. I'm not a witch or an old mad woman," she said. "I have received a gift when I arrived in this world. They call it premonition."

Kara, half-surprised, half-amused, asked her, "What's that? Well...I don't want to be rude but...you mean you need to make money today. I didn't see too many customers coming in the last hour." She paused and looking around added, "However, it's a shame because all these lovely things here from the past are still in excellent condition. I know it is good quality. Now, tell me how you knew in your forecasting that I would be coming in your store today?"

The Danish lady laughed loudly. "You're good!" she replied. "Okay, the only thing I know is it seems to happen more frequently these days and it feels more natural each time. Well...about the premonitions. Let's say I got an insight just before going to sleep and after it, I got a glimpse about how an event will show up. Then during the night in my dreams, I can picture the whole scene. For example, last night I saw you exactly the way you are, coming in my store and buying this camera. Shortly after, I heard a voice telling me very gently, "This is the one we were waiting for in order to close the circle. Please do help her." And here you are.

Kara nodded. "Well, interesting!" she said.

"I know what you're going to say," the woman replied. "Are you nuts? But believe me, it's true. I am a kind of medium if you prefer. I don't often talk about it. I got most of my hunches while dreaming. It has been that way all my life. Many years ago, I dreamed about moving from Denmark to Canada one night. One week later, I was here. I could give you many other examples but the time is inappropriate for the moment. I know you'll be back anyway."

Her face was glowing with joy. In that instant, Kara thought that she must have been a beauty when she was young.

"Let's put your things in this bag which had been waiting for you all this time, my dear Kara," the woman whispered.

Astonished, Kara tried to say something but no words would come out. So speechless, she paid the lady. That one accompanied Kara to the door.

"See you soon," Kara said. Once outside, she thought, I don't know why I let her think I would come back.

She kept walking in the street without stopping—she felt that the old lady was still watching her from the door. When Kara was sure to be out of sight, she stopped and sat on a bench. She felt dizzy. She began to breathe deeply. That was her way to come back fast to reality and clear up her mind in a split second. She felt so much energy there—she wondered if it was coming from the Danish lady or from the old objects displayed in the store. Well, anyway. I am glad to be out of there and I have the firm intention to stay away, she thought. She got up. While walking, she started visualising the whole scene. Everything felt like being in slow motion in that store, And...she knew my name. It's so strange.

The sun was getting hot. She stopped by a terrace bar and sat at a table in the shade. The people sitting next to her were having fun and laughing heartily. It put Kara at ease. She ordered a glass of white wine. She took the camera out of the bag and started checking it closely. The woman's words were still in her head. She smiled inside. This lady is good! She knows how to sell things. I'll bet she sings the same song to anybody who ever comes to her store. It must be her way of attracting them to her. Her accent and language are very colourful too. Unfortunately, she must feel very lonely in her museum. That's her trick to get you I suppose...Kara stop! You're crazy thinking it might be... At that moment, she remembered that as soon as she met her eyes, something clicked in her head. The Danish lady's blue eyes mesmerized her. They sparkled and became almost intolerable in intensity to watch. That is why she decided to look around in the store. She felt inside that she was very attracted to her aura so to speak. An hour later and a second glass of wine, Kara tried again to rationalize her feelings. She then became sceptic about the whole thing. She reminded herself. I was out of control right after mom died. The memory of it came back. It was at that moment that she developed a deep interest for life after death. She read anything she could find about parapsychology. Then, she started juggling with phenomena such as telepathy and telekinesis, and later on she experimented with different rituals. Unfortunately, she was too young to go in that unknown world by herself without any wise direction. After swallowing too much stuff, she became nauseous and stopped for a while. After all, Kara just wanted to communicate with her mother—let her know she was sorry for what she did and how much she loved her.

She smiled at the thought that she was certain she would succeed but nothing happened. She did not get any answers.

Then years after, while going to the university, she started again her interest for the thing. However, after a while, she became afraid of it and put it in the same basket of black and white magic. To her, it became clear—that was just a mix of prehistoric superstitions and rituals that allowed a person to enter a trance state. Those actions and practices based on the supernatural were not for her anymore, and scepticism won hand up. Right after it, her rebel side put everybody in the same box—charlatans, shamans, gurus, sorcerers, astrologers, preachers, impostors, healers and spiritual leaders. The only one being who won her heart and respect over the years was the Dalai Lama.

Kara took a sip of wine and reflected on it. I've never fully recovered of my spiritual addiction I guess. I was still looking for something. After that phase, she went to New Age, a less dangerous thing. She liked the light and positive approach of it. It gave her a sense of comfort and freedom for a while. People were also more interesting, nicer and less weird. That helped the Cause.

Again, she went through it very seriously—she wanted to know. She read many books on Spiritual Teachers and Traditions on Buddhism, Judaism, Islamism, Christianity, Hinduism, Karma and Zen and so on. She made hers the principles she liked the most as simplicity, love, harmony and freedom. And one day, she suddenly stopped reading about all that stuff—she was done with it. Overdose had done its job.

An inner feeling of denial grew more and more each day. God was dead and there was nothing after life. Big silence replaced it instead—she believed she got the big picture at last. The only thing she couldn't explain to herself was the fact that she had seen the murderer's face so vividly on that frightening night. However, with the time she began doubting that too—that could have been anybody's face—what a cosmic joke it was.

Pure coincidence, she repeated silently to herself. It was a fluke when the police arrested him that day. I've never had any experience of visions afterwards.

She finished her glass and put the camera back in the bag. On her way home, the therapist's words came back to her. "You have to forgive the man if you want to move on with your life."

She remembered. The abominable idea of forgiving him was so repelling—she closed her heart and sealed the file instead. Later on, she made her move. She rejected her beliefs all at once—religion, old traditions, spiritual theories and the man. In doing so, she turned her eyes to the Big Reality—accepting the fact that she was born to live and die like any other species on that earth. She would make the most of that surviving time—existing in the moment was her only truth and celebrating life, her only religion.

She would be her own master no matter what would occur in that space and time. She would be the only thinker and doer in her life and if the Living Universe wanted to back her up, well—that was fine too.

She knew she went too far in one way or the other. But deep down, she understood the reason—she needed to go to antipodes in order to find her balance and experiment what worked and what did not.

In the evening, she looked at the stars on the terrace. She thought, something is holding all these heavenly bodies in that empty space, this void is full of cosmic energy. This same energy keeps me all together and makes me breathe, think and move. Therefore, it means there is something there but what?

CHAPTER FOUR

A NEW BEGINNING

One week after, she saw an ad in the morning paper about a photography course for beginners—how to develop a good foundation in basic photographic concepts, camera handling, use of lens, film exposure controls and dark room. She said to herself, "Hum...that could be interesting."

She went to register in the afternoon and paid the fees. After it, she headed for a bar to join some friends. On her way, she thought about them. Inseparable friends at the university, they had succeeded to stay in touch through the years. However, they had not seen each other too often in the past two years—everybody was too busy to get a life.

Even if they called each other occasionally, she missed their presence very much. So she had called them the night before. They all agreed to meet in their favorite bar.

Quickly, she summarized in her head what went on with them. Jason, the happily divorced anthropologist was at a crossroad like her. Kate, the authentic geologist worked part-time and had a hard time to find long-term contract. Cloe the historian who liked more the past then her present was still struggling with the difficulty to make a living at doing just that. Articulated and witty, she had a way of digging in the past to bring up stories they had never heard about but knew these tales were closer to the truth. Her research deep and elaborate, sustained with many examples always captivated them. Cloe was a passionate and interesting woman.

Kara entered the place and saw them having a drink at the bar. They waved and she joined them.

She kissed each one on both cheeks. "It's so good to see you guys," she said joyfully. "It reminds me of the good times we had together when we were studying and trying to help each other with the so-called expertise we thought we had at that period. Remember! We thought we were so smart...It's been a while since we have not seen each other. We have lots of catching up to do my friends!"

They all agreed with Kara that it was refreshing to be together again. After ordering a beer, she asked Cloe, "Why don't you start Cloe, I missed so much the storyteller in you—it will be a good warming up for us."

Cloe replied with a crazy look. She took a dramatic voice and began, "Once upon a time, there was a neurotic historian who wanted to fall in love so badly that she decided to go one night to a poetry evening. There she saw a guy, a poet who was not particularly handsome, but after seeing him performing on the stage with two musicians for an hour, she fell in love with his voice. The voice, the words and the music were so harmoniously intertwined together that the historian closed her eyes and said to herself, "This is the man I've been looking for." After the poet performance, she directly walked toward him and let him know she liked his poetry. He then asked her what she was doing for the rest of the evening—bla-bla-bla—they loved and saw each other for six months. Unfortunately, during that period, the historian changed from neurotic to lunatic and the poet stayed alcoholic. As she couldn't stand seeing him drinking first thing in the morning before facing the day, and couldn't afford to pay his bills either, she took her love in her hands and put it back in her heart again. End of the story."

They stayed silent for a few minutes. Jason broke the ice. "I'm sorry it didn't work for you Cloe. But you know that you deserve better than that."

Cloe looked at them. "Don't feel sorry for me, guys. I came back to myself since that. The sadness is still there but the hurt is long gone. I met other guys after him...but...I was not very attracted to them. So I became more interested in my work, fell in love again with my passion for the past, and now I feel more rejuvenated than ever. Okay Jason, it's your turn now. What have you been doing for the past two years, young fellow?"

With a big smile, Jason said, "You know that after the divorce, everything went blurred for at least three months in my life. Remember girls, I didn't stop calling you. Sorry about that, I couldn't face you before me but sharing over the phone my sorrow with you helped me big time. By the way, thank you for listening to me and never giving me a piece of advice. I really appreciated it. You know that I don't like shrink too much, so the best thing to do was working. It helped me go through that confusing time and kept my sanity together." He paused. "I'm feeling much better and ready to take whatever life throws at me. I now enjoy my freedom. I also realize that I cannot live an intimate relationship with a woman three hundred and sixty-five days a year even if I love her. I know it will sound selfish...what I'm going to say...but I prefer to be on my own and deal with people and events the way I like without compromising, arguing and fighting. What can I say...I love my freedom."

Jason seemed relieved. He added, "I feel like a brand new boy now. At the moment, I'm working on a big project with my students and next year if everything goes well, I'll take a sabbatical year. I don't know where I will go yet but I'm sure girls that you'll help me clarify the choice of my destination. Okay, that's all for me and what about you Kate, the earthly lifter of all." He smiled. "Did you make new discovery in geology lately or are you on drugs or something? You look so serene."

Kate always looked fresh like a rose even after spending three days in the field—she had that Feminine Mystique that eluded Cloe and Kara. She always told them that finding joy in nature had been her best cosmetic under the worst conditions.

Kate laughed at Jason's comment. "Big boy, I may look content but I must admit that I still have a hard time to make ends meet each month," she said. "However, the only thing I'm certain of is that I'm balancing between heaven and earth—the stars suddenly interest me." Rising a hand, she continued, "Okay...okay...let me explain. Last year, I went up North during the summer for a geology study. We settled down our camp in the middle of nowhere. That night, I decided to sleep outside and glanced at the stars for a few hours. The sky was so clear and the stars so bright that I started to feel very little in that big space and out of the blue, I went out of reality so to speak. It felt like being propelled in the cosmos without a chance of coming back. I still can recall the thoughts going on inside, "Are you happy with your life or is there something bothering you at that moment? Life is so big and mysterious—do you know who you are anyway?" Coming back from that waking dream or whatever, I felt asleep like a baby. The day after, I thought about that but didn't make much of it..."

Kara chuckled. "Ha! I see that you have had your first spiritual experience. Interesting!" she said.

"Please, don't make fun of me?" Kate replied. "You know that seeing and touching are more important to me. Okay, to make a long story short, I came back home and one night I went to a bar with a colleague who introduced me to a girl he knew very well." Kate began blushing rapidly. She went on, "I feel a little embarrassed telling you that...after all those years of denial. All right! I finally came out. I'm gay...I realized that my relationships with men at work were and still are very good but the intimate ones with them were awful and painful. I never had this sex drive toward guys anyway. I always felt very comfortable with girls at all times though inside myself I couldn't stand the thought I could prefer women to men in a sexual relation..." Kate stopped talking to catch her breath. She looked at them. "Would you like me to finish?"

With ears hanging out at her mouth, they all nodded at the same time. Yet, Kate seemed unsure about going on.

"Come on, Kate. Of course, we want you to finish what you started. We are waiting...what a news!" Cloe said.

"Well, I had lots of weird dreams where I was involved with women and the day I met that girl; it clicked in my head. I was sexually attracted to her. Then, I met her again and we saw each other for a while. I now understand even if it didn't work between us that I am a lesbian. That's it for me. And now, I'm expecting some comments from you, guys. You don't know how glad I am to be done with it."

She smiled and then said, "All right, do you still like me? Shoot!"

Jason, Cloe and Kara appeared a little taken aback.

"Do we know this girl?" Kara said trying to stay serious.

Jason added gently, "For a surprise, it's a big one but I want you to know that it doesn't change a thing in my friendship with you. I love you the way you are. I hope you'll be happier in whatever relationship you are in."

"At last, you've told us—I won't make a big deal out of it," Cloe said. "The only thing that saddens me is you've just missed a few years of good sex but now it's time to catch up with the stars...Of course, I still like you and will always like you." And laughing, she succeeded to say, "Thank you for sharing this terrible secret with us and from now on, I want to know everything about your encounters in the future, little lesbo-starry-geologist."

Cloe glanced at Kara. "Okay, Kara. It's your turn. Well...we are waiting. It's better to be juicy to beat that."

"I have not much to say. Okay, okay...I have a confession to make." Kara replied. She articulated slowly, "Cloe, Kate and Jason, I'm not your darling counsellor or the wanted-to-be archeologist anymore. I quit my job a week ago and I didn't look for another one yet. It was time to take a break and think about a new beginning. It has started last year...I began getting tired and fed up of listening to others. It sounds harsh but that's the way I felt emotionally. Now, my priority is to rest and renew myself for the next big wave. However, this afternoon before coming here, I went to register for a photography course. I'll see what happens. About my love relationship...hum...I didn't get lucky either, even if I think that I'm wide open on the subject of the counterpart..."

"What do you mean?" Jason asked.

"All I can say is I'm never satisfied," Kara answered. "What happens is every man I meet is too skinny or too fat, too poor or too rich, too young or too old, too idiot or too smart and the list can go on and on. I even tried with girls, pleasant but not enough for me to be sexually attracted to women. I like best men."

And looking at Kate, she added, "Just too bad Kate, I'm not a lesbian. You know it could have worked wonderfully between us because I like you very much. However, I prefer men even though I find them contemptible. Sorry Jason for that one. Well, I think I'm done here."

After that last comment, the fun began. Cloe and Kate intoned together. "At last, our feminist is back."

"Kara, I hope you'll stay in touch and tell us what your plans will be... and where you are going to on your next crusade" Jason added.

The time flied so fast that evening that they decided to continue the celebration in a Chilean restaurant. Before leaving, they promised to each other they would meet once a month at the same bar and that, no matter what happened in their life, they would be there. They swore and said goodbye to each other.

In the taxi, Kara thought she was lucky to have such good friends in her life. She had other friends too; however, these persons were real, not phony like the rest. And for that reason, she would cherish that friendship forever.

#

After a seven-month attendance to the photography course, Kara began enjoying it so much that she carried her camera wherever she went. On sunny or rainy days, there was always something to focus on. She took pictures of anything susceptible to reveal the inner reality of the big illusion she lived in—but before getting it right, she knew she needed to practice a lot.

So practice she did. The first models to volunteer were her friends. On them, she tried different lights, different angles, sometimes just close-ups of their faces. Then later on, she specialized almost on taking shots of people faces. The happy ones were good; however, the most interesting ones were those where you could read every feature—the sadness of the eye or the misery of difficult lives. And then with the time, she learned that every face had something to tell—face full of wisdom and serenity, the one with pride, the other with resignation, the shutdown face or the photogenic one. Satisfied with the result, she kept going on. The camera lens seemed to have a life on its own—Kara let it work for her.

Her friends encouraged her to pursue that new interest. Kara gratefully accepted their positive criticism and praise, love and care. At school, classmates were also very involved in their crafts—they share many tips with each other while exchanging cameras. Their teacher taught them how to read a landscape and used it in the creative aspects and techniques of outdoor photography. He often reminded them to explore the art of seeing with the emphasis on observation, imagination and creativity.

Just before finishing her photographic course, Kara transformed her living room into a studio. That day, Mitsou the cat was the model. She had disguised the feline as a rock star. After a patient hour, she finally obtained what she was looking for. The cat didn't mind eating all the treats but at the end, she had more important business than pleasing her master. Sighing, Kara translated it as—this is the last séance. I won't dress up anymore. I'm not a circus freak cat, you got it!—Kara stroked the cat and let her go. Now I know how difficult it is to take pictures of children and animals, she thought. But it's easier to make a quick buck with them. She expected that her new clients would want their children or beloved animals' pictures taken.

#

That was a lovely day. Kara decided to go out for a walk. On her way, she thought she should go see that Danish lady and thank her for the camera which helped her take a new direction in life.

The weather was still warm for October; the store door was wide opened. She looked through the entry and saw two peoples in—three others were outside discussing in front of the store. She heard them speaking a foreign language but couldn't detect what country they were from. However, as soon as she entered the store, she understood they were Danish. When the owner recognized her—she switched in English. She welcomed Kara and kissed her on the cheek.

Surprised and flattered by that affectionate gesture, Kara said, "I was just walking by and wanted to say Hi."

The Danish lady took her arm and introduced her to the couple. "They are from Denmark. Unfortunately, it's their last day of vacation—they will fly home tomorrow." Looking at the man, she added, "I know his mother very well, she was my childhood friend. It's such a pleasure to have them visit me."

Kara didn't want to interrupt their conversation any longer and said, "I'll come back another time—"

"No...No stay. They were about to leave anyway," the Danish lady replied.

The couple nodded. "Our friends are waiting for us outside," the man added.

"All right...I'll check around a little," Kara said.

They went back at where they were, and ten minutes later they left the store.

"Have you used the camera yet?" the Danish lady asked.

"Certainly, I have," Kara answered. "I came over to thank you for giving me the opportunity to use this camera. I've been attending a photography course for several months now. My teacher told me..." She got out the camera. "It's a very good quality camera and the price was more than fair. I really enjoy taking pictures, particularly with that one...and I must say the results are not bad for a beginner. Of course, I need more experience and practice but it will come. Well, thank you again for the camera.

Delighted to hear that, the woman smiled. "When I make a customer happy, that makes my day too Kara. You see, I still remember your name after all that time. I knew you would be coming back."

"You have a good memory," Kara said. "It would be nice to know yours."

"My name is Angela Taylor."

While talking, Kara realized that woman had lots of interests and culture. She could talk about history of art, theatre, music and dance with a remarkable ease. Kara appreciated her wit, sharpness and intelligence.

"Would you like a cup of tea?" she asked Kara.

"That would be nice."

The woman went to a tiny kitchen behind the curtain at the back of the store. She came out with a tray and put it on the counter. She then pulled a stool towards Kara and went sitting on the other side of the counter. Once again, they were facing each other and nobody came into the store. Kara thought that was strange—she could see through the open door people walking by and yet, no one stopped.

She asked Kara lots of questions about her birthplace, family, studies, work and life.

Kara told her what she needed to know without revealing too much of herself. However, Mrs. Taylor was always coming back to the time after the death of her mother. She wanted to know how she coped with it the following years. At that moment, Kara felt like she also knew about her cousin's murder, although she had never talked about that after the therapy. Even her closest friends did not know about the tragedy. Kara tried to change the subject. Seeing her reluctance, the old lady stayed silent for a moment.

Kara checked her watch. "Well, it's time to go home and feed the cat," she said quickly.

"Mitsou the cat, you mean," Mrs. Taylor added.

Taken by surprise, Kara asked, "How do you know her name, I've never mentioned it to you before?"

"I know many things about you...even your secrets deeply hidden in your unconscious. Don't worry...I didn't spy on you in order to get this information. I just know."

She looked at Kara in the eyes. "You remember...I told you that I have a certain talent and natural abilities to look in the past, present and future. I didn't ask for it—it was given to me. I have to use it if I want to stay at peace with myself even if sometimes I don't like what I feel or see. The only thing I know is the more I use it, the better I feel. Don't you see that you are a blessing sent to me by God."

And almost in tears, she continued. "Now, I understand the reason why I've moved here and opened a store. I was waiting for you and you came."

That time, Kara wanted to set the record straight and firmly said, "I want you to know that I have stopped believing in that stuff a long time ago but—I will continue to respect you for whom you are no matter what. Each of us sees life differently and has the right to express it the way they want." Kara got up.

"I'm sure you're thinking that I am an old crazy woman with too much time and imagination on her hands but...you will come back," she said. "Well, I'm getting tired now but before you go, I want to tell you one more thing—keep practicing your skills in

photography. You're going to be very good at it—that
will serve you well for many years to come. One day,
you will see the puzzle coming together. Right now,
you're just a little confused about which way to go.
Don't worry—just be patient. By the way, it's a quality
you have to work on. Everything will unfold at the right
time and place. Another thing, start using and
developing slowly your gift sent by God—you know
exactly what I mean by that. Bye now. Come see me
again."

In the street, Kara felt ambiguous, perplexed and
angry. She asked herself aloud, "Which one of us is
insane?" The person behind passing her by said, "It
must be you."

Embarrassed, Kara walked rapidly home. She put the
answering machine off and spent all evening listening
to Opera with Mitsou by her side. Usually, the cat used
to come and go but that evening—she stayed close to
her as if she wanted to protect her from a bad spell.
Kara thought about the Danish lady.

The first thing that came up in her mind was can I
trust her? If so, will I see her again? I really don't feel
like having something special and I do remember how
hard I tried to get some proves from the metaphysical
world with zero success.

The flash I got that night was pure coincidence. I am
convinced of it, she thought. And if I have some talent,
abilities or whatever, why had I never experienced
anything before or after it? Oh, yeah, I had heard these
women talking to me in my head; well! I was young
and I had a lot of imagination. That's all.

At the end of the evening, she made a decision. She
would see again the Danish lady in order to test her
abilities. That time, she would be the one asking
questions. She got up and went to bed. Just before
reaching the dreams world, she thought, "Ask her about

that night—was it fiction, illusion, reality or pure luck?"

CHAPTER FIVE

THE MAN WITH THE PLAN

Kara was on her way to the third monthly friend's reunion. She knew that everyone had been anticipating that gathering. The first hour was devoted to a kind of monthly report. Each one had to tell where they were at in their lives. They were allowed to bitch, swear and moan about anything they could think of—free speech was welcomed. The only rule in effect was that nobody could give any advice to anyone. After doing it, the atmosphere would lighten up almost magically—they would then proceed with the real issue of having fun and enjoying each other.

That night, Jason was late. He looked tired when he entered the bar. After kissing each of them, he said rapidly, "Don't you mind if I first start talking about my horrible week."

They all nodded.

"It seems that this month will never end. So many things to do, so little time to make it happen." He stopped to catch his breath.

"What's going on Jason? You look like a total wreck! Anyway, go ahead," Kate said.

"Okay, girls. Sometimes life appears to me like a big never-ending job. Working, sleeping, eating—sleeping, eating, working over and over again. I know that as soon as this project at the university is over, it will be time to think seriously about a larger life plan where my dreams and goals will be met. Seven months to go now...and if I want to keep my sanity, I'd better see you more often. I also need to keep dreaming about where I want to go in nine months. I already have many places that I am interested in but cannot make up my mind yet.

Kara asked him if he was done. He nodded.

"Poor little boy, so tired and so rich..." she said. "Jason, tell me immediately without thinking where you would like to go right now?"

"Well...California, Mexico, Guatemala, Peru," Jason answered right away.

Kara replied, "You see Jason, you pretty well know where to go without being aware of it consciously."

Jason agreed with her. "I guess you're right. I'm so exhausted this week. I don't know if I'm coming or going. However, what I just said is very revealing to me—I would love to go to these places. As you know, last year I decided I would take a long break from the university. At first, I thought about this trip in a more intellectual way. You know...going to Europe, visiting museums, studying old architecture and art. However the idea of going there alone felt so boring that I didn't even try to prepare an itinerary. Of course, I know that by going there on my own, I would meet people—and it would force me to interact with them but the feeling of being alone...You see, what I would like is going on a trip with friends and sharing together the experience of unknown places."

Suddenly, Jason appeared less tired. He smiled. "Why don't you take a break, girls?" Come and reinvent the world with me. We would have such a good time."

They all looked at each other. Jason went on. "None of us has a serious love relationship in the moment—no attach so to speak. We are still young—early thirty is the beginning of living and...we would remember it for the rest of our lives...something to talk about when we'll be eighty. That would be so great!"

Cloe's eyes brightened. "I hope you're not teasing us," she said. "I admit that you succeeded to get my attention here. Last week, my boss told me they wouldn't have any budget left to continue the project next year and I'd better look for a new job. As you know it costs me a fortune where I live. I could move back to my parents' house and save money...and look for another job after the trip. Well Jason, it sounds good to me."

She put her arm round Jason's waist, "Yes! I need a change in my life too. I need an adventure before rusting and I dare say that California, Mexico and South America would meet that need. We will be free of work almost at the same time. What a good opportunity to grasp."

Kate shook her head. "No Cloe and Jason, you won't get away with that one. You can't keep dreaming without me in the scenery. I've been fantasizing for years about travelling with good friends by my side. I did go to Japan, China and Europe...remember, it was ok. I had many good memories about these trips but it's really better to travel with people you can trust—can share intimacy of thoughts and interests. And of course, it makes a big difference to be with friends who are not afraid to climb mountains—try new ways of exploring the world. That would be such a good experience to be together once again."

She stopped talking and ordered another drink. "You know Jason, travelling alone isn't so terrible either because it forces you to be more open to people and deal more rapidly with the events that occur to you. On the other hand, you have to think about your safety and learn about whom to trust. I remember times when I spent my time checking everybody around and whatever they were doing. In short, I was always on the lookout. I also recall having been easily ripped off by the merchants at the market or by taxi drivers in the first two trips. Then after, I made sure that I lived in a good place and in the right area. However, it becomes annoying because you miss a lot about the reality of people living out of the nice spot."

Kate took a sip and continued. "As a geologist, I'm interested to go to the fields wherever I am. One time in Japan, I found two guides and paid them very well in order to go to the places I wanted to see in the country. Unfortunately, during the whole trek, I could feel I was not taken seriously by them and it hurt my feelings a lot." Then, her eyes lit up. "Yes! I can visualize being on a trip with different experts who happen to be my friends, discussing with them about whatever I discover and taking the time to enjoy the journey. What a treat! No schedule to follow, no supervisor to report to, no pressure of deadline. You see these days, I feel more like a prospector than a geologist. My job is exploring and searching on behalf of big companies. Unfortunately, they give you part-time contract in the hope that the team survey finds something interesting like a gold mine in the allowed time. If not, you   are history my friends."

She finished her glass in a stroke. "Would you like me to go on because I'm not done yet?"

Jason said, "Go on Kate. It's interesting to see that I'm not the only one that has a miserable life."

"Thank you Jason for cheering me up," she replied. "Nevertheless, the truth is everyone is downsizing these days. Lately, the government has cut its budget in the research department. So it means that I have no chance to get a job with them this year, and I am fed up to apply and go dancing for big companies that want you to find the bonanza for them. I always feel that I'm on trial—if the results are not sufficient to their scale, they don't renew your contract. Of course, I know I'm not the only one in this world that faces the sad reality of economy and its bad effects. However, I want to take a break from fighting and surviving for a while."

She paused, and then kissed Jason on the cheek. "Jason, you just said what I need to hear. I want to broaden my horizons and go see the world in good company." Then chuckling she added, "I might find the map and the treasure that would answer my cravings for love, a better life, better working conditions and a decent living. Okay...I'm aware that I didn't stop talking—it's time to let someone else do it but before that, I just want to say that it's the first time in my life that I succeeded to save money. So it would work perfectly."

She put her arm around Kara. "What about you, Kara?" Kate asked. "You're in a transitional period too. Imagine the four of us on a trip. That would be fantastic!"

Kara observed the trio for a short while. "Stop staring at me that way!" she said.

"Anything you could say can be held against you, madam. So be sure to choose your words carefully in order to give us the answer we are expecting from you," Jason said.

They all laughed.

"Listening to you guys and feeling your enthusiasm are very infectious. I admit I got the virus too." Kara said, and then she asked, "Are you serious about going on a trip next year? Because if you are...it would be the perfect timing for me too."

They all said at the same time, "Yes!"

Kara went on. "I would have enough time to improve my photography skills and make money. About my apartment, I can easily find someone that'll be interested to stay in for six months or a year. Now the question is—will we survive it?" I know that we're good friends but even with the best intentions; what would happen if we couldn't get along with each other? That's a possibility. I suggest that if we want to have some fun, we need to plan and organized well this trip. For example, it's important not to be preoccupied all the time by where we are going to spend the night—how much money we have left and so on."

Her friends agreed. Then, they all began talking at the same time.

After a while, Kara made them stop. "All right! While everyone was babbling, an idea came up to me about how we would like to travel. Would it be by plane, by train, by bus or on bikes? Then, I thought about my father's RV, which he only drives now to go fishing with his friends. He used it a lot the first years but his wife got tired of it. So now, he wants to sell it and buy a smaller one. Think about it...and if you're interested by the idea of a RV, I'll get in touch with him to know how much he wants for it. I'm quite sure that my father will let it go for a good price and we could sell it back on our return. Perhaps, he'll let us rent it. It's just an idea, a suggestion..."

Jason immediately responded, "Eh! Kara, that's a good idea. I once thought about travelling with that kind of vehicle. There are many advantages with a RV. For example, no hassle to look for a room and—we can save money by eating on the premises most of the time. If the driver gets tired, there's always someone who can replace him or her. Moreover, we can stop anywhere we want. It seems like a very convenient and comfortable way of camping, don't you think?"

Kate and Cloe approved.

"Please Kara, call your father and ask him about the condition of the RV," Jason said. "And if everything's ok, I'll go meet him with you and check out the RV."

Kara gladly said that she would.

Seriously considering the whole idea for a while, Jason went on. "Well, I'm very interested. Therefore, if everything's fine, I suppose I'll ask a motor mechanic to have a check on it. I will also bring my father and a friend who know more about it than I do...getting their advice will be wise..."

"I never thought about travelling with a RV," Cloe observed. "However, I must admit that when I go camping and see a big caravan of RV's entering a camping site, I feel a little envious of these semi-retired people in their miniature mobile homes." She laughed. "At first, I thought I was too young for that; most of them are in their sixties but since you put the idea in my head...well, they seem to enjoy it very much. The only thing is I'm not certain that I'd like to be part all the time of the caravan and follow the herd or flock wherever they decide to go,"

Kara smiled at Cloe and replied, "I think they stick together for security reasons...but we don't have to be part of it. We are four grown-up people. We can defend ourselves—we're three big girls and we'll have a personal bouncer at our service. What can we ask more for?"

They all looked at Jason. They started examining him from the top of his head to the bottom of his feet. They then all burst out laughing. Jason was a big and tall man—he could scare anyone that would make a quick one on them.

"Stop it, girls. I feel naked," Jason replied. "And by the way, don't forget that the challenge for me will be..." He sighed. "Travelling with the most beautiful and nasty women on earth. I don't mind to be the big brother but...if you get yourself in trouble; don't count on me to get you out of it if I see you did it on purpose. You see... I do remember the university years when...All right."

"We are too old for that," the three girls said at the same time.

"That's not the same type of adventure we are looking for, big brother," Kara responded. "Big sisters will take care of themselves. We're not eighteen years old anymore."

And the conversation went on filled with laughter about the foolish years they had shared together.

Jason then reminded them about the present and the RV. They all liked the idea. The electricity was in the air. Each one brought new ideas, and Jason appeared to be reenergized.

They agreed that they would meet twice a month in order to plan and organize whatever they decided to do about the trip—like people to see, phone calls to make and information to look for.

It was close to midnight. Jason got up. "I'm feeling better than three hours ago but it's time to go home," he said. "Tomorrow is another big day. However, I now have something to look for. The reward is waiting for me. It's not anymore vague or blurred—it's tangible."

When kissing Kara, he added, "Call me as soon as you get some news. I guess...I'll see you in two weeks. That gives me enough time to think about the idea. Anyway, if you don't change your mind during that period, it means we go for it...right! Bye girls,"

Cloe, Kate and Kara went next door for a bite. After it, Kate drove Cloe and Kara home. Before getting off, Kara said to Kate, "Have sweet dreams about finding the map and the treasure that you heart holds for you. Imagine four maps and four treasures to discover. We'll always have something to look for. See you next week for your photographic séance. Bye now."

The day after, just before going to her photography class, Kara phoned her father. They gave each other some news. Her father didn't know she had quit her job. He sounded quite surprised of learning her new interest in photography.

Kara felt cheap. Her father left often messages on her answering machine but she didn't call back. "Sorry...sorry dad about not returning your calls," she said a little embarrassed. She seemed to have always a good reason—too busy, overscheduled. She tried to get out of that faux pas. "But now I have more time on my hands to get in touch."

As soon as he heard it, he asked, "When will you come Kara? We miss you so much. Victoria is not so far...I hope to see you before Christmas this year!"

"Of course, you will dad."

After asking him again how things were at home, she decided to be honest. "Dad, the reason I'm calling you is to know if you are still using the RV."

"Not right now. I want to sell it and as soon as it's sold, I'll buy a smaller one. Why are you asking that?"

"Three friends and I are talking very seriously about going together on a long trip next year. I thought about you RV, and Jason...you remember him?" Kara said. "Well, he would like to have a look at the RV. He might want to buy it—so if he does, he will probably try to negotiate for a reasonable price." Kara laughed. "It's for a good cause. It's now up to you dad."

"We'll see Kara." And wittily, he said, "It's just too bad that the cause is not for a honeymoon. Oh! Well, you're still young; you have time. By the way, have you met someone interesting lately?"

"Dad, the day I'll meet someone like you, I'll get married without hesitation but unfortunately the ones like you don't exist anymore," she replied.

Her father laughed. "Keep looking Kara, they hide. They are afraid to be eaten raw."

He teased Kara for a little while, and then she asked him, "Would it be ok if Jason and I see you in two weeks...let's say on Saturday in the afternoon and I promise dad, I'll be staying home for two days.

Her father welcomed the news. "It sounds good to me. Remember Kara, you still have two brothers alive who will be happy to see you too..."

After hanging up the phone, Kara thought about her family. She didn't put too much effort on that. In fact, she wanted to distance herself from them, and succeeded very well at it. On the other hand, she knew that Morgan, Dave and Steve did not mind; they had their own lives and friends. Her father was the only one who appeared to miss them.

She thought about Morgan and the distance of hearts and miles between them. She said to herself, "What can I say? We are not the family-oriented type—the clan is not a priority in our lives."

#

In the evening, Jason called Kara to let her know he would pick her up at seven o'clock in the morning. "I know it's a little early but I don't want to miss the ferry and wait for the next one," he said. "After checking the RV, my father and my friend want to drive around the island. By the way, Cloe and Kate had made up their minds."

"And what's the answer?"

"The answer had been positive. What about you?"

"It's wonderful," Kara said. "You can be sure that I'll be part of the gang. So see you tomorrow at seven." She hanged up.

Her father was outside when they arrived. He greeted them warmly. All went well, Jason was glad to see that the RV was still in good condition. Kara reminded him that her father always took great care of his toys.

Later on, Jason's father, his friend and he made a detailed inspection of the engine. After that, they all drove the RV with Kara's father as captain of the ship. He gave some tips as how to park easily, how to use efficiently the side mirrors, what was the best speed of cruising and so on. Afterwards, Jason discussed the price with him.

Jason was in a very mood; they all knew that he had already bought it in his heart. After an hour of walking around the RV, Jason shook her dad's hand and said, "I'll give you an answer next Saturday." And then, they left.

Kara enjoyed her stay. She was happy to see that her father still had a good relationship with his wife Jody. She also had a good time with her two brothers that dropped by. The weekend was great and went fast.

#

Kara, Cloe and Kate bought some bottles of champagne and drove to Jason's father house. In the alley, Jason was waiting for them. As soon as he recognized the car, he waved and told them where to park. The RV was taking all the space in the backyard.

After they got off the car, Jason introduced them to the people there. Then, they all looked at the marvel on wheels. Kate asked Jason's mother for some glasses and opened a bottle of champagne. Cloe opened a second one, and served the people who wanted some. After it, they all raised their glasses and cheered up. Jason went kissing the RV and the celebration began.

Cloe and Kate kept going in and out the RV during the whole evening while Jason and Kara talked about the preparation of the trip to Jason's parents and friends. Everyone had a good story to tell about travelling. It was a magic and charming evening. At midnight, everybody went home but the quartet.

They all sat inside the RV and had a coffee with dessert. Cloe observed. "It's nice. This RV looks like a little house and it's amazingly comfortable. I know that there will be times where it will feel cramped here but we just have to pitch a tent outside in order to give privacy to whoever requests it."

"Thoughtful, Cloc," Kate said. "I really like the way they display everything, very compact but at the same time very cosy. And for the rest—I assume we will be outside most of the time when we are not driving."

"I would enjoy spending the night here tonight. Wouldn't you?" Kara said.

Cloe and Kate joyfully nodded. Jason sighed. "Will you grow up one day girls? You're so girlish!" he stated. Then, he grinned broadly. "Got you! I know you would say it. I brought four sleeping bags? Give me a minute; I'll get them in the house."

Kate, Kara and Cloe rose and jumped on Jason. They jostled him until he asked for mercy.

"Bad girls, I can change my mind you know," he added in a scream.

#

The last month before the trip, everyone rushed to terminate unfinished business.

Kara succeeded to make some more money by taking some family portraits, wedding photography, modeling portfolios and graduation pictures. She even touched the commercial side and did advertising pictures for food, products and clothes. She was happy about the results but she thought that she'll have to practice those skills all the time on the trip to get better at it.

Dave's girlfriend Nancy told her that her sister Candice would be interested to sublet her apartment while she was away. It was her first year at the University of UBC. Everything worked well. Even the owners, Mr. Andrew and his wife were home. They had decided not to travel that year. Kara usually took care of the house when they travelled, so one thing less to worry about.

The last thing to plan was Mitsou the cat. She thought about bringing her on the trip but changed her mind. Two months would have been possible but a year in a RV was too long. She was happy when Candice offered to take care of the cat.

Cloe and Kate more motivated than ever, were busy too to make last arrangements. Jason had just finished his university project. He too found someone to sublet his apartment for a year. Everything seemed to be in place.

One morning, Jason dropped by Kara's apartment. He confessed to her, "You know that that project was not such a big deal after all. I worked hard but it appeared easier and lighter because I was looking forward to this trip."

Kara agreed with him and added, "As far as I'm concerned, rewarding myself, deserving it or not is the difference between my parents generation and mine. Working is nice but there is time to smell the roses. Those overachievers who choose not to stop in their lifetime in order to accumulate more wealth will probably be rewarded sooner than they thought by being the richest ones of the cemetery."

"You got it right sister. Amen."

They kidded each other about their down to earth wisdom. After he left, Kara called her sister Morgan and let her know she would be stopping by on her way to California. She explained they would stay two days at the most. She also pointed out there was no need to prepare anything; they would sleep in the RV.

Morgan sounded relieved and they chatted for a while. However, they did not have much to say to each other. Kara hoped that the presence of her friends in LA would help the encounter. After the phone call, she thought that they were both the same...very independent.

In the afternoon, Kara decided that it was time to go see Mrs. Taylor before leaving. Once again, nobody was in the store when she came in. The Danish lady looked tired. Sitting next to the counter in a big blue velvet armchair, she was reading a book. She looked up and at the view of Kara, her face changed dramatically.

She stood up, hugged Kara and invited her to sit down. Minutes later, Kara joined her at the back and helped her with the coffee. She let her know that she would be leaving in a week with three other friends. They would travel in a RV and go down to the Pacific Coast to most likely South America.

Mrs. Taylor seemed upset when hearing it. She sighed. "Well Kara, even if I tell you not to go, I already know that you have made up your mind about it," she said. "Therefore, the only thing I can say is take great care of your friends and yourself. You'll travel through dangerous lands and you will have to keep an eye on each situation more seriously than the others will. Kara, promise me that you'll take special and extra-care wherever you go and in whatever you do."

Annoyed by that, Kara replied, "You scare me. Why are you telling me these things? I was just happy to come here to announce this good news to you." She looked in her eyes genuinely. "All right, tell me what you see..."

The Danish lady shook her head—she looked sad. "Sorry if you think that I try to scare you. I hope you will have a great time with your friends. I just want you to be extra-careful. I'm sure that you will learn a lot from this travelling experience and..."

Kara interrupted her. "It always sounds that you know more about me and my life than I do...and that drives me crazy." She immediately apologized.

Then Kara thought that it was time to test her ESP skills before she rambled too far. So she changed the subject quickly.

Kara asked questions about her life—where she was born and how she lived in Denmark. She experienced a weird feeling. Mrs. Taylor talked about her past the same way herself did at their first encounter—telling her just what she needed to know. However, Kara did not stop asking questions and finally, Mrs. Taylor gave in.

She learned that Mrs. Taylor was born in Copenhagen. Her mother, Mary Taylor was English— her father Ned Jensen was an authentic Dane. Before moving to Canada, she changed her last name for Taylor. She told Kara that she had a wonderful childhood and got married at a very early age with a man she loved dearly. His name was Jens Philpsen. They both loved children but unfortunately could not have any. Therefore, each weekend they would receive nephews and nieces and treated them like their own.

"My husband and I had a life full of life," Mrs. Taylor said. She laughed.

And she continued, "My husband opened an antique shop right after our marriage. He succeeded very well to make a decent living with it. Unfortunately, he died of cancer at the age of fifty. After it, I sold the house and the car and bought an apartment in the Latin Quarter." She pointed out that though Copenhagen was a big city, it was surprisingly easy to get around.

"I loved living in that part of the city," she said. "I met many artists of different spheres and I became aware of new forms of art. However, I must acknowledge that my love of learning came first from the past when working in the antique shop with my husband. After two years of mourning, I began enjoying my new freedom by going out a lot, watching new cultural trends and making new friends. I went often to the theatre and cinema." She stopped talking and stayed silent for a moment. She then looked at Kara and said, "You'll be very interested by what I'm going to say now... I know that you're waiting for it."

With a defying voice, Kara replied, "I want to know everything about you. You see I don't have your powers."

They both laughed.

The woman continued. "One day, I decided to know more about my capabilities in predicting the future, and I began meeting people that were interested in spiritualism and metaphysics. Most of them had different skills or psychics powers if you like. Together, we shared our knowledge and decided to form a secret society called—The Midnight Circle—it still survives these days but it's less intense and active. Well, many members had died and newcomers are rare."

Smiling at Kara, she added, "You see, at ten years old, I felt a little crazy about having these capabilities. I didn't talk about it for a long time—not even to my family or at the beginning with my husband. I was afraid they would think I was nuts. Three years after getting married, things went out of control. I was having those dreams about plane crashes, criminal activities, people deaths, floods and earthquakes and so on. I would usually read my dreams in the newspaper the following week exactly the way I saw them happen."

She paused. "One day, I had enough of that non-sense—I couldn't deal with it anymore. I had to tell someone—I wanted to know if I was crazy or not. So I saw a psychiatrist for two years. Let me tell you that that man was a blessing sent by God to me. He saved my sanity by taking the time to explain to me that nothing was wrong with me. He even became very interested about writing down the so-called—prophecies dreams—to measure the accuracy of the predictions—I usually got right nine of ten on his scale. After that, he introduced me to different experts who were studying ESP and together they tried to assess my skills for a year. Then knowing that I was not crazy, I stopped the therapy—those measurements tests were exhausting. However, it gave me courage and finally, I told my husband and family. They accepted me for what I was. I became more relaxed and comfortable with myself. What a big relief it was."

"Do you want me to continue?" she asked Kara.

"It's getting exciting. Please, go ahead," Kara answered.

"After the death of my husband, I had a lot of time on my hands and began reading on the subject. Let me tell you that I met lots of strange people from mystical to pure fake..." She stopped talking.

Why have you moved to Canada?" Kara asked.

"I like Copenhagen but one day, at the age of sixty-five, I got a hunch, a very strong feeling—almost an order telling me to move to BC, Canada. After moving here, I was informed in my dreams to be waiting for someone very special that would be later the link between the Midnight Circle and the Upper One. Okay, I don't want to lose you here...there is a Higher Circle who is in control of..."

She observed Kara for a while. This one was in awe. The woman hesitated to go further but the truth had to come out—Kara had to be prepared for the trip. So she went on. "Don't ask me what it is or who they are; I have no idea. In my dreams, this voice is and always had been very clear. One night, it strongly said, "You must wait for her... and let her know what you know. When the time comes, we will contact her more significantly and prepare her for the assignment." She stopped and took a deep breath. "Okay Kara, you must have understood by now that the one is you. The time has not come yet for you—they will let you free of doing whatever you want to do for the moment but know they will keep an eye on you."

After carefully listening to the Danish lady, Kara didn't know what to say—she was just stunned. However, denial came back and rejected it. She didn't want to hurt the woman's feelings but succeeded to do so.

"This is a big surprise to me...You got me by the hook here and it's quite flattering to know that you think that I am the special one but...I don't think so," Kara said. "You see, I was very interested in that stuff fifteen years ago but nothing relevant happened to me. I didn't have like you those dreams or predictions of the future, nothing at all. Therefore, I gave up and decided that it was not for me. I also learned that most people who tried making me believe they had special powers were big fakes."

Mrs. Taylor gave her a hard stare and raised a brow. "Kara, you have come here today with in mind to know once and for all if I am a fake or not...It's time for the truth now—remember at the age of four, you climbed up a stool to see your face in the bathroom mirror and then, you saw yourself and the whole universe at the same time in your body—you were sure of your existence and very aware of the Big Reality. You saw your soul in her inner reality but couldn't explain it to yourself—you were too young."

Her eyes sparkled and she added, "That state of being went blurred and vague with the years. Your rational side got stronger than your sensitive one. It's good because you must be strong at all levels before doing what you are supposed to do...Now, the question you are burning to ask me since you have been here is: was it an illusion, a coincidence or pure luck about that night or was it real?"

Mrs. Taylor closed her eyes and continued. "You were in the house when the rapist came in—he went directly upstairs to the room you were sleeping in. In the dark, he touched your shoulder. He stopped when he heard your uncle coughing. Then he decided to go back downstairs to check the knives in the kitchen. On his way back, he saw you cousin sleeping in the living room. At that moment, he chose to kill her."

She paused. Kara observed that her eyelids moved rapidly.

"That same night, you went through a very strange experience. You saw the man first in your mind and then, you envisioned him in a fetal position sucking his thumb. The police arrested the same man you saw in your vision the morning after."

Mrs. Taylor opened her eyes. Kara was staring at her. "Yes Kara, that was real. Now you know that I can read your mind. I have to say no for the second question, you couldn't prevent that event. And don't worry for your cousin and your mother—they are at the right place. You see, everything happens for a reason. I know that you begin hating this expression...but you will learn to live with it as I did in the past. Once again, I repeat—you saw him and then, you made it happen. He will be living in this position for another two years and then he will die."

And firmly, she added, "The reason why nothing happened to you before and after that traumatic event is because your job will be for later. I'm just the messenger but trust me, you will know when it is time. I hope that I answered all your questions clearly enough."

Speechless, Kara got up. She walked back and forth in the store for a while. Then she sat back and closed her eyes. The Danish lady was observing her behaviour very attentively. Suddenly, Kara felt a warm loving energy coming in, the same one she felt when she was four. That state of total well-being penetrated each cell of her body. Then that energy expanded around. She opened her eyes and looked at Mrs. Taylor.

With tears in her eyes, Mrs. Taylor said, "You just got a glimpse. It's a reminder—you have to live accordingly to the Prophecy from now on." She stood up and added, "I will talk to you as soon as you come back from your trip—so far, that's all you need to know."

Kara kissed the woman on both cheeks. She looked at her differently—she deeply sensed she got the answer or the revelation to what she had been looking for all those years.

Still troubled, she said, "Forgive me, Mrs. Taylor. The only way for me to believe you was that you had to answer those questions correctly. I had to make sure in my mind that you were not a liar. Please, forgive me again. It's so big what you just told me."

Mrs. Taylor interrupted Kara. "Take it easy and relax about that. They know what they are doing; they will give you what you can take, no more no less...Well, one more thing, don't talk about that with anyone, not even with your trusted friends. Just be aware of your thoughts and actions. One day at a time and all will go well. See you next year my dear Kara."

At the door, she hugged Kara. "I love you very much. It's a pleasure to know you."

"I love you too," Kara replied. "Bye bye now."

Kara went to the closer park and sat on a bench. She could not think anymore—she just stared at the lagoon before her.

Shortly after, a second wave of warm energy invaded her body.

CHAPTER SIX

VOYAGE OF DISCOVERY

That day was the big day. Cloe, Kate and Kara joined Jason at his parents' house. They arrived loaded with luggage, dried food bags and other little things necessary for the enjoyment, comfort and needs.

In the golden light of the morning, the RV shone. It looked like a big boat on wheels waiting for the captain and its passengers to embark and sail away.

Everyone was in a good mood and in excellent shape. Cloe, Kate and Kara had been jogging for the last two months while Jason had been going to a fitness center. Mentally and physically prepared for the trip, they were more than ready to go.

Cloe and Kate's parents were already on the premises—they wanted to say goodbye to their daughters. Jason's mother was very emotional that morning—tears were flowing down her cheeks. He tried to reassure her concerns. "Mom...please, we are going to take great care of each other—there is no need to worry." He added, jokingly, "After all, we're going on this trip to have fun. We are not going to war. Please mom, stop it." And he kissed her on both cheeks.

His father checked the tires pressure a last time. He then walked up to Jason and the girls. "Have a good trip everyone. And girls, please don't be too hard on Jason even if you think he deserves it. I don't want to be the one that will fix him up when he comes back," he said.

Everyone had a good laugh. They all said a last goodbye to their children. Then the quartet got into the RV. Jason and Kate sat at the front—Cloe and Kara at the back. They all put their seats in the most comfortable position as if they were riding first class. They waved everyone off and drove away.

Jason and Cloe had done the grocery the night before in order to have plenty of food for the next three days. They wanted to drive long hours without stopping. The only halt would be at the gas station to fill up the RV.

However, the day was so beautiful that they changed their minds on the way and decided they would drive to Olympia and then spent the night in a RV park at the outskirts of town. Kara and Cloe were busy at the back putting together atlas, details maps, forestry maps and books while Kate and Jason were enjoying the landscape of the Pacific Northwest. They had planned to explore the Sunset Coast after getting to Portland. The coastline road would be more interesting than driving in the interior.

The following day, driving on the northwestern shore of the coastal Oregon road, they savoured slowly the scenery of sea on one side and local farms on the other. Oregon was wonderful for its state parks, wayside dots along the coast and easy access for the RV. They all agreed to stay longer at Newport. The campsite was close to the ocean and the view beautiful. That night, Kara and Cloe pitched their tents and slept outside. They would often be doing that afterwards, not only to give space to each other but simply because it was so pleasant to be outside most of the time.

Each one drove in turn, so the others could have a relax look around or read or just take a nap. They drove slowly all the way, stopping at many seaside little towns. They loved buying fresh vegetables, fruits and seafood on the way while enjoying the view of the summerhouses where artists spent the hot season and exhibit their work. Some of them lived there year round. It gave a lot of cachet and colour to those lovely small towns.

That day, they went to visit an art gallery in the afternoon. As soon as they got out, Kara said, "This place is a little paradise. No wonder why they are so many creators living on the seacoast. I got the impression that this place speaks to people in so many ways. You can feel the mystery of earth and heaven at the same time. Don't you feel the same way?" she asked.

"I'll bet Kara, you are already dreaming about living here in a near future." Kate observed. She smiled. "Now, it's time to start practicing your art by taking some shots of the beautiful models you brought with you."

"Yes Kara, get your camera. I'm ready to give you my best shot." Jason added. "You're lucky; it won't be hard for you to get the best of me because I'm a natural beauty."

He stopped talking and took a muscular position.

Cloe told him, "Forget about that one; you look goofier than handsome young man."

Kate and Kara nodded. Jason wasn't done yet. He took his light jacket he had around his waist and put it on his head transforming himself in a kind of guru. He joined his hands first and then opened his arms.

He took a guru voice. "Mark my words young ladies. We're just beginning the journey. We are going to discover some spots on this earth where we will be dreaming and yearning for long after finishing the trip. So take heart, enjoy the scenery and let the Spirit of Discovery whispered to your ears where to go. Amen."

Jason joined his hands again. Cloe knelt to him. Kate showed him the finger, and Kara pleasurably took nasty shots of them.

Kara thought that it was so good to be with people that liked life and each other. Everything was easier to take—even the pain and its weight she carried around seemed lighter, less frightening. Savouring life in the moment was the only truth.

They walked through the town. Cloe agreed with Kara about the people living alongside the coast. "It looks like people don't really retire here. It's such a marvelous place to live," she commented. "I have come here once before with some relatives but we travelled so fast—I had no time to enjoy or taste it."

They all cooked together that night. They had a feast of seafood, fried rice, fresh salad and baked bread accompanied with good wine. Some campers from California joined them in the evening around the fire and let them know about the best spots. Before going to sleep, Jason a little drunk, said while hiccupping, "I think that I'm already in paradise...here and it's just the beginning. Well, it's true that on vacation...we see the world differently...being by the sea most of the time is also very relaxing." Then, he stuttered, "I will sleep...sleep...well again tonight with the sounds of waves...whispering to my ears. Good...good night."

When they got out of the RV the morning after, the girls smiled at the view of Jason. He had not quite made it to his tent—half of his body was out, and the sun had already reddened it. Kate picked up a pail full of water and threw it on him. "You might have slept in paradise last night but you wake up in hell this morning," she shouted.

#

The weather was on their side too; it rained two hours on their first three weeks. They drove in the state of California on the road 101. They watched all along the way miles and miles of vineyards and wineries and then entered the beautiful redwood forest.

They spent three days in San Francisco. The first day, Cloe and Kara went visiting museums while Jason and Kate rented bikes and rode around the city. Then, in the evening, after dining in a nice restaurant, they went dancing and drinking in outrageous bars. They also woke up with terrible hangovers but didn't care—they had so much fun that they agreed to pay the price.

At Santa Barbara, Jason wanted a last checkup on the RV before taking the road again. At the garage station, he let them know, "Nothing is wrong with it; it just for safety measures. I'll stay at the garage. The mechanic told me it would be done by five. So you're free to do whatever you like this afternoon. Enjoy!"

Santa Barbara possessed its own distinctive essence—a well-preserved early Spanish settlement positioned between a curving bay and the Santa Ynez Mountains. The girls walked in the cobbled pathways the whole afternoon, enjoying the red tile roofs and studying the old architecture. On their way to the garage, Kara had the impression that someone was following them. She began checking behind her. A little worried, she told Cloe and Kate to go ahead while stopping at a phone booth. She stayed there for a while. However, she did not see anyone suspicious. She then called her sister Morgan and let her know they would arrive the day after late in the afternoon. When Jason saw her, he gladly said, "The RV is still in a very good condition and ready for its passengers."

Driving a RV in Los Angeles was not an easy task. Jason was glad to park it in Morgan's large driveway. Morgan welcomed the whole company warmly. Her husband being out of town for the week, she told them right away that she would refuse to let them sleep overnight in the RV. She added that she had two guest rooms plus the basement to offer.

Jason, Cloe and Kate replied that they would be all right sleeping in the RV and plus, they would be out all day visiting LA. But Morgan insisted. They finally complied. After all, a good mattress was welcome after a camping trip. Kara really appreciated Morgan's willingness to please them.

Morgan put her arm around Kara's shoulders. "Tomorrow, we will spend the day together sister," she said. Looking at the others, she added, "I'm sure Cloe, Kate and Jason will find on their own a lot to discover about this beautiful city." She then asked them, "Is it you first time in the city?"

Cloe and Kate shook their heads and told her they both came in LA once before with their parents when they were children.

"It's my first time in LA and I'm already excited— I've planned lots of things to do and see," Jason said.

Morgan's dog Rodo started barking. "Sorry but it's time for his walk," she said sighing.

Right away, Jason offered her to walk the dog, saying he was eager to look around anyway. She gave him the leash with pleasure. "I see that you're not only handsome but courteous too. Thanks Jason."

It was getting late and they were all hungry— Morgan invited them to have dinner in the backyard. She had created a wonderful garden around the pool with the help of her expert friends. The sight of it was stunning. The design of the house, furniture and decoration amazed the guests. It demonstrated an exquisite taste. Kara understood that Morgan had left behind the pinky room.

Cloe, Kate and Jason felt immediately comfortable with Morgan. It helped break the ice between the two sisters. Kara thought, they might be wondering why

Morgan and I don't see each other more often but first I have to make sure that none of them will know about that tragic night. I'll have a serious conversation with Morgan tomorrow. She cannot mention any of it to them.

During the meal, Morgan asked them to talk about their trip from Vancouver to LA with the RV. "How did you manage to get along with each other?"

Jason started first. With a serious look on his face, he said, "Well, it was not easy at the beginning...You see...they didn't want to listen to me when I taught them how to drive the RV, and then—where to go, what to do and see—what to eat and where to sleep. However the second week, they began behaving better as soon as they understood that I was their god, their guru and they were my followers. Now...they know what to do just at the look of my face, don't you sisters?"

Kate still chuckling with a hand on her mouth, winked at Kara and Cloe and in the twinkling of an eye, Jason was skyrocketed in the pool with his clothes and shoes.

The scene was deliriously funny. They were still laughing when Jason sat down with a towel to dry out. He approached Morgan's ear and murmured, "See how they learned well, I also taught them to defend themselves." And loudly, he said to the girls, "I decided that my mission is over—you're now ready to be on your own." And with a childish voice, he added, "However, you miss something here. Remember what my father told you before leaving about not hurting me and you did bad girls. I'll let him know about that..."

Morgan couldn't stop giggling. Finally, she succeeded to say, "I can visualize the four of you travelling and acting all along that way. People around must think that you're deliriously crazy but thanks for the show; it was well received."

After the meal, they talked about the likes and dislikes they encountered; to them, the little inconveniences were so trivial compared to what they had lived up to till then. Cloe pointed out to Morgan that they wanted to stay longer on site in Mexico and Central America—it would give them more time to organize their settlement. However, if things were not working out between them on the way, they would be free to go on travelling alone if they wished.

They spent the rest of the evening in the pool. That night, the tired travellers really appreciated to sleep on a good mattress.

Cloe, Kate and Jason left the house early in the morning, Kara alone with her sister in the kitchen talked about everything but the family. They had a second cup of coffee by the pool. Then Kara brought up the subject. Morgan assured her that she wouldn't say a word about it. Both relieved, they changed the topic quickly. The matter was closed.

Morgan smiled. "I'm glad you're here," she said. "I missed you very much, you know."

"Thanks Morgan. So tell me what have you been doing these days?"

"Oh! Well, I've been very busy, involved in one hundred things at the same time in the community over the past years. I also helped Roger with his new business while preparing my courses and teaching at the college. But—two months ago—I gave up many things...Time to take care of myself and spend more time with Roger. Knowing that you were coming, I decided to take a week off." She smiled. "I want to spend time with you and make it special."

She got up. "For this reason today, I'll be your guide. First of all, what about the best breakfast in town in my favorite restaurant?"

"Great! I accept with pleasure," Kara enthusiastically said.

They drove close to Long Beach. Sitting in a trendy restaurant, Kara observed to Morgan. "Everyone looks like a star here, they may be just extras in a film...but I can feel pretty well the hollywoody atmosphere—it's colourful, glamorous and most of the people are good looking too which helps..." Lifting her head at the same time, she stared at a young handsome man who was walking by their table. He looked back at her and smiled.

Morgan replied merrily, "This is just your first glimpse at LA...Fortunately, there's more to come than the Hollywood mania."

After breakfast, Kara confessed, "It's nice. However, I don't know if I would like to live here. I guess you get used to it with the time—you don't pay too much attention as I do right now.

"At first, I thought like you but now I like this city very much—I find it very stimulating. I have good friends. Roger and I go away often so it's always nice to come back home. My life is here now—I couldn't even think of going back to BC." She then asked Kara, "What do you think you'll be doing after that trip?"

Kara took a few seconds thinking before answering. "I'm pretty sure that it'll be in photography. It reminds me that I have some pictures that need to be developed. I'll do it tomorrow. Today, I just want to be with you and relax."

For the first time in years, they enjoyed each other a lot. Morgan drove everywhere she could think of—asking Kara what she would like to see. Then they went shopping for a few hours. Later on, Kara took many pictures of her sister. After a while, Morgan let her know that it was more than enough.

"You make me think that I am the star of the day. Give me this camera and show me how it works; it's my turn to take some shots of you," Morgan said. She did her best she could under the circumstances—Kara took unimaginable positions playing the clown and making a fool of herself.

Then Morgan took her to a fancy starry bar on Sunset Boulevard where some friends of her were having a drink. She introduced Kara to them and quickly explained the reason of her visit. They became intrigued about the places Kara and her friends wanted to visit.

One of them insisted that she should call her friends to join them. They were so nice, interesting and funny, she did not hesitate. She got up and went by the washroom where the paid phones were. She called at Morgan's house wishing they were there. She informed them on the answering machine to pick up the phone and waited a few seconds. Cloe answered. Kara let her know what was going on. Cloe asked Kate and Jason if they were interested to go to that place. Then Cloe told Kara they would join them and wrote down the address.

While talking on the phone, Kara could feel a presence behind her listening to what she was saying. Before hanging up, she suddenly turned her head back. The man looked right in her eyes. She hung up the phone without changing position. Looking up at his rough face, she asked, "Can I help you?"

The man grinned. He stayed silent and continued to stare at her with his steel blue eyes. She assessed quickly the man. I'm sure he's not a nice person. He was tall and well-dressed. With his large shoulders and bully face, he looked like a hit man, the perfect Mafiosi type you see in movies, she thought.

The man came very close to her and said with a nasty voice, "No, you cannot help me. I just wanted to see for myself who was the special one. You don't look too dangerous at first sight." He smiled obnoxiously and went on. "I just want to let you know if I were you—I would be very...very careful about every move."

Two men were coming up to make a phone call. The man backed off and Kara immediately left room for them. At that moment, she wanted to forget Mrs. Taylor's warnings, her life was too good. A few minutes later, she tried to convince herself that it was just another nutcase loose in LA.

The two men were then on the phone talking. It gave her courage. The man was still scornfully looking at her, so she made her move. She came close to him, touched him on his right arm and softly said, "It will be better for you to forget about me. Choose well...because you have a few choices left. It's up to you—if you do something harmful to someone, I will know about it and...it will be too bad for you."

On that, she turned back and walked to her table.

As soon as she sat down, she looked around for a while. The man seemed to have vanished without a trace. He's a sick man; that's all, she thought. She started to relax and ordered a scotch on the rock. She then told them that her friends were coming.

Minutes later, Kara lost touch with the conversation at the table—her thoughts were elsewhere. She could not comprehend why she acted that way. She actually surprised herself. It felt like someone else was talking on my behalf to that man. I'd better check what's going on inside and around me tonight.

The conversation was becoming very animated at the table and nobody was paying attention to her. She closed her eyes for a few seconds and saw in her mind the Danish lady face. She could read her lips. "You have done the right thing."

She opened her eyes. Morgan murmured to her, "Is everything ok Kara? You look a little upset."

"It must be the travelling and the emotion to be with you...and the drinks I had. I'd better have a coffee next," she casually said.

At that same moment, Kate, Cloe and Jason appeared at the door. They were looking for her. She got up and took them back to the table. She introduced them to Morgan's friends. Then the waiter joined another table to theirs—they all sat down and ordered a drink. They connected easily with these people; the mood was light and joyful.

After the happy hours, the music got louder in the bar. "It would be nice to finish the evening elsewhere," Morgan said. She suggested a good Indian restaurant that was not far away. They all agreed—they could not hear each other anymore.

It was just beginning to get darker when they came back at Morgan's house. The dog was ready for his walk. As everyone looked tired, Kara said to Morgan, "I'll walk the dog to the park."

Morgan gave her the leash and showed where the park was. Kara needed to be alone to figure out what exactly went on that afternoon. She watched the spaniel running loose in the park—she thought that he had a funny look like his master...large dropping ears and short legs. Morgan had told her that Rodo was more Roger's dog than hers. Kara was actually glad that the master was away for the week; so they wouldn't have to deal with each other. They were reciprocally unable to communicate with each other. She admitted that it was another reason why she didn't visit Morgan more often or invited them. However, it was ok—they both accepted the fact they didn't get along and that was it.

She sat on a bench while keeping an eye on the dog. She then shifted her thoughts to the man met at the bar. She wondered if he had followed her from BC or if it was simply a coincidence. After it, she asked herself why she had seen Mrs. Taylor. She then closed her eyes thinking about her. Nothing happened. If I have a gift, it means that it only works sporadically and not on request. So it's worthless, she thought. The second question she asked herself, "Am I losing it?"

That one demanded more attention. However, looking back at the trip from BC to LA, she felt that she had never been happier in her life—in good shape and relaxed—she was on vacation with wonderful people and had a lot of fun. After that little check, she knew without a doubt that she was more than all right. But at the background, her mind was saying be more alert from now on. Shortly after, the idea came to her about the possibility that Mrs. Taylor might be crazy enough to send someone just to scare her—she discarded it immediately. No, on the contrary, she really felt in her heart that she saw her and read the message. She looked up at the sky. God or Universe, what do you want from me? Please, be specific and clear so—I can get it! She waited a few seconds before saying to herself. "As usual, I'm talking alone."

She tried to remember clearly the man's face. He was the kind of man she despised the most, the "macho" one, the chauvinistic type with too much testosterone to handle on his own. His cold eyes gave her shivers too. She felt so much hatred from him. Why did he say that to her? Was he a nutcase as she assumed him to be?

Different scenarios were playing in her mind. The man might have had a bad day and he didn't like my face. He looked like the perfect example of the man capable to batter his wife and children without guilt.

Then her thoughts went further. The soldier on a battlefield who kills for the pleasure of it, hidden under the cover that he is defending his country. The police officer that kills on a regular basis, giving always a good reason why he did it—he had no choice and no witness either. The Mafiosi type who doesn't have to hide his reasons, the hit man or the serial killer and... Those thoughts began feeding more and more her wild mind. These bad apples use violence and force to get what they want—they treat women like dirt, second-class citizens. Consequently, these women become a shadow under their tyranny. These men like to take control of any situations at all times because they are overwhelmed by their desire of power. They cowardly control their victims by using verbal abuse, physical threats—that way; they prevent the "shadow" to counterattack. Their way of manipulation is to break them down by criticizing whatever they do and use it to punish them.

Kara took a deep breath. She forced herself to stop thinking about those awful scripts. She slowly came down by saying, "Thanks God, there are some good men on this earth too." She got up and called the dog.

In the street with the dog under leash, memories of childhood inundated her psyche. The little ten-year-old girl she was took over the mind and shouted, "You know it's unfair and what have you done about that yet?" "Not too much," she replied. The little voice began grousing at her—Kara had enough. Stop it little brat, I do what I can with what I got. You want me to save the world or make it a better place to be. I like your courage and temerity but I decided that it was not my Cause. I'm not ready to fight for it. I'm even tired of it. By the way, I'm wondering if it's you that attracted that weirdo into my life today. Stop it! You see, I didn't receive the call yet. Even if Mrs. Taylor told me that I'm special, the problem is I don't feel it inside. It is a lost cause—you got it! The little entity evaporated.

They stayed longer than they thought. Days went fast. Jason and Kate rented a car for two days and drove everywhere in LA: Beverly Hills, West Hollywood, Malibu, and Santa Monica while Cloe, Kara and Morgan visited the Music Centre, Chinatown, TV Studios, and Sunset Strip—ending with other great museums.

The last night was quiet. The quartet prepared the maps for the next destination: Mexico.

Before they left, Morgan said to Kara, "Stay in touch sister. And I hope that after this adventure, you will come more often." Kara promised. They hugged each other. Then she said, "Wishing you all the best on the road. It was nice to meet you guys."

They said good-bye to Morgan and Rodo the dog and drove away.

In San Diego Country, Kara and Cloe found on their park sites map a place to spend the night close to the border. Kate was the one at the wheel—she had fun practising her Spanish with Jason. They were the only ones who could speak Spanish fluently. They teased Cloe and Kara a lot when they tried to talk Spanish with them. In a half-smile, Kara let them know that as soon as they found their spot on the RV site, Cloe and she would be busy studying Spanish and would not make any dinner for them even it was their turn to do so. Cloe, the best cook of the group went even further. "I back her up. Stop making fun of us when we speak Spanish or you would cook on your own for the rest of the trip."

Jason laughed. "That's all right with me...the way you talked to each other in Spanish...Poor you! You actually need to work on it for long, long hours," he replied.

Kate and Jason were now raving. However, she succeeded to park the RV right. They immediately got out leaving Cloe and Kara mumbling inside.

Five minutes later, their neighbours, a Canadian couple, came to introduce themselves. They told Kate and Jason they were just back from Mexico. Very interested by their comments, Jason invited them for dinner. They happily accepted the invitation and went to get some bottles of wine in their RV.

Kate came back in the RV and took some food from the fridge. She announced solemnly to the girls, "Just too bad that you have to study. Our neighbours, a very nice couple, are coming for dinner. The man even told Jason he would help him cook.

One hour later, Kate opened the door, had a quick look at the girls and said in Spanish, "It smells so good. See you later guys."

Kara who had just learned a new expression, answered back, "Get lost little devil."

Kate frowned without saying anything, then smiled and closed the door.

The students listened and repeated with their Spanish tapes for another hour. Then they made some lemonade and had some hot dogs. Right after, they joined their friends and the Canadian couple around the fire. They learned that these people had a great time in Mexico. The couple told them that they had many friends that spent all year round in different parts of Mexico. So it was easier for them to get friendly with the locals and use their good advice about where to go. They also talked about the conditions of the road and safety measures.

Early in the morning, they checked out all the papers they would need to cross the border. They put on the table their passports, birth certificates, tourist cards, automobiles and RV permits. Be prepared was the motto of the day and prepared they were.

They had little trouble crossing to Mexico in Tijuana. However, it did take time to get through the paper work—they waited over two hours for someone to come and complete their fifteen minutes inspection. In order to make a good impression, Jason and Kate talked only in Spanish to the agents who were pleasant and helpful. After checking carefully the RV, the agents left satisfied. The quartet was relieved—they knew the custom officers were sometimes suspicious of young people travelling in RV.

#

The first month in Mexico was special and nice. Everyone had received what they heavenly asked for— completely uprooted. They drove the RV from villages to villages interacting along with the natives and locals. Elderly people and children were particularly helpful by taking the time to explain whatever they would ask them.

The following months, they stayed longer on the premises. It was more enjoyable to all of them. Kate and Jason who had a lot in common went out most of the time for a field trip while Cloe and Kara visited farms, village markets and churches—they also learned a lot from the elderly in the village. These women taught them how to weave fabrics and baskets—and how to cook properly the Mexican food.

Kara and Cloe did improve their Spanish but not enough to feel easy about it. Luckily, they always found someone that could speak English and translate to them immediately what the women were telling and showing. They secretly bet between them that they would speak as well as Kate and Jason within two months. They knew that it was a big challenge.

The quartet bought two bikes with baskets—so they could ride for getting things they needed without taking the bus or taxi. After the purchase though, they were not sure which means of commuting were safer. People drove fast over there—the road was a dangerous place to be, on foot or on bike. But with the time, they overcame the fear of speedy drivers.

Cloe and Kara liked to get fresh products and prepared Mexican dishes to Kate and Jason. Their new friends met on the camping site, also appreciated having a bite while dropping by. Life was good, good...

#

It was hot when they arrived in Mazatlan. Tequila and Siesta welcomed the tired travellers.

They found a very nice spot—they all took it easy and reminded each other that they were still on vacation.

That morning, they were on the road again. Kara had almost forgotten about the Danish lady and the man met in LA. She was having such a great time. She swore to herself that nobody would take it away from her; if so, that person would be in big trouble. She entertained the idea sometimes while driving the RV, don't mess up with Kara or you will no longer enjoy your stay on this earth. She knew that it was a crazy idea to bear in mind but that was her way to overcome her frustration on the road. However, Jason relaxed when she drove—Kara was a good driver.

That was something else with Cloe. Jason reminded her often like an old brother, "Take your time Cloe. Driving in Mexico is easy when you know what you're doing. Drive alertly and defensively, and please! Keep your eyes on the road."

Kara, Kate and Cloe all agreed on one thing—they didn't like driving in the mountains. The motor home, in second gear, would take forever to get on the top of the hill. They learned too to take precautions when filling up the RV. Each time, Jason the guru took pleasure to remind them, "Look at the gas cap, watch the meter carefully and avoid talking to the employee when doing it."

They drove for three days heading for Mexico City.

Tired of that long driving, they decided that the big city would wait—they took a country road. They found a perfect spot—a sheep farmer let them park in his field. They could get water from a village well not far away.

The following mornings, Jason made them delicious and elaborate late breakfasts, sometimes with tortillas; other times, bacon and eggs accompanied with a dish of sliced mangos, papaya, plum apples, bananas and oranges. The girls couldn't be happier.

To them, the RV was a wonderful travelling lifestyle. When it rained, they could sit under the awning or go inside to read or play games. They also learned not to be at the same place all together for too long. When they had arguments over stupid things— they would go out with other people for a couple of days. It was a harmonious exit and the right way to keep peace.

Being at that place for a while, the villagers got to know them and invited them for a wedding. The quartet all dressed up for the occasion. Kara took many pictures and promised the couple and villagers that she would send the photos as soon as they would be in Mexico City. Before leaving the morning after, they had breakfast with the groom family. To them, interacting with the Mexicans was the best part of the trip.

And life continued on the road again. They chose to spend three days in Teotihuacan before going to the big city. When they got off the RV, Jason said to Kara, "We'll see if the wanted-to-be archeologist will decipher what went on here."

"I'll certainly do," she replied. She touched her backpack. "I've brought some books with me to refresh my memory," she informed him. "And I'll check dear anthropologist, geologist and historian, what you can tell me about this site with only what you see on the premises. Of course, it'll be a pleasure for me to correct you. I also want to remind you that I had to change my orientation in life when I realized that I couldn't make a living of it...okay...I want to see if you have developed your sense of observation with the years. Do you want to play a game? If so, I'll prepare a little questionnaire. She looked around. "Ok, I'm waiting..."

Jason the performer answered, "That sounds good to me. I'll probably be the best at it." He smiled proudly. "I remember having read about this place—well, a long time ago but I have an elephant memory, so...be prepared to lose Kate and Cloe..."

Cloe cut him right away. "Do you want to keep score Kara" she said.

"All right," Kara answered.

"It's fine with me too but I would like to know what the winner gets for her or his expertise," Kate said.

Kara smiled largely, "Going to see the best show in Mexico City with me."

Everyone said, "That will be me."

Kara took fifteen minutes to write down the questions. Then, they walked on the site. Kara felt great—she was finally living her dream—she was there. Jason made them stop. He took his teacher voice and said, "Teotihuacan displayed the ruins of the largest and most important city in pre-Columbia Central Mexico. It was a major religious, political and commercial center that had been developed in the Valle de Mexico..."

Kate was making faces behind him. Cloe and Kara were sniggering.

Then, they stopped him. The girls told him that at least they already knew it about that ancient city.

With a grin on his face, he casually said, "I know I'm going to win."

In the middle of the complex of ruins, before they had a chance to check the signs, Kara made them stop. "What's the name of the avenue?"

"The Avenue of the Dead," they all said quickly at the same time.

They went on walking until they reached the great Pyramid of the Sun. Kara kept asking questions. They all tried to answer the best they could just by looking at the remnants. And Kara continued to mark points on her questionnaire sheet.

After it, they visited the large building known as the Citadel that contained impressive sculptures carved out of stone. They gazed at the murals of plants, animals and geographic features that decorated the wall of many of the surrounding structures.

"How about climbing one of the two pyramids?" Kate asked.

They all nodded and there they went. After that effort, they walked around the other. They all took pictures while Jason filmed them on the site for quite a while.

Finally, Kara counted the points and revealed that Kate had the best score and would get her reward as soon as they would be in Mexico City. They then met the archeologists on site and had lunch with them.

The archeologists answered all their questions. They were extremely nice and polite. The three young women knew that those men were flirting with them and let it be.

At the beginning, Jason left alone at the back seemed amused and watched the whole scene. However, the day after, he let them know that the game was over. The girls did not argue; they had enough too. It was time to hit the road again.

They spent two weeks in Mexico City, Kate and Kara rented a room in a hotel downtown while Jason and Cloe stayed on a campground—those two did not mind. From the RV site, they had choice between the bus shuttle to go visit the town or ride their bikes.

As soon as they arrived in the hotel room, Kara started checking all the film rolls and made her 'to do list" for the day.

Kate and Kara used often the metro during the week—they even mastered to get around town without problems. They visited the Country Capital, which was a modern and ancient city with many sights and sites to see. They learned that the city was built atop ruins of the once powerful Aztec city Tenochtitlan. The Aztecs had chosen that site on the island of Tlateloco in Lago de Texcoco for its defendable position but then Spanish explorer Hernan Cortez conquered it in 1521.

During the day, Kate walked with her camera and filmed many parts of the city. She loved the grand boulevards and big skyscrapers mixed with scattered narrow streets and colonial facades. Kara preferred to take shots of the city's centre, the expansive Plaza de la Constitucion, called the Zocalo, which at the beginning was the Aztec center of government and religion. Slowly, she savoured through the zoom lens the architecture of Mexico City. In the afternoon, on her way back to the hotel, she had again the feeling that someone was watching and following her. She decided to enter a store and checked it out—but the streets were so overcrowded with people, she finally gave up. She just stayed more cautious thereafter.

On the fifth day, they all regrouped in southeast of Mexico City to see the floating Gardens of Xochimilco.

Jason contemplating that extraordinary garden asked the girls to ponder over that ancient lake system. Then, he informed them. "The Aztecs and other peoples who built rafts on the lake created those floating gardens called chinampas. They covered them with soil and planted flowers and vegetables on them. Later on, the rafts became islands rooted to the bottom of the shallow lake. It created a network of waterway..."

Then, Cloe continued. She gave them a sense of history and put them in the context of the making of creation. Kara and Kate really enjoyed the experience of visualizing these people doing it.

After the flower-line canal, they went visiting the sixteenth-century Church of San Bernardino.

In the evening, Kara kept her promise and brought Kate to the best musical comedy in town. The losers went to see a movie.

Leaving town, Kara and her friends reflected on Mexico City. They agreed with the experts studying the city—the rapidly growing population had created severe housing, transportation, and air pollution problems with the time—the smog was really bad. Yet, they all survived through the days with good memories of their stay in one of the largest urban centers in the world.

Once again, they had no problem at the border when crossing for Guatemala. After changing some money for Guatemalan cash, they drove the Pan American Highway for a while and then took the little roads. They liked so much the country that they spent two months there. They rented motorcycles, sometimes scooters to ride around the area. Colourful walking rainbow women and smiling children filled up the air with just their joy of being. People were friendlier too, less aggressive in stores and in markets.

In Turicentro, they found a wonderful campground not far from Guatemala City, full of hook-ups, big swimming pool, Jacuzzi, wet sauna.

"What a luxury!" Kara marvelled.

They all nodded in awe to have found such a paradise. The view was fantastic—plenty of abundant and riche green hills getting along with dormant volcanic cones. A hidden active volcano spurted steam and smoke every ten to fifteen minutes. They learned that the volcano provided the thermal energy that heated the pools and saunas. They stayed there for quite a while before hitting the road again.

That day, they drove for hours. They finally stopped at Antigua. On the campground, they met many backpackers. Lost in the flower power, these young people delightfully refreshed their minds reminding the quartet that they too once were nice, cute and enthusiastic about changing the world.

Early in the morning, they went visiting the Caves of Languin. On the premises, the guide first gave them a good gas lantern and waterproof flashlights. He then talked to them about safety measures on the site. He explained that they would discover several large high domed caverns with many huge stalagmites and stalactites through the rocky pathway. As it could be very slippery, he warned them to be cautious while walking. At the last minute, two men and a woman joined the group. They introduced themselves quickly. The guide repeated his little speech and then the group entered the caves.

Kate was the first one to follow the guide behind, then Cloe, Jason, Kara, the woman and the two men. The caves were impressive and the natural ambiance terrific—everyone seemed to have gotten for their money. The guide was helpful and skilful; he knew his caves. At the end of the journey just before coming out, Kara stopped to look at the walls. She had seen something moving but when she turned on the flashlight on the spot, nothing. The woman and the man behind passing her asked if there was something wrong. She told them to go ahead—she would join them in a minute. However, the last man stopped and watched Kara checking with the flashlight everything on the wall and on the ground.

Surprised that he was still there, she turned the flashlight on him and said, "I was sure that I saw something...well...it seems to have vanished. I'd better go join the others."

The man blocked her passage. "You should give up what you've been looking for or else...it will kill you. You got it!" he said abruptly.

"What are you talking about and who are you?" she angrily asked.

"I am your dark side and let me tell you that you're very ugly," he answered back.

"Very funny," she replied, becoming very tense.

He laughed. He then punched her in the face and pushed her strongly on the wall—her head knocked forcefully the rock. The man watched her pass out—he then picked up her flashlight and gas lantern and ran away.

Although still very dizzy, she came back quickly to her senses and tried to assess the situation. This man is crazy, she thought. I'd better get out of here fast. Be cautious, he might still be around, hidden in a corner. As she couldn't find the flashlight either the gas lantern on the ground, she began moving forward in the dark very carefully. Then, she heard Kate calling her. Kara shouted out, "I'm over here."

A few minutes later, she saw the lanterns. Kate and the guide were coming toward her. "What happened?" Kate asked. Kara didn't answer. "We were waiting for you outside when we saw that guy running out. We asked him what was going on but he kept running, got in his car and disappeared. The guide and I thought we'd better check on you and here you are. Now, tell me what happened?"

Kara said, "I believe the man lost his mind—after punching me, he pushed me on the wall for no reason and...he laughed while doing it."

As soon as they came out, the group surrounded Kara. They all asked her the same question. The guide told them, "Just a minute, please." He looked at her eyes, then at the back of her head. He got out of his backpack a first aid kit box. He helped her to sit on a flat rock next to the cave entrance. He poured peroxide on the wound and dry it out with a cotton wool pad. "You're lucky, it's just a little bump and some scratches; nothing to be worried about," he said. "However, you'll have a black eye for a few days."

Kara looked at the woman and the man still there. "What's wrong with your friend?" she asked. "He's weird."

The pale woman answered, "Actually, my husband and I don't know this man. We have met him yesterday afternoon at the bar of our hotel. We talked about coming here—he seemed very interested and asked if he could join us. He looked all right...we did not see anything wrong with him. He came to pick us up at the hotel this morning." She took Kara's hand. "I'm so sorry about what happened."

Her husband said, "I cannot believe what he just did to you. We deeply apologize about that." Looking around, he added, "Now about this weirdo, I know for a fact that he's not living at our hotel. He told us that he had rented a house by the beach but I don't know where. At least, we know his name, Peter Henderson." Then he asked Kara, "Do you want to charge him for assault?"

Kara answered rapidly, "No, I don't. However, I have the feeling that Peter Henderson is not his real name. Anyway, I'm ok—he just pushed me but if I see him again, he'll have a piece of my mind, that...bastard."

The guide excused himself and went to his jeep to make some phone calls.

The couple looked miserable. The man told his wife that it was the last time he would trust a perfect stranger asking him for a favour. None would make a pass at him anymore. Hearing that, Jason told the couple that they should continue to trust people even if they had a bad experience. Kara added, "Trusting people is something we have to believe in. I know that we all have to be aware and concerned of new people we meet—however, that go to a certain degree...Listen, we all are on vacation here, why not enjoy the rest of the day. I'm just fine; don't worry about me."

The couple asked the guide if he could give them a lift to their hotel. He nodded.

Looking at the girls, Jason said, "We would be pleased to give you a ride if well...you trust us."

The couple laughed at the comment and accepted the offer.

The group was then in a better spirit and the guide, relieved. He signalled to the group, "First, I called the police and informed them about the incident. I told them everything I knew—I gave them the car mark and colour but unfortunately not the license plate numbers..." When a pickup truck arrived, he said more lightly, "The second call I made was to my sister, she has prepared something special for you—a little surprise in order to change the atmosphere. Don't forget that things were just fine at the beginning of the day and we're going to finish on the same note if you don't mind."

Smiling at them, his sister brought two big baskets full of Guatemalan food, fruits and drinks. She told them in English with a light accent, "Everyone must be hungry after a big day of walking and exploring the caves and a little bit more! So I brought you a little snack." They all sat on the ground. The woman looked at Kara. She picked up some ice cubes from the icebox, put it in a small towel and gave it to her.

"Thanks a lot," Kara said and put it on her eye.

They all appreciated the gesture and thanked the guide and her sister for their courtesy. Everyone was more comfortable. The guide let them know he had another surprise for them. At dusk, he led them to a place where they all sat on the ground to watch hundred of bats pouring out of nowhere looking for their evening meal. Everyone enjoyed the spectacle but Kara. She could not care less about the bats. She thought it reminded her of her dark side.

The day after, it was time for them to move on to El Salvador.

As soon as they crossed the border, they changed their money from one country to the other. The people, Los Salvadorenos were also friendly, helpful and pleasant waving and smiling as they drove by. When they arrived on the Northern beaches, it felt strange to them to walk on the beach made of black volcanic sand but they got used to it quickly and did not mind at all after a while.

They liked a lot the local cooking in El Salvador. They got lost on the road from time to time. However, comparing to other RV drivers, they were lucky in general to find rapidly their way back. Jason and Kara often thanked Cloe and Kate because they made sure they bought the right maps, large and detailed maps.

After assessing the situation in El Salvador, they decided that they would not go any further—the country highways had too many potholes and the RV could not take it any longer. They also saw too many civilian arm guards along the road—and it rang a bell. They voted and decided to go back to Mexico. After driving back hundreds of kilometres, they stopped first in Acapulco to spend the weekend.

On their way out, they visited other cave complexes. Kate in her element, tried to cheer up her companions when explaining how these waterfalls of frozen ice had been created over the years to form the coned shaped stalactites and stalagmites.

They finally told her that they all learned their lessons very well and thanked her adding that was all they could take. It was time to do something else. Back in Mazatlan, they took it easy—horse riding and playing golf were the activities of the day.

After eleven months of RV, it was time to go back home. They drove to USA with no regret—satisfied of their journey and aware of their smaller bank accounts.

CHAPTER SEVEN

THE RED FOREST

Back to California's North Coast Region, they camped in the Redwood National Park, home of the world's tallest trees. It was peaceful and the hiking trails were great.

Kara benefited from walking alone in the wood with her camera. She spent her time taking pictures of whatever presented itself to her—catching the light through the trees, birds on a branch or a deer running through the forest. That day, Kara mulled over the fact that they would be home soon. Before getting the blues, she joined the trio and talked about that.

On her request, the others began sharing about the ongoing vacation. They recalled the good time they had and discussed what was coming up right after the trip.

And then, Cloe started talking about their friendship. She declared that it would be eternal. Very touched by that comment, Kate, Kara and Jason raised their beers and made the promise to Cloe to continue to have that kind of respect and concern for one another as long as they lived.

Kara confessed that she never fully understood the reason why when the four of them met for the first time at the university; it clicked so deeply between them.

Together, they ignited that extraordinary sense of lightness, humour and sparkles that she never found with other friends. After thinking about their past, Cloe, Kate and Jason realized that they never experienced either that kind of good connection with their childhood friends or family members. They had good experiences too but never at that level.

After a while, Jason thought that it was enough and teased them, "Once again, you're becoming too emotional. Don't analyse it; just take it."

Cloe, following his advice, poured a full cold-water pail over him. "Cool off a little...and just take it," she said.

He went after her while Kate and Kara cheered up for Cloe.

After a copious meal, Kara prepared the fire camp. They sat around without a word as if they saw through the flames, the special closeness and authenticity they had developed when they were together. It was getting late—Kara got up and went to the RV. Jason, Cloe and Kate chose to sleep outside.

In the middle of the night, Kara began feeling sick. She wondered why—she felt so good a few hours before. She got up, took some aspirins and went back to bed. She started dreaming about an old woman...this one was sitting on a brown building porch...it looked like a kind of entrance to an old building...everything around was in a blurred brown colour, even the woman wore brown clothes from head to toes...the old woman was busy cutting some branches.

In her dream, Kara walked towards the building— she then could see better. On the second step, she saw an old brown kettle propped by a big rusty bucket upside down and bottomless which seemed to serve as a fire container—and she understood—the woman was feeding a fire in order to boil the water. She stopped and simply observed the woman. That one did not pay attention to her, focusing only on what she was doing. Kara got closer.

The woman looked up at her. "Be prepared for what's coming up," she said.

"For what?" Kara asked.

The woman ignored it and continued, "No, you cannot stop it. You cannot comprehend it at this moment. This event will make you very sad but you will eventually survive it. Don't blame yourself for it..."

It did not sound good to Kara, and she thought, they will get me right this time.

"Now listen very carefully to what I'm about to tell you. You cannot refuse it anymore. I repeat, you cannot refuse anymore the power given to you and by the way, this is not a dream—it's simply a different reality. My task is letting you know that you have a job to do—you know what it is. The Light be with you, Kara. See you later."

Kara opened her eyes and checked the time. It was eight in the morning. She heard Cloe and Kate talking outside. And then, she heard the light wind through the branches—and the birds singing a strange melody. She imagined what the lyrics were, "Life is a long dream, my friend. When you wake up, you understand that is all it was, a dream and then you forget, you go back to the illusion of earthly reality, and you never quite get out of that confusion. This reality mocks you my friend by sending you misleading messages but you're still dreaming. Wake up my friend." She thought that she was really confused that morning.

She had a shower and got dressed. She looked at herself in the mirror—I looked like I have a terrible hangover. Paying attention to her face, she thought, Vision or dream or parallel reality, I'm not the one you think I am. I would be the first one to know it, wouldn't I? So what's wrong with you people? I have no idea of what you're talking about. For God's sake, whoever you are, leave me alone. All right!

After massaging her face and looking at the results, she gave up. She went out. Her friends had already had breakfast—they observed Kara preparing hers.

"You look funny this morning Kara," Jason said. "Did you have a nightmare or did you cry all night—maybe you're still missing the Mexican guy. You know the one you ran away with for two days letting us in the dark with a little note, "I'll be back soon.""

"Ha-ha-ha...very funny but you're right Jason—I had a weird dream. That's all."

"Would you like to talk about it" Cloe asked. "You look terrible! You might feel better."

Kara agreed to share part of her dream. "You know, it's the kind of dream in which a perfect stranger is telling you not to blame yourself about what's going on around you but because you're the observer, you know perfectly well that you're the creator of that dream...I don't know what it means...May be, that has to do with returning home. Anyway, I'll have some adjusting to do when back in the real world. You see, vacation to me is living in a fantastic world but it's not the real one..."

Jason pointed out to Kara, "As soon as I have a dream I can remember, I'll ask you to interpret it for me. It seems that you don't need too much information in order to explain a dream. I'm sure Kara that your dreams had more details than you want us to know but that's all right. The truth is I...did not...get...it at all."

Kara stayed silent. Jason added, "But it's ok."

"I just want to forget about that. All right!" Kara replied and she changed the subject.

However, Kate came back to it, "I think Kara that you're a little hard on yourself. I see you as someone who can succeed at whatever she puts her mind to. Moreover, you're not alone; I'll be there for you if you need help."

"Thanks Kate. I know you will."

Jason and Cloe backed up Kate. Kara said, "Thanks guys. What are you going to do today?"

"I'm going fishing," Jason answered.

Cloe and Kate let her know they would go hiking.

"All right. I'll stay here and read a good book I started but never had time to finish," Kara said.

Around eleven o'clock, Jason left with his fishing rod. Five minutes later, Cloe and Kate were on their way and told Kara they should be back by six o'clock.

At seven, Jason came back to the campsite. Kara was feeling very uncomfortable. She checked her watch and informed Jason. "The girls were supposed to be back around six."

Jason tried to make her feel better. "Calm down Kara. They must have met people on their way and are still with them."

Kara didn't buy it. She walked around the campsite looking for them. She finally asked everyone on the site if they saw two women heading for the hiking trail or coming back from it. Three persons told her that they had met them in the wood in the afternoon but that was all. She told Jason about that. Together, they went to see the ranger. They explained to him that they were very concerned about their friends.

Two forest guides were in the office. After listening politely to Kara and Jason, the ranger wanted to talk privately to the guides. "Can you wait outside please; we will be shortly with you."

Five minutes later, the two guides asked Jason to walk the hiking trail with them. They mentioned that it would be easier for them if he could recognize anything they might have left behind on the road. It was getting dark. However, the guides were well equipped for the search; they had powerful flashlights and radio transmitters.

The ranger walked back to the campsite with Kara. He kept communicating with the guides by walkie-talkie. By midnight, having no news from the girls, they all knew something went terribly wrong. Therefore, the ranger called the police and then, some volunteers who knew very well the area. They showed up thirty minutes later.

First, they began searching on the campsite and then all around for clues. After that, they entered the wood. They walked in large formation wherever it was possible on both sides of the hiking trail, looking for any traces that Cloe and Kate could have left behind.

At seven in the morning, the number of volunteers got bigger. They were prepared to search the entire area. The police asked Kara to give them pictures of Cloe and Kate. Before leaving, the officer in charge told Kara to stay at the camp and to try to get some rest.

Jason came back exhausted and worried. Kara gave him some coffee and sat at his side. She tried to comfort him but was not successful at it. A wreck herself, she decided to go lie down in the RV. There, she tried to figure out what could have happened to them. Perhaps, they had a confrontation with a bear or perhaps, one of them lost footing on the trail causing her to slide down the hill—or fell down from the edge and the other one tried to help her and was pulled by the other. Those tormented thoughts went on and on until the tiredness of her body couldn't take it anymore—she fell asleep.

At four in the afternoon, two volunteers found their bodies fifteen miles away from the campsite. Both bodies had been mutilated. They would learn later that Kate had been raped and then murdered. Not far away, they found Cloe, also dead and covered with bruises all over her body. Two fingers were missing on her right hand.

A police car stopped by their campsite—two officers got off and gave them the terrible news. Kara and Jason were devastated, crying their hearts out. One of the officers asked them to follow him in order to identify the bodies. On the way to the morgue, he told them that they also found two men five miles away from the crime scene. One was dead, the other alive but in a terrible state. The officer added that those men could have been involved in the crime but they would have to investigate more deeply to know what really happened.

The day after, the FBI was on the case. They asked Kara and Jason lots of questions. They both answered the investigators everything they could. Cloe and Kate's parents arrived the same day, Jason's father got there in the evening. Kara chose to wait before calling home. The FBI asked everyone to stay near the police station for at least three days. They also asked Kara and Jason to be available on request, which they did. After four days, they released them with the advice to go home. They added they would contact them as soon as they had information. However, Kara, Jason and his father, Cloe and Kate's parents all chose to stay there until the truth came out.

The autopsy had been done on the two bodies—but there were many other tests to be conducted. The FBI needed further investigation.

A week after, the police released some information—apparently, the two men they found were from Texas and on vacation. They were in their late thirties. One of them had been discovered dead in his black pick-up truck in the middle of a logging road. The other one had been found fifty feet away from the road under a big tree, lying in a fetal position sucking his thumb—he was unable to speak or to move. They were not sure yet if the dead man killed himself or if the other one did it.

After investigating the past of those two men and doing all the tests, the police and the FBI concluded that the two men had killed the two women. Later on, the forensic evidence backed them up. Still speculating on the reason, they reported that it was likely a heinous act of random. However, they couldn't explain why a man died and the other, paralyzed in that bizarre position.

They assured the victims' families that the case was not closed for them. They would let them know of any new developments. Therefore, the best thing to do was then to go back home.

Cloe and Kate's parents made arrangements to bring back home the bodies. Jason and his father drove back the RV to BC. Kara flew to LA to be with her sister. They cried together. To them, it was the third nightmare of their lives. Their father and brothers were in constant communication with them over the phone. Morgan offered her all the support she could give.

Kara and Morgan flew back home to attend the funeral. Their whole family and Jason received them at the airport. Then, they drove to the church.

Back in her apartment, Candice offered Kara two choices. The first one was she could stay with her for a while if she didn't want to be alone. The second one was simply to move out if Kara wanted to be by herself. She had a friend who was looking for a roommate—so there was no problem. Kara let her know she would prefer to be alone. Candice respected her choice and moved out the day after.

Kara felt unsettled in her apartment for quite a while. Mitsou the cat was the only presence she could relate to. Running everywhere in a playful manner, the cat sometimes, succeeded to steal some smiles from her. This cat is a godsend, she thought. Kara did nothing for two months except going out to get some food for the cat and her. Jason often visited her. And slowly, Kara went back to work.

#

One day, two FBI agents showed up at Kara's door. She let them in. As soon as they sat down in the studio, they told her they wanted some answers to their questions. It seemed to her that that afternoon would never end. First, they were very interested to know if she had any idea or explanation about the man found in a fetal position, sucking his thumb. They informed her that after checking out with the RCMP, they discovered that in another case, the police had found a man in the same manner.

One of the agents looked directly in her eyes. "We find it strange that after making the connection with those two cases, it happened that you were very close to the people killed in both events," he said. "Don't you find it a big coincidence? Can you help us with that, please?"

Kara put all her courage together. "Unfortunately, I cannot help you with that. It's just a horrible coincidence. I told the police and the FBI agents before everything I could," she answered.

The other agent opened the file they had on Kara. He started reciting the facts the FBI knew. Then, he read aloud all the questions they asked her two months earlier and all the answers she gave them. Kara listened carefully and remained calm. He asked her if she would like to change her statement.

She waited a few minutes before talking. "No, I won't change my statement. I have either no explanation to offer about those cases. I'm myself amazed by that, and petrified by those terrible events. I thought about that for a long time and I cannot find any answers for it."

The first agent, who talked to her, watched her face when he pointed out that it was bizarre that the two men could not even express a sound. "According to doctors and psychiatrists, this kind of dysfunction has no name yet because...no one in the world had ever recorded a case like that. After performing many tests on both of them, doctors indicated that they have a normal and healthy organism; even their brains seem to operate normally." He paused and observed Kara. "In the medical world, that form of physical distortion would be the first one to be recorded. I'm asking you again...what kind of trauma could have caused them to stay in that vegetable state."

"For the last time, I don't know why they turned out that way. After all, I am not a doctor," she said. Then she suggested, "Those two men were probably mentally ill before committing such terrible crimes and therefore, strange things happened to strange people."

They continued to bombard her with questions and each time, she answered, "I have no idea; I don't know." But in her mind, something different was going on: you cannot confess to them what happened. They won't believe you anyway. They will put you away thinking you're insane and dangerous—drag you in an institution for mentally ill people. You'll finish your days there. Just keep telling them that it was an extraordinary coincidence and they'll give up on you.

After three intense hours, the two agents finally got up. They looked around checking the pictures on the wall. Before leaving, they informed her to contact them if she remembered any other facts concerning the two cases.

She closed the door, turned back and leaned on it for a few minutes. Then, with tears coming down her face, she walked directly to her bedroom. She felt down on her knees and once again, she asked the Universe to take her back.

"God, I cannot live like that anymore," she screamed. After raging for a while, she cried until she could not feel anything inside. The cat observed her distress with detachment. He knew that Kara would survive it.

CHAPTER EIGHT

THE BLUE BOOK

One day at a time, Kara slowly came back to life. Feeling better, she put all her energy in her work. It paid off. She became in demand as a freelance photographer.

Her family also played a role in her recovery. She often visited her dad and brothers on the island and her sister in LA.

She appreciated that her family never talked in her presence about the strange coincidence of the two deranged men, alive and still in that fetal position. Of course, her father once admitted to her that there was an astonishing connection between the two cases but denied any link with Kara. To him, his daughter was a survivor and nothing else. Kara was relieved—no need to justify herself anymore.

#

It took Kara two more years before being ready to see the Danish lady. Even if that woman was always at the back of her mind, she never let her have priority in her thoughts. The reason she wanted to see her was she had had a recurring dream every night during the week. In that dream, Mrs. Taylor smiled and said, "My dear friend, it is time to come to the store now. I have something for you."

With the years, Kara had learned not to deny those dreams anymore when they happened that way. The wise thing to do was to go see what they meant.

Kara tried to open the door but it was locked. She stepped back and looked through the window store to see if Mrs. Taylor was there. She saw a man busy at putting objects in a box. She decided to knock at the door. The man opened it. He asked her with a Danish accent, "Can I help you?"

"Yes you can...well...in fact; I was expecting to see Mrs. Taylor. Is she there?"

He did not answer the question. Instead, he asked, "Do you know her?"

"Yes, I do. Please, can you tell me where she is? I'd like to talk to her."

With a calm voice, he said, "She passed away a month ago."

Kara looked so pale that the man invited her to come in and sit down. After choosing the old chair Mrs Taylor used to sit down, she introduced herself. "My name is Kara Lewis. I was simply an acquaintance, a client but I used to have tea and good conversation with Mrs. Taylor. I went away for a long period. So this morning, I decided that it was time to see her again but unfortunately...it's too late. Do you know what happened to her?"

"She died naturally in her sleep. The doctor told me that she did not suffer at all. Old age was actually the only reason of her death."

The man presented his hand and said, "Let me introduce myself. I am Neil Mayhagen, her nephew. I've been here to close the store and take care of whatever that needs to be done. I really loved my aunt Angela. She was cool and funny, maybe a little eccentric but that just added to her charm. Everyone who knew her loved her. She will be missed by all her nieces and nephews."

Kara acknowledged. "Mrs. Taylor often talked to me about all her lovely nieces and nephews when having tea or coffee with me. It's nice to hear that it is reciprocal."

Neil stared at her. He suddenly said, "Wait a minute, you told me that your name is Kara Lewis. It reminds me that I have something to give you. Three days ago, I went through her desk at the back, and I found a big envelope with a note on it saying: If Kara Lewis does not come this week, send it to her. The envelope was addressed to you. That's a good thing you're here; no need to send it now."

He immediately went to the back and reappeared with a large blue envelope. He read the address aloud and asked her, "Do you still live there" Kara nodded. He added, "She must have known you would be coming around that time because the date on the note is exactly today! It is strange that she put a note on it. Well...Aunt Angela's memory was probably failing her those last days.

Kara rose up and took the envelope. "Mrs. Taylor was a very special woman. She always seemed to know things about people before they even did," she said with a low voice.

Neil laughed. He agreed with her. "I have to confess that sometimes she scared me with her special abilities to foretell but on the other hand, she was so lovely in doing so that I forgave and forgot easily about that. I must admit though that I still have a hard time to believe in that kind of power or ESP skills." He went behind the counter and brought back some pictures of Mrs. Taylor in her forties. "She was still a beauty at that age...beautiful... and her blue eyes, so intense..."

Giving her the pictures, he continued. "To come back to the ESP skills, I would rather consider my aunt as a remarkable observer of life—she could easily measure the strength and weakness of human being. But that's true...she had an extraordinary capability to see through you, the same thing with an object." He stopped. "I must bore you."

"No...No, continue please," Kara said.

"My aunt was an avid reader of history under all its forms. I saw her more than once sitting in front of an old object—and just by looking at it or touching it, she would tell us its history, its use, the people that made it and those who used it. As I was studying history at the university at that time, I had fun to do some research and check if she was right and each time she was..."

Kara gave him back the pictures. He had a last look at them and then said, "I can give you another example of her so-called powers. As you know, my cousins and I were often at her house on weekends during our childhood. Sometimes, it happened that someone broke something—it could be a glass, a vase, whatever. I remember very clearly that if my aunt was not present when that took place; she would come in, looked at the broken object and tell us who did it, how he or she did it and why. She never reprimanded us but gently and firmly told us to pay attention to what we were doing... my aunt always mesmerized me with her extraordinary sense of observation."

Lost in his memories for a few minutes, he came back with a smile on his face and recognized, "Well, I realize that I keep you—you must have better things to do than listening to a family story of people you don't even know."

Kara replied quickly, "On the contrary, I found it very interesting." As she was not in a hurry, she asked him if she could have a last look at things in the store before leaving.

"Please feel free to do so."

He looked around him and added, "I'd better go back to work; there's still a lot to do here."

Twenty minutes later, seeing how much work Neil had to accomplish about trying to clear up all those books, objects and other things, Kara offered him some help. He accepted with relief.

"That would be nice. I got lots of boxes to pack up. Fortunately, someone who knew my aunt bought everything she had. He will pick it up in two days. So I think I'll be ready to leave next week."

They worked all afternoon. Tired, Neil stopped and sat down. "Okay Kara. Thank you for your help. You did enough. You must be hungry by now..."

They went to a small restaurant not far away. After dinner, Neil asked Kara if she wanted to see his Aunt Angela's suite.

"It would be great!" she answered immediately.

Delighted by the idea of seeing it, she followed him with the blue envelope under her right arm.

When she entered, Kara was not surprised. It was a replica of Mrs. Taylor's store—a collection of heterogeneous art objects coming from different countries, some of them dating from seven hundred years or more. The only difference with the store was the order and harmony in the display—a strange symphony of art.

Neil offered a drink to Kara. He then showed her the rest of the six-room suite. In the living room, Kara went to have a look at the bookshelves. She took at random a book from it. Neil came closer and looked at the book still in its case.

"I recognize this blue book and the case." He smiled. "I think Aunt Angela would have liked you to have this book. Please, keep it and take the time to read it. I remember...one day, I asked her what this book was about. She answered that it was a book about women— a tribute to all goddesses, prophets, priestesses, witches and ordinary women like her. Noticing my curiosity, she told me, "My young man, this book is about women who know who they are and where they are going. However, this book can be understood just by the wise one; the one who knows." She got my interest there. I begged her to let me read it, telling her that I wanted to know what women want in life." He laughed. "You see, I was sixteen years old at the time, naive and very attracted by the opposite sex. I thought that I would know about their most intimate secrets—that sounded exciting enough to me."

"And..." Kara said candidly. "I want to know." She smiled.

"Well, I thought that I was very smart. I started reading it, trying to understand what they were talking about. I finally lost interest at the fifth chapter and gave it back to her. In fact, I was ashamed of my ignorance about how women looked at life. But...but just for saving the face, I told her that I gave up reading it because I assumed that was girl stuff and therefore not very serious. That's how stupid I was thinking at that age. Aunt Angela took the book back and smiling at me replied that it was the first and last chance I got if...My aunt couldn't finish her sentence because she was laughing too hard. Seeing her react to it that way, I laughed too, though uncertain if she laughed at my stupid comment or simply at the ignorant young man before her who had no clue about life and its mysteries."

They sat on the couch. Kara asked, "What are you going to do with this suite? All the paintings, books and the rest..."

"Well, it will be taken by the same man who bought everything in the store. His wife and he have a big antique store downtown. My aunt had already made all the arrangements with him six months ago. I guess she knew...Would you like some coffee?"

She followed him to the kitchen. "Can you tell me more about Mrs. Taylor?" Kara asked. "How would you describe her? I mean...at home with you." She listened with deep interest. She discovered she was not only nice to her relatives but also to total strangers like her. Kara felt guilty about having waited so long before deciding to see her. That woman was damn right about many things concerning her life. And sitting there with a cup of coffee, she thought that it was the 'rendez-vous manqué.'

It was raining; Neil called her a taxi. She thanked him for his time, kindness and the book. Then, she gave him her phone number and address. "Just in case you feel like dropping by before leaving for Denmark."

Mitsou greeted Kara when she opened the door. She gave her some dry food and fresh water. It was late— she left the envelope and the book on the kitchen table and went to bed. She had a last thought for Mrs. Taylor, and with tears in her eyes, she fell asleep.

In the morning, she woke up with the cat on her stomach. As soon as she opened her eyes, she saw two little wild black bars facing her. The Mitsou morning game—Surprise! Surprise! I got you again. Get up, feed me and play with me lazy girl. Kara smiled. She liked so much that fur ball—always ready to give freely love and energy.

After feeding the cat, she went to have a bubble bath. Later on, Mitsou joined her. She sat on the toilet coverlid next to the bathtub and watched every move that Kara was making under the bubbles with her hands and feet.

"Let's the game begin," Kara joyously said. She threw at Mitsou bubbles of soapy water. Surprised, insulted, and amused at the same time, the cat ran out as fast as she could to come back in the same speed. Kara did the same thing again. That went up four more times.

The scene was hilarious. "Time to stop that nonsense before killing yourself, little brat," she warned the cat. However, Mitsou came back so fast that time that she misjudged her manoeuvre, jumped on the edge of the tub and dove right in the water. She got out very fast, landed on the bathmat, shook herself and gave a hard look to her master. Kara laughed deliriously. Getting out of the tub, she started singing, "I got you little lioness. That was my turn and I did it very well..." Mitsou could not take it anymore. Defeated, she went to hide behind the couch and dried off her misfortune.

With a cup of coffee, she sat at the kitchen table. For a few minutes, she stared at the blue envelope next to the bookcase. She finally took the envelope and read the note on it. Then, she weighed it in her hand, turned it back and opened it. She found two blue handwritten pages plus a smaller blue envelope. She murmured, "I suppose that Mrs. Taylor liked the blue color. I do remember that each time I visited her –she always wore blue clothes—maybe different tones, nuances and styles but always blue. Even her big chair was blue. Well, she honoured that color anyway. She read the letter. And then she reread it over and over again.

Mitsou showed up in the kitchen, all dry. She jumped on the table and sat there. She looked at Kara's eyes and then at the blue letter. Kara's face was so serious and grave that the cat took a solemn posture— she wanted to share that precious moment with her lovely roommate.

In that letter, Mrs. Taylor went right to the point.
Dear Kara,

I will be gone when you read this letter. Do not be upset, nor sad; just remember and cherish the good moments we had spent together. I know that it has taken you a lot of courage to go through all these ordeals without losing your mind. "WE" had to put you to the test. I wrote "WE" because I had not been alone in having interest in you. We had been watching your every move, even sometimes thoughts when you allowed us to sink into your spirit.

Kara, read the book you have taken from my suite with an open mind (I know I surprise you again). Do not judge, just think. Practise thinking and think again about everything you have done since you were brought on this earth. I declare that from now on you will not run away from your past anymore.

Remember the people you have met, the things you have done for other people and for yourself. The thoughts you had when doing it. Look at your dark side before the bright one. It's very important to do it in that order because light comes from the dark.

Life and the Universe are more powerful than your six senses can reveal to you. You already had that experience when you looked at yourself in the 'special' mirror for the first time, remember! Later on, you have contemplated that power in your dreams—then, in real life events. Unfortunately, you have denied it because you were too afraid of that powerful force.

I simplify a lot here for you in order to begin understanding that you cannot deny it anymore. You always knew it but tried to disconnect from it. The more you refused it, the more the Universe forced you to take it back. You see Kara this power is like your past—it belongs to you and only you.

About this power now, it can help you to know that "We" do not want you to save the world and you will not be a martyr either BUT YOU WILL HAVE A JOB TO DO and you must be prepared for it. Read the blue book until every word and sentence is part of every cell of your body. That will be a good beginning.

Concerning the smaller blue envelope, you must wait before opening it. YOU WILL DO IT ON YOUR

FORTIETH BIRTHDAY. Then you will start operating at full speed. Meanwhile, enjoy your reading and your life. You know deep inside that the life you received is not there for you to struggle with it. Life is given to us for the purpose of being celebrated. However, there are people on this earth who disagree with it. Your soul will guide you—contact it for further information.
Love to you Kara,
Angela Taylor, your Danish Lady

Kara finally put the letter on the table and tried to relax by saying, "I'm thirty-four, so it means that I have six years left to fool around before...going to no woman's land...interesting..." She stopped there; she knew.

On that same day, she began reading slowly the blue book. After two chapters, she was impressed by its philosophical tone. I'm glad that this book is not a form of religious obsession written for those spiritually overdosed or mentally constipated, she thought.

The phone rang and she got up to answer it. After introducing himself, the man told her that he got her phone number from a good friend of his. He then let her know that he heard about her work and would be interested to meet her if she was available. He explained that he wanted to sell his house, the furniture etc...Therefore, he would like her to come and take some pictures of his house to show its best assets. He added sighing that he was a very busy man and wished she could come that day if it was possible.

Kara asked him some questions relating to the house. She decided to go for it. They made an appointment for two o'clock in the afternoon.

She drove in a very nice area. The autumnal light seemed to enhance the splendour and authenticity of the big old houses, tall trees and magnificent gardens. She had a last look at the address.

At the gate, she saw a camera installed on the left side with an intercom. She pushed the button, and the voice asked her who she was. She introduced herself and the gate opened. After parking the car in the driveway, she took a few minutes to check the exterior of the house. Big and loveable, she thought. She walked to the entrance and rang the doorbell.

A man in his early forties opened the door and welcomed her. After helping her to take off her jacket, he introduced himself again. His name was Kevin Conte. He was slender and tall with very short grey hair and green eyes. A handsome man, she thought, he has a smiling face, charming. I like that. He asked her to follow him—he wanted to show her different rooms of the house.

After seeing the second floor, they came back downstairs. Kevin smiled. "What do you think about it?"

She smiled back. She looked around. "What a lovely house you have and you want to get rid of it!"

He sighed. "Well, I already own too many places. I realize that keeping track of all the things I need to do in order to maintain them is a full time job by itself. And time...I have no more."

At that moment, Kara could not understand why he called her. He sounded as he could afford the best professional photographer of the world.

"Of course, I had people who did take care of this house and the other ones but the day I got serious and checked how much money I was spending on it—I knew I was losing too much for the time spent in each place. So this month, I decided to keep up the ones I really like to live in and sell the rest of them."

Kara kept staring at him. <u>I cannot understand why he chose me for taking the pictures of this beautiful house,</u> she was still thinking.

He seemed reading her thoughts and added right away, "You must be wondering why I did choose you to do it. First, I have to say that the fellow that referred you is an old childhood friend who has eye for talented people. He urged me to call you and give it a try to see firsthand what you are capable of doing with a camera. Second, I like to give a chance to new talents..." He started chuckling, then he continued, "But what convinced me the most to contact you is...well...my friend showed me the pictures you took of him and his dog. You have succeeded to make him and his ugly dog look so good on these pictures. So it means to me...that you could make believe anything to people and therefore sell everything with your pictures."

He paused. And with a large smile, he added, "Selling dreams to people is what I do for a living. Now you know. Would you like something to drink?'

Not knowing what to say, she answered, "A coffee would be great."

She followed him to the kitchen. While Kevin was preparing the coffee, Kara couldn't stop thinking at what he said. She didn't know if he was serious or just joking around about his friend's pictures. So she hid her embarrassment. Kara had learned that surprise played a big role in her life and had to get used to it. The little voice inside whispered, <u>what the heck! Go for it.</u>

"Do you have any questions about the house?" Kevin asked.

She knew she had to say something. So she asked him awkwardly, "Why did you buy this house in the first place?"

He put her cup of coffee on the counter and then, took an innocent look. He admitted like a little boy he had to live somewhere when doing business in the city. They both laughed.

After the coffee, she let him know, "I don't know if I can meet your expectations but I'll give it a try and—we'll see. I have my cameras in my car. The light outside is perfect to take pictures of the house's exterior. So if you don't mind, I'll start right away."

"Fine with me," he said.

She went out and took two cameras with her. After taking several shots from different angles of every side of the house, she came back in and checked again every room. Then, she joined Kevin in the living room—he was leafing through a designing home magazine. He invited her to sit down.

Looking at the magazine he had in his hands, she pointed out. "The people that took those pictures would certainly do a better job than I would."

He shook his head. "I already pay them too much for the results sometimes," he replied.

She was stunned. "There's a question I usually don't like to ask when I first meet someone for the first time but this time I will. Can you tell me what on earth do you do for a living?"

He smiled. "I wear many hats Kara. First, I'm a businessman, a publisher of different newspapers and magazines. For example, the one I hold in my hand is one of them. I'm also an art collector, a mountain climber and bla-bla-bla...Let's say that I like to explore many sides of life as I go around on the planet. Enough of me, what about you Kara?"

She wished to talk about anything else but her at that moment. So she simply informed him that after the university, she worked as a counsellor in the social work, and then decided to do something else with her life. Therefore, shortly after, she attended a photography course and discovered that she really liked it. Since that, all she wanted was to make a decent living doing it and that's all she could say about her.

Kevin noticed that Kara looked uneasy. "Thank you Kara, I would like to know more about you but I guess that's all I'll get today. That's all right; I respect it."

She was surprised by his comment but remained silent. Kevin realized that he went too far, he tried to correct it.

"Did you take all the pictures you wanted?" he asked.

She answered positively. And looking around, she added, "Now...about the interior of the house, I would prefer to take them in the morning—the light would be better."

He nodded.

"Will tomorrow be a good day for you? If it's a sunny day, of course," she asked.

He got his agenda and opened it. "Tomorrow is Friday. Sorry, I can't. I could leave you the keys but while you were outside, I looked everywhere for the second set and couldn't find them. I have to leave early tomorrow morning. May I ask you if Saturday morning would be ok with you? At the same time..."

Kara saw that he suddenly looked shy.

With a stuttering voice, he continued. "Heu...I mean...Well, would you be interested to have breakfast with me on Saturday morning? I would make it myself..."

He behaved so odd that Kara mischievously cut him. "With pleasure, if it's sunny of course," she answered.

He seemed relieved.

Then, he let her know that he would be in town for only a month. So he would appreciate to have the pictures of the house as soon as possible. Kara nodded. She put her small jacket on and walked to the door. She could feel his eyes looking at her body. She turned very fast to get his last look, which seemed to have stopped at her butt. <u>Got you,</u> she thought. They shook hands and she left.

On the porch, Kevin watched her driving away. He began whistling and then put his left hand in his pocket where he could touch the second set of keys.

Kara stopped by the mall to do some grocery and errands. On her way back to the car in the parking lot, she unexpectedly met the client who referred her to Kevin Conte. The man got out of his car. His eyes brightened as soon as he saw her. "What a coincidence it is! I was just talking to Kevin about you on my car phone. He told me that he met you and there you are."

"Yes, I did," she replied. "Well, thank you for this new contact. I just hope the results will satisfy your friend. Can I ask you why you thought about me when you already know that this man could have his own staff doing it for him in a more professional way? Please, explain it to me—I must say that I'm baffled by this one."

He didn't say a word. He smiled instead.

Kara put the bags on the ground. She crossed her arms while waiting for an answer. His face became serious but she knew he was faking it—he liked to tease. His name was Don Robert; he was a tall person with a big stature. Although, the same age than Kevin Conte, he looked older.

Finally, the man said straightforwardly, "I know what you did for the dog and me. No one could have done it nicer than you did. You're already a pro as far as I'm concerned. Moreover, I like what you do. My friend was looking for a new talented photographer and I thought about you. That's all."

His dog was barking in the car. While opening the door, he continued, "Kevin and I have grown up together in Italy—our families were very close friends.

He is now a successful businessman. Kevin is always in search of new talents and new things to do. He's also a very nice person—no matter how busy he is, we manage to stay in touch and this time, he asked me if I knew a good photographer in town. I showed him the best samples I had...Well, something like that."

He stopped talking and put a leash around the dog neck. Then, he added, "Kevin became quickly a very rich man in the publishing business. All those years, I have checked all the magazines published by his firm. It's wonderful to see what they could do with a picture. Now, to come back to your first question, I saw your work displayed on the walls when I went to your studio. I was amazed by the diversity of your pictures: nature, people faces, animals, products, advertising...And then, the miracle happened, you took a picture of my dog and me." He laughed. "When Kevin saw it, he was so taken aback that he asked me immediately, "I want to see that person, she succeeded to make you look good, man! She is a magician and I want to know her." Now Kara, you know the real reason he wanted you to take some shots of his house."

She just nodded.

Don Robert continued. "By the way, I let him know that you were not the type of person that would beg in order to earn a living as a photographer. However, if you are interested to work for a big firm, Kevin would be the right person for you. He would open doors for you Kara."

She answered back, "It could be very interesting. I'll think about it...I have to go now. Well, thank you for thinking of me." She stroked the dog, shook his hand and left.

Alone in the parking lot, Don Robert thought that Kara was a very special woman. However, he sighed admitting he was not her type but secretly hoped that Kevin was not either.

After dinner, she walked to the studio with a glass of white wine in her hand. She looked at the man and dog's pictures on the wall. She thought that they were hilariously funny, delightful and real at the same time. "I did a very good job, yes! Now, would I be able to meet the challenge? That's true—we didn't talk about money yet," she said to herself. "This is an important issue—money. How could I forget to talk about that? He's going to think that I'm not business-oriented, just a dumb photographer."

She sat on the couch, picked up the first magazine on the pile that was on the floor. She checked the second page where the publisher's name was—Kevin Conte's name was on it. She looked at the pictures very carefully—they were beautiful. These two men are crazy, she thought. I will never be able to compete with these shots. Anyway, I hate competition with a passion but on the other hand, I swear to myself that I'll make a decent living of it. Nothing will stop me!

She grabbed the address phone book and called a friend of a friend who had just started in the publishing business. Kara explained to her what she did and went to the point without mentioning Kevin Conte's business name. The woman gave her a rate and Kara satisfied, thanked her for the information and hung up with contentment.

After having a shower, she looked at her naked body in the mirror. She whispered to Mitsou who was observing her, "What do you think? Does it want to test my photographic talents or my bum?" The cat couldn't care less and walked away from the bathroom. She mumbled alone, "Well, just do your job the best you can girl."

That thought drifted away, and she surprised herself thinking, is he married? He's got everything for him: old pal's network, power, fame, health and money. Women must gravitate around him like flies. Hey! Kara, what's wrong with you? Remember...you gave up on that kind of relationship a long time ago. At that moment, she tried to memorize all the guys she went out with. Bad memories and broken hearts came back to trouble her again—those relationships were filled with lies, cheating and loud arguments. There were times when no words were spoken—however, feelings of heavy dullness were worse than shouting or crying. She concluded that she had tried very hard but Mr. Wrong appeared too many times disguised in Mr. Right. Freedom and peace of mind seemed more appealing to her. In case of a biological need, a nightstand could suit her very well. Before sleeping, she read another chapter of the blue book. When closing her eyes, she entered almost immediately the dreamy world.

She woke up early that Saturday morning. She opened the back kitchen door and looked outside. The sky was blue. She sang to herself that it would be a lovely day in Paradise. At eight o'clock, Kevin called her. She told him she would be there in twenty minutes.

He sounded once again embarrassed but happy at the same time. This guy is very shy with women or perhaps, he has a wife or girlfriend and feels guilty for having me for breakfast. Don't worry about it, little boy, I will do my job and bye-bye, she thought.

After breakfast, Kara and he became more relaxed. She told him that she really appreciated his culinary talents.

They talked about art, books and films for a while. Then, she checked the time. She got up and smiled. "Well, by the time you will be done with the cleaning in the kitchen, I'll be ready to take some shots at it." She left and went upstairs with three cameras.

While washing the pots, Kevin thought, <u>an independent girl—with dark eyes—they looked fierce sometimes. Perhaps, she had a troubled childhood or simply because she had worked with difficult people as a counsellor, who knows! All I know is she doesn't like to talk about herself but on the other hand, I kind of like it. It's refreshing. Everyone thinks he is so important including me. I could use more of her wisdom in my way of dealing with people. She is also very attractive and appears not worry about that either. In fact, she looks real and I like it a lot. I wish I could spend more time with her this month.</u>

Kevin had been so busy with his life lately—he had no more time to date women. But he recalled having gone out with lots of women when days were less frazzled. He smiled at that thought. He knew that nice collection of beautiful women at his side in the limelight proved only to his peers and to the business world that he had made his place in the high society.

However, life had another meaning since he had succeeded at all levels. He did not need to show off anymore. Being wealthy was the passport to enter the financial circle and his two feet were solidly ingrained in the circus for the past five years. To him, the word rich meant that he could afford many things without having a feeling of deprivation. That was the only good thing about having money.

Kevin Conte was a lucky and determined man. His motto was a credo of being at the right place at the right time with the right people and doing the right thing in order to get what he wanted and what he wanted, he needed it and would have it.

Kara appeared in the kitchen and took a picture of him by surprise. He was giving a last touch at his spotless kitchen—still wearing his apron.

A little disconcerted at first, his sharp sense of humour came back fast. With a high pitch voice, he said, "First, you should not take a picture of me when I'm not ready for it and second, my hair is all messed up." Passing a hand on his short hair, he added, "Oh! No. I forgot to put my wig on this morning! Really, I cannot win with you."

Kara decided to go with the music. She shook her head. "I took this shot to prove to other women that Mr. Right exists..." she responded. She started giggling. However, she knew she had just showed up her colours and tried to fix it up by adding something silly but unfortunately, it didn't work. Busted, she thought.

That gave ammunition to Kevin. He replied right away, "I would like you to tell me what your definition of Mr. Right is?"

"Well, I didn't have time to think about that yet. It's just a lousy expression—it seems very popular these days. That's all."

Kevin didn't push any further. He changed quickly the subject. "Are you going to take some pictures of the kitchen now"?

"Yes I am."

She took five different shots and that was it. The phone rang and he answered. Kara checked all her cameras and equipment. Seeing that she wanted to leave, he stopped talking and let her know that he would be with her shortly after. He resumed his conversation rapidly and joined Kara in the hall who was looking at the beautiful paintings on the wall.

"Sorry about that. I think it's time we talked about money now. Isn't it?"

"Yes, it is," she said. "But first, let me develop all the pictures, and after revising my work, I'll give you a price. It's that makes sense to you?"

"Fine with me. When would that be ready?"

"Give me three days. I'll call you at your home or office; whatever..."

Kevin gave her his business card with a phone number at the back and told her she could reach him at this number at all time. "Please, use only this one when you call me."

She acquiesced. "All right then, see you later." She shook his hand and left.

Days later, Kara was happy with the results of the pictures. She thought they looked as professional as the ones found in magazines. She concluded, "Good enough for me. If he doesn't like them; just too bad for him."

Dave was in town and paid her a visit. They sat in the kitchen and had a cup of coffee. After it, she took his hand and brought him to the studio. She asked him to have a good look at the pictures and let her know what he thought. "This is a very nice house with a lot of cachet and charm," he commented. "I didn't know you were exploring the real estate field sister. Well, if so...Let me tell you that these pictures should rather belong to a designer home magazine."

Delighted, Kara shouted, "You hit the spot Dave. I like the idea of designer home magazine; however, they will instead end their days in a real estate office somewhere..." After explaining to Dave the contract she got and with whom, she admitted that the only thing she had to figure out then was the price she should charge him.

She told him the price. "What do you think? Well, you look surprised. Nevertheless, I feel confident that the price is fair; I made some phone calls before and..."

"I guess you're right," Dave said. He gave her a kiss. "Hey sister! I'm proud of you and I hope this will open another door for you. After all, making a living at what you like to do is something you have always believed in." He took her hands. "Listen, I'm in town for business. I'm free for the evening. Would you like to eat something somewhere with me?"

They dined in an Italian restaurant. Dave talked about his girlfriend, the family and the children he would like to have some days. He then asked her about her projects in the near future. He listened with interest. She looks better, she looks good, he thought. The sadness in her face seemed to have faded a little bit with the time. Then, they talked about what was going on in town. An hour later, Dave went back to his hotel and Kara to her apartment.

The following morning, Kara called Kevin Conte on his personal phone letting him know that the pictures were ready. He asked her if he could drop by her place in the evening. She gave him the address while looking around her. After hanging up, she had a consciousness attack and screamed, "What a mess!" She picked up what she could to put the place in order. After it, she ran to her afternoon business appointment.

At eight o'clock, Kevin showed up at the door. She welcomed him and put his coat on a hanger in the closet. She then invited him to follow her in the studio. He glanced around discreetly but carefully. To him, the place looked colourful but not blatant—instead, it was simple and alive.

He knew that Kara needed money to go on with her business; therefore, he decided not to be a shark that time—that time, he would be more interested in her dealing skills. After reviewing the pictures, Kevin was impressed with her work. "I'd like to know exactly how many years of experience do you have in the photographic business?" he asked.

Kara took her time before answering. She looked right in his eyes and with a smile on her face, said, "Enough to know how much it is worth," and then told him the price.

Smiling back, he replied, "I think you've done your homework before telling me your pricing. I admit it's a fair game." He checked again the pictures, "Well, I'm very satisfied with the results. Okay. I'll bring them with me tonight. I want to show them to some of my people downtown tomorrow."

Kara went to get a big envelope, put the pictures in it and gave it to him. He asked her if he could pay with a cheque.

"No problem," she said.

He immediately wrote down a cheque. Kara took it and read it. She looked surprised.

"There's a mistake."

"I just want to thank you for a job well done. Please...take it that way."

She thanked him and put the cheque on the desk. They stayed silent for a moment. Not knowing what to do, Kevin went to have a look at the pictures on the walls. After it, he turned around and said, "I'd better go. Thanks again for the pictures and your time. It was a pleasure to do business with you."

She nodded.

Just before opening the door, Kara suggested, "I know you're a busy man but if you're not in a hurry, would you like a drink?"

Again, he looked pleased and shy at the same time. He stammered, "If you have no plans for the evening...particularly with this nice jazz music in the background...it's very inviting. I accept with pleasure."

She offered him a glass of scotch. She thought that they were both interested to know more about each other. However, she was not sure of the parts, the brain or the body. She would know soon.

Before leaving, Kevin asked, "It sounds a little awkward but do you mind if I call you for going out? I still have three more weeks in town and I...I really enjoy your presence."

"It'll be a pleasure Kevin."

He looked relieved. He went out and disappeared in the darkness of the night.

The last thought Kara had on mind before sleeping that night was about the song "Taking a chance on love."

CHAPTER NINE

BETWEEN THE LINES

Kara had a good time with Kevin Conte. However, she wondered why they did not get physically involved. To her, he was certainly a very attractive man but she guessed that the chemistry was not there. On the other hand, she really liked his witty side—they laughed a lot together in those past weeks. Then, she contradicted herself once again; it would be nice to have sex with him—no, no, no—I'd better take it slowly. We'll see.

She asked herself out loud, "Am I getting smarter or wiser with the time or am I too sick and tired of the same tragico-comedy soap opera? Then she thought, act one, meeting the guy—act two, getting to know him—act three, having sex with him—act four, we are so different, it won't work—act five, dumping him before being dumped and act six, meeting another guy to forget the last jerk.

She ended up laughing and then, thought about her dear lost friend Cloe. She would add to back her up, "Don't try to change a man; it is a lost cause. You'd better change completely for another one instead. It is simpler, easier, and more efficient that way!"

Nevertheless, Kara was getting tired of the same scenario. It is like a bad habit you want to get rid of. And looking at her reflection in the studio mirror, she added, you know it does not do any good anymore—but you're in denial—and you hope it will give you the same pleasure you had the first time you tried it. Unfortunately, it always fails and you keep repeating it until it hurts so much—Oh! That's true—your pain always liberates you of yourself. She pulled the tongue. I'm sick.

That night, she went to bed continuing her inner monologue in her sleep. She reached the state of dream. She saw on a big screen a blurred reddish silhouette enveloped by a golden light. The entity asked her physical body, "What would you choose to experience from now on, pain or freedom? The answer to it is in the second part of your training. Observe your mind. Do not judge or hate—you will get stuck if you do. You know damn well that a love relationship is not necessary in order to define yourself anymore. Love is good but it takes two to tango. Kara, it's time to get used to your new you."

The picture on the screen vanished to give place to a voice talking softly, "After becoming more comfortable with the stranger in you, invite her to stay as long as she wishes. She will bring you the sacred gifts and start refurnishing your empty mental house with real things like peace of mind, wisdom and freedom. After unveiling her, you will discover that she is the light of your heart demanding you to treat it fairly. We know that you like fairness...When will you start doing it to yourself?"

In the morning, before going to work, she read another chapter of the blue book. She found it odd that the words written in it, although presented in a different way spoke the same language to her than the dream she had. However, those words were clearer and deeper in meaning—no one could miss the point. She understood. Those women involved in that book went through hard times and came back on their feet with a different approach of life. After meditating on that, she had breakfast and went to work.

That was the last evening of Kevin in town—he would be flying the day after to London for another three month and then, come back to Vancouver to close the deal of the house. He got the price he asked for and had no reason to stay there any longer. He invited Kara at his home that night. They had a nice dinner but did not talk too much during the meal.

After it, he invited her to sit in the living room. He let her know he had something important in mind. He offered her another glass of wine. Then, he walked back and forth in the room without a word and finally sat down. "Would you be interested to work for me as a free lance photographer?" he asked her.

"Well..." She took a sip of wine.

Kevin said quickly, "Before answering, let me explain what this work would demand from you. At times, you could be going to London, Paris, New York, LA, Tokyo or Hong Kong—of course, all business expenses included with the air flight tickets, hotels etc..." He paused. "You will also work closely with me on some projects..." He stopped talking and looked at Kara very seriously. "What do you think about that?"

Kara expected that he would ask her about doing some contracts for him in the city but no more than that. She had prepared herself mentally for the first proposition but not for that one. Then, she realized that Kevin was death serious about the offer. Still overwhelmed by the idea of working for him in London—she drank off her glass. A dialogue went on in her mind, think about that, travelling everywhere in the world—oh, my God! it sounds surreal. Look at the big picture. Remember, you have dreamed about that kind of life since you were a little girl and at this moment, someone is offering that opportunity to you, grab it! I will, I am...

She got up and walked toward the bar collecting her thoughts as quick as she could. She turned and leaned back against the counter. "I accept at one condition—as soon as you'll have some work for me to do, I'll do the job—see how it goes and after it, if we are still both interested to continue working together; fine with me. If not, I'll let you know right away and I assume you'll do the same. What do you think about that, Kevin?"

"That makes a lot of sense. I totally agree with this condition of you. Now..."

He started explaining that he wanted to widen his field in that coming year. It would not only touch the design home magazine but also the Real Estate guide magazine—these two last ones would be presented in a new format. In addition, he made part of his interest for the internet market. He informed Kara that he was presently thinking about a new concept of selling what he had to offer to the public by the means of websites.

"You would be the perfect candidate for the job. I need your creative touch on these new projects," he said. In order to convince her, he pushed the last straw, "I also know that you like to take pictures of nature and people. I assure you that you'll have time to do so—you will not always be working and living in big centres. I'll allow you enough spare time to do whatever you want to...How does it sound?"

Kara smiled. "Not bad at all," she said.

"Oh, yes! Last thing that I haven't mentioned yet is you will be paid immediately after each contract. Okay...you may live between two planes at the beginning of this venture but after it, you'll be able to go back home and replenish yourself before the next assignment. If everything goes well according to the plan, you'll be capable to afford many things in a very short-term period."

With a nervous little laugh, she replied, "It's difficult to refuse such an opportunity presented that way. However, I repeat myself—I accept the first contract offer and see if it works." Taking a more serious tone of voice, she added, "There's one more thing I would like to clear up right away before going any further."

She tried to compose herself. "Of course, it sounds great! You give me the chance to enlarge my horizons but you see Kevin, I have gone out with you many times these past weeks. I know...nothing serious happened between us and I appreciate your way of being professional and gentleman...but...don't get me wrong, I like to be in your company but I'm afraid if it goes any further than that—well, it won't work at all for me because..."

She paused, sighed and continued. "I know it will not work if it's more than a business relationship."

"I know what you mean and I have no expectation whatsoever about you sleeping with me in order to get the job," Kevin said. "The truth is...I have learned my lessons well too. I prefer having a good worker like you that I can trust and...know that the job will be done. You see, I have had many women in my life—don't worry, I know how fragile is a love relationship compared to a friendship." And with a reserved smile, he added, "I must confess that I would be a fool not noticing that you're very attractive but I can keep my distance when it's about business. Now Kara, do you have any other question?"

She really liked what she heard. Her reticence vanished. "No further questions, Mr. Conte. I'll take the job."

She looked at her watch. "It's getting late—I have to get up early tomorrow morning. I'd better go."

"I should follow your example—I have a plane to catch tomorrow."

Kara reached for her coat. Kevin helped her to put it on. She smiled inside. Nobody does that better than this Kevin. He's so charming. He took her hand, kissed it and said in French, "Au plaisir de vous revoir madame."

With a British accent, she replied, "I'm looking forward to seeing you again Sir Conte."

On the porch, he said, "Expect a phone call from me within two weeks and please, don't take too many contracts this week. I'd like you to be available any time next week. The reason is that as soon as the deal is made, the big machine will start operating at a very fast speed and—I'll need all my people around me. Good night now."

She turned back. "It sounds good to me Kevin. Good bye."

#

On the tenth day, Kevin called her. The project was on. "I'll need you in two days. Is it ok with you?"

"Yes, it is," she answered enthusiastically.

"All right then. My assistant will make the necessary arrangements, the flight reservation, the hotel etc...She will meet you at the airport, drive you first to your hotel and then to the office."

Two days later, Kara left Mitsou to the owners of the house. She put the blue book in one of her suitcases, closed everything in her flat and drove to the airport.

The rest is history. Kara traveled a lot and worked on several projects brought in by Kevin. He introduced her to important people all over the world. With the time, she dealt with other private contractors. These new contacts brought her more work and consequently, she became extra-loaded with many datelines but miraculously succeeded to meet them all. Busy, busy, busy was life.

She understood what Kevin meant by saying he was a busy man the first time she met him. The passion he poured into his work was close to perfectionism. He was the one who took care of every final detail of a project before exposing it. He actually had no time for a social life but he did not care—he loved what he was doing.

Having more experience behind her back, Kara felt the same urge to perform than Kevin. The fire going on inside seemed to lead her in the right direction. On that stage of competition, she retained just the joy of performing at what she did best—getting to know people at another level. She had incredible encounters with people of all walks of life and from different ethnic groups and ages.

The blue book always followed her wherever she went—she read it whenever she had a chance. However, she was not sure if the radical change in her life was due to Kevin Conte or the blue book but one thing was certain—her life had taken a quantum leap, an inner shift in reality.

Everything was different—she could see, hear, smell, taste and feel more acutely than before. She knew when people were lying to her or themselves because she had acted that way herself for a long time before getting the clarity necessary to understand her own voice. She did not have any desire to look back anymore. She grasped the present intensely. It was the only point of power where she could create her reality. And the blue book was backing her up all the way.

Her business relationship and friendship with Kevin Conte deepened with the years. He often invited her on his boat which cruised between Italy and Greece. Sometimes, they spent the weekend together in Paris, New York or Hong Kong. Yet, they never had sex together. The more they got to know each other, the better they enjoyed and respected their friendship but...

In New York for the New Year's Eve, Kara and Kevin were looking at the lights of the city from the thirtieth floor balcony of his suite. He slowly turned his head and looked tenderly at her. He kissed her lightly on the cheek. "Happy New Year Kara; it's lovely to be with you to celebrate it," he whispered.

Kara smiled. She saluted him with her glass of champagne. "Happy New Year to you too; it's nice to be here tonight."

Then the big Midnight blow resonated in the air. They cheered up and greeted with other New Yorkers that were on their balconies.

It took quite a while for the hubbub to calm itself. In the frenzy of excitement, Kevin suddenly embraced Kara and kissed her on the mouth that time. Then, he declared his love to her. "I would like to be with you forever. Would you marry me?"

Stunned by that sudden declaration, Kara stuttered something that sounded like yes and no. Kevin looked upset. So she took his arm and brought him in the living room where they sat. It was time to be honest with him. She declared, "I love you a lot Kevin but getting married would change nothing between us. Let's face it—you and I love too much our work. Look! We would still be living in different houses around the world. Marrying you means to me that I would expect to see you more often..." She paused. He did not seem very happy. She added, "I know in advance that it would be impossible to demand it from you and because I don't like to wait for anybody...and I confess... I like my freedom too much..."

She took his hand. She hesitated before saying. "Why not leave things the way they are. We're always happy to see each other, not expecting anything only unconditional love. Kevin...I...I am infinitely sorry if I hurt your feelings but you asked me a big question and

I can just tell the truth. You see, I...I already appreciate what I have with you."

Kevin stayed silent for a while. He finally got up, went behind the bar and brought a bottle of champagne. He poured some in both glasses and sat back beside her. He smiled. "I thought about that all week. I was quite nervous tonight—not sure of your answer. The only thing I'm certain now is the answer came right from the heart. Your wisdom amazed me. However, I have to confess that you are part of my dreams more and more."

He stopped and took her hands. "In these dreams, you present yourself as a kind of spiritual being always smiling at me and leading the way. Sometimes, you take my hand when we walk in the wood and you show me how wonderful life is. I also remember vividly seeing at different occasions, a little girl in a yoga position next to you while I talk to you." He described the child the best he could to Kara and asked her, "Does it ring a bell to you"?

Disconcerted by what Kevin has just revealed, she drank off her glass. "I don't know anyone who could fit the child description," she answered. "But it's very sweet to hear that you dream of me that way...It sounds like a fairy tale, don't you think?" She burst out laughing.

Kevin let Kara tease him. He then put his arm around her—he was just happy that he had the guts to ask her to marry him. Somewhere in his mind, he knew that she would refuse. That was against everything she believed in a relationship. To her, the ultimate goal to reach between two people was unconditional love and marriage licence was just a fake label to put on. He also recalled that she once said to one of his friends that getting married was just a waste of time and money— she would get tired quickly to wake up three hundred and sixty-five days with the same person on her side. Kevin recognized that she was right—the right thing was offering to each other the best of themselves when they were together.

They talked all night on that New Year's Eve, trying to understand each point of view. Kevin finally said, "I agree with you that the relationship we had is excellent but—I want more than that. After all, we are not brother and sister—I need to feel you physically too, you know..."

Kara laughed. "I thought you meet these needs with your dates," she replied.

"You know damn well that you are the only one in my life since I have met you little teaser, and what about you? Am I the only one in your life? Maybe, someone else out there is waiting for you."

Happy to hear it, she immediately said, "I sense a little taste of jealousy here. It never occurred to you big guy, that I have been in love with you since the beginning but you and I were so busy. So I decided to hold on love, take my time and give you time too. However, it was highly time to make your move because I would have jumped on you otherwise...got it!"

He kissed her. "I got it!" he said and kissed her again.

He then grabbed the bottle of champagne and filled the glasses. More relaxed, Kevin came back to his recurring dreams he had and described it with more details that time. She listened—half-surprised, half-amused—but then a flash of memory came back—she had the same dream about a little girl. She interrupted him. "Wait a minute. Since you've started describing her so well, I do remember now having dreamed about a little girl but you were not there and I can tell you that

I did not feel like a spiritual being in those dreams. I rather looked miserable...Isn't that weird?"

Kevin observed, "Yes it is."

He got closer to Kara—he could feel her entire body. He kissed her on the neck. "You can say anything you want but you're still my angel, my little rebel and my beloved at the same time," he whispered. And he kissed her again.

"I didn't know you were such a good kisser. If I had known it, I wouldn't have waited so long."

Kevin put a finger on her lips and said, "I'm not just a good kisser. Would you like to know more?"

"I would love too."

They kept drinking and kept laughing hilariously, just happy to share their little secrets and bad habits. He finally got up, led her to the bedroom and while hiccupping said, "Little angel, please take me to heaven with you tonight."

After all those years of unfulfilled desires, they really enjoyed making love to each other. In fact, they did just that during the whole week. Before leaving New York that day, they promised to each other that whatever happened, they would always be available to one another if an emotional or physical need showed up and that was it.

CHAPTER TEN

ROCKY ROAD

Six months later, Kevin let Kara know he had decided to take some time off. His friend Jerry Brown had convinced him to go climbing the Everest in the Himalayas with him. Kevin seemed so enthusiastic about that that Kara backed him up. However, she reminded him that he had better come back with all his body parts. He promised.

Kevin and Jerry saw each other often in the last two months of preparation. They really put all their energy on organizing the journey and getting in shape. However, during the training, Kevin began to have some doubts. He said to Jerry, "Half the Everest would be enough for me."

His friend did not want to hear about that, "We will go to the top or nothing," he replied.

"All right, my friend—whatever you say—don't forget that you're younger and in better shape than I am," Kevin responded.

"You can do it, Kevin. Come on...we talk about that before...it's not the first mountain you climb. We'll take our time, that's all."

The day after, while looking at the map for the third time, Kevin said to him, "What about just trekking the Everest region first and if we like it, we'll climb it next year."

Jerry saw that Kevin was serious about not being able to make it to the top. He knew too that they should have prepared long before that. A little disappointed, he said, "What can I say...okay; that makes sense. We'll be more prepared—Old man!"

"You realize as me that by the time, we would actually be in top shape on the site—it will be time to return home," Kevin said.

Then they prepared judiciously their itinerary. They chose to go by Karta, the Everest East base camp, elevated at 5050 m. They would start trekking from Kathmandu and after that, they would move to Lhasa.

The idea that they chose Tibet for destination really thrilled Kara. She encouraged Kevin and Jerry to go all the way

In the last days, they were all at Jerry's house. The two men in great shape teased Kara and Jerry's wife, Jennifer by offering them to join them.

"You're lucky that I'm not physically fit to meet such a challenge," Kara responded. "However, we never know, I may join you at the end of the trip."

As for Jennifer, she made it clear to them that she would never allow herself to participate in those foolish undertakings. Seeing how tense she was, Jerry said, "Jennifer, relax! Okay, it's time to go downstairs now."

They all went down to the basement, Kevin and Jerry spent the whole afternoon explaining to Kara and Jennifer the itinerary they had carefully prepared. The big day was coming.

That morning, they all sat in the living room before leaving for the airport. Jennifer and Kara warned them to take great care of each other and gave news whenever they could.

Jennifer insisted strongly on some points while knocking her little fist on the table in order to make them understand that she was dead serious. "Please, if one of you becomes exhausted or get injured, swear to me that you stop the whole crazy thing right there..."

They both assured her they would do exactly that if something serious happened. Jennifer was not convinced—their cloudy minds were already gone for the top of the world.

At the airport, Kara told Kevin, "I'll be going to Paris for a few weeks. After that, I'll return to Vancouver." She gave him the hotel phone number. "Just in case," she said.

"I'll certainly call as soon as we make the first part of the trip to let you know what you'll be missing Miss Lewis."

She pushed him gently. "Enjoy every minute of it Sir Conte."

"I will angel. Have fun in Paris but not too much..."

They smiled at each other and then kissed.

Ten minutes later, Jennifer with tears in her eyes finally let go of Jerry.

And there they went. They arrived at Kathmandu early in the morning. Their guides were waiting for them. On the premises, they were informed that some treks had been closed in the past three days. Therefore, they took the entire day with the guides to assess different treks and prepare the equipment.

Two days later in Paris, Kara began working. Her client, a top model named Elaine Duro, had heard about Kara's unique view of taking pictures. She offered Kara the challenge to make her look completely different of what the Press, women magazines, fashion world and public would expect from her. Kara responded very eagerly to her demand. Elaine Duro did not look quite like the other models she met before. Moreover, that woman wanted desperately to quit the fashion file to enter the cinema world.

The photographer tried to carry out the order during the following days: showing people that Elaine Duro was more than a pretty face. But—finding authenticity in a marketing face was not obvious. Kara had to find a way to reinvent Elaine Duro. First, she spent as much time as necessary with the model. On the third day, she brought her to one of the city big markets and there, she took shots of the model most of the time by surprise. Then, Kara suggested to her if she really wanted to be an actor, she had to act as if she was unaware of her presence and began to do whatever she felt like—right in the middle of that crowded garden. She let her go and five minutes later, Kara went spying on her. She patiently waited for the right moment and after a while, the camera lenses succeeded to get in touch with the natural beauty of Elaine. She took shots of her, looking at an object, talking to a vendor, buying fruits and flowers or simply walking through the alleys among that sea of people. Elaine and the market ambiance were amazing. Finally, Kara ended up taking some more pictures of the busy colourful bazaar.

Days later, Kara took some more shots of the model in a rented studio, and that was it. After developing the pictures, she met the want-to-be actor for the last time at her apartment to show the results. Very satisfied with the pictures, Elaine Duro thanked deeply Kara for the wonderful work. She went as far as saying that Kara was not only a super talented photographer but she had inspired eyes for capturing the reality of things.

Kara spent the rest of her time in Paris walking around, enjoying the city. However, Kevin was always at the back of her mind. At the hotel, late in the evening, she called her dad to let him know she would fly home the day after it. She knew that her father had prepared something special for her fortieth birthday—he had strongly insisted the month before to see if she would be there that day.

At the Vancouver airport, she was surprised to see her two brothers waiting for her at the arrival gate. "What's going on? Someone died?" she asked.

They welcomed her but were not too talkative. Dave just informed her that they wanted to make sure she could drop her things at her place and not worried about it. Then, they would drive immediately to the ferry.

Kara sat at the back of Steve's van. Delighted and suspicious of their delicate intentions, she shouted to them, "Shoot it! Guys. Does dad have in mind more than an invitation in a nice restaurant as he used to do each time is our birthday."

The two brothers stayed silent.

Kara did not stop nagging them. "What kind of surprise party is he organizing? Please, tell me boys or I'll get mad if you don't talk."

Dave said, "Don't try to manipulate us. It may have worked when you were young but now..."

"Get lost," she replied.

Steve looked at her in the mirror. He tried to take a natural tone of voice. "First of all, at your age, you should not behave that way. Dad just wanted us to pick you up at the airport on time. It's not a big deal sister. You already know that you'll eat at the same restaurant that all of us, fortunately or unfortunately had to go when we turned the big forty."

Dave in the front passenger seat, turned his head back and mockingly added, "It is like an obsession with dad. He went to that restaurant when he turned forty. Well...something memorable must have happened there because since that—he had dragged there, Morgan, Steve and even the nicest of the family who is of course...me...but this time my darling; it's your fortieth treat! Enjoy the ride and take it easy Miss Spinster."

"What a lousy comment to make. Of course, it's coming from..."

They all laughed hilariously, each one visualising the scene at the restaurant with their father—they would try to stay cool without laughing—an impossible feat to accomplish but they hoped they would.

"Wait a minute, guys, my birthday is only tomorrow," Kara said. "You know, this morning on the plane I was hoping to go home, relax all day, and hit the road the day after. So, it means that you expect me to drop off my things home, run and take another one hour drive plus the ferry...At least, tell me, this is for a good cause...just guessing..."

Steve suggested, "After dropping your things, poor little Kara, if you are so tired, just take it easy and have a nap at the back of the van. On the ferry, it will be..."

"Yeah...Yeah," she said sighing. "You always have the right answer for everything, don't you Steve?"

He agreed. "You got it right sister. Dave might be the nicest of the family but when you are the smartest, you have to lead the path all the way to your siblings in order to show them how privileged they are to have such a brother. Sometimes, it's boring though—it's lonely up there you know."

"Okay smart ass, your ego will smother you one day; mark my words!" Kara mumbled.

Kidding each other was the favorite pastime of the family, so they went on and on and on. Kara was happy to be back in the game and reunited with her two brothers, a rare occasion in those past two years. She appreciated greatly that after all those years, they had kept intact their sense of humour.

After opening the front door, she walked to the kitchen and turned on the light. The first thing she saw was Mitsou the cat on the table with a party hat on her head. She said right away, "What's going on here? Mitsou is here?"

She walked to the studio. Looking up, she saw a banner suspended above the living room arch that said, "Happy Forty Kara." Dave turned on the light at the same time she entered. They were all there—her dad, his wife Jody, Morgan and Roger, Nancy and Michelle—even the Andrews. They all began singing "Happy Birthday to you". Dave and Steve were harmonizing at the top of their lungs behind her.

Kara's fatigue disappeared rapidly. Enchanted, she applauded. "Thank you so much for being all here; it's lovely," she said. "Now I know the reason why Dave and Steve played jerks with me. Big surprise—I was not expecting that one. Thank you again."

She hugged and kissed everyone. Mrs. Andrew told her, "We have prepared a barbecue in the backyard; everything is ready."

Her dad embraced her again. "I hope you're not disappointed," he said. "Last week, I was going to make the reservation for...you know...my favourite restaurant but your brothers and sister insisted to celebrate your birthday in your own place. Something different they said. I thought that was ok but..."

Jody came to his side smiling. She concluded, "Finally, your dad got the message."

"What do you mean? What's wrong with tradition?" he replied.

It was funny. At the background, Kara could see her sister Morgan and two brothers laughing madly while they were going out on the terrace. But she succeeded to keep a straight face before her father.

After refreshing herself a little, she stroked Mitsou for a while. Then, she went to the kitchen, poured herself a glass of champagne and joined people in the backyard. It was nice to be out on that warm summertime afternoon. Her dad sitting beside her at the picnic table asked, "What is Kevin doing these days?"

"At this very moment, he's trekking somewhere in Tibet," she joyfully answered.

That got the attention of her two brothers. "Are you kidding us?" Dave said. "The businessman is now a climber in the Himalayas. Will it be his new career?"

Her family had met Kevin a few times. They knew that Kara and Kevin were a very good team at work but never assumed anything more. Of course, the secretive Kara had never mentioned to them her love relationship with him.

"This man has many strings to his guitar," she said to Dave. "However, he's not climbing the Everest but trekking around with one of his good friends. They had prepared for four months for this endeavour and –I hope everything goes well for them up there."

She paused, pensive. "He has been gone for two weeks now. I'm expecting to hear from him soon."

Around ten o'clock, Morgan and Roger were the first ones to leave. They had rented a hotel room in the city and then, would take the first flight in the morning. They let her know they really enjoyed spending the day with her. She accompanied them to the car and gave them a last hug.

Steve, the designated driver, had a last cup of coffee before asking the rest of the family if they were ready to go. After many hugs and kisses, they all got into the van. They waved her goodbye before disappearing into the night. Kara returned to the backyard. She gratefully thanked the Andrews for their kindness and for having taken care of Mitsou and her plants. She wanted to help Mrs. Andrew clean after but that one refused categorically. She told her to get some rest instead. They said goodnight to each other and Kara went to her apartment. She grabbed the luggage left in the living room, put the suitcases in the corner of the bedroom and fell flat on her bed undressed. She slept at the minute she touched the bed.

When she opened her eyes in the morning, she was happy to be in her bed and see the familiar things. To her, being on the road was exciting and fun but waiting for a flight and sleeping in strange beds were the lousy side of it.

After having a shower, she went to the kitchen. She opened the fridge and stood there, flabbergasted. The fridge was full of her favourite food. She found a note inside written by Morgan—when I checked your empty fridge, I knew you would not feel like doing a grocery this morning. See, I still remember what you love eating. Enjoy. Happy Birthday Kara. Love, Morgan.

Kara thought aloud, "Thank you lovely sister. I am spoiled and I like it a lot."

After a nice breakfast, she walked through her little cosy place. She had decided years before, to keep permanently the flat even if she could afford a better spot when coming to the city. She loved it exactly as it was. She had nice people around and the area was very quiet. To her, that apartment was a temple, a shrine, a place to replenish body and mind when away for too long.

She went back to the kitchen and washed the glasses left the night before. After placing everything in order, she went to the studio to check some new cameras she had bought in Paris. She was busy to put them together when she heard the cat mewing. She looked down. Mitsou was sitting on something blue. Her eyes widened with astonishment. She walked toward the cat and then stopped, mesmerized. The view of the blue envelope immediately rang a bell. That's right. I must open it on my fortieth birthday.

Kara knelt down, stroked the cat and pushed her gently on the side. Before opening it, she tried to recall where she had hidden it in the first place, and then the memory came back to her. She had put it behind one of her pictures frames in the studio.

She got up, checked behind the frame and saw that the back had loosened a little. It has probably fallen due to the vibration in the room of all the people here yesterday, she thought. But I'm sure that I didn't see it last night. Sighing another time, she said to herself, "Once again, coincidence and mystery...the blue envelope fell on the floor exactly this morning. Oh! Well, you must be used to it by now..."

She picked up reluctantly the envelope. Her rebel spirit murmured, "Can you give me a break whoever you are?" Then, she opened it slowly still swearing to that whoever...It contained a few typewritten pages:

Nothing after death is an intolerable thought
Immortality in the world is an intolerable thought
Take the quantum leap
Hang out there
Between Earth and Heaven

Kara, this is your wake up call, time for a reality check. You will experience from now on a deeper shift in reality. Sometimes, you will be very upset by what you see or feel but we urge you not to give up. Keeping going is the only way to comprehend the world. You will start remembering why you chose to live on planet earth. This process will be painful at the beginning; however, if you keep your eye firmly on the target, you will understand that it is a requirement necessary for the job you were assigned to do.

Kara, your mission is TO FIND THE ONE THAT WILL CHANGE FOR EVER THE WAY HOMOSAPIENS THINK ON THIS PLANET. THAT

PERSON WILL BE COMMITTED TO BRINGING CLARITY ON EARTH.

The Universe has sent some special beings on this sphere before in order to prepare the field to the planet itself and then to all living creatures. Their missions were making sure that the GUIDING LIGHT OF ENERGY would enter the stratosphere without distortion. Jesus and Mohammed were the last ones who spoke the truth about LIFE-ENERGY. We named them because we know that you have taken long hours to read about their lives and accomplishments while contemplating the situation of the world.

Keep reading the blue book. It will help you understand why you have to do exactly what we are asking you. Don't worry—you will not be turned into a fanatic blind nut believer; on the contrary...

Some people will help you along the way in your search. You must be thinking why you and why we are not contacting this person ourselves.

The reason is we do not know anymore than you who this human being is. However, our mighty guide recommends that you should start looking for her. Yes, it's a She...Put all your doubts aside while doing that. All the facts you need to know will be revealed to you as soon as you begin looking.

Our work ends here—it was to prepare you spiritually, mentally and physically for this great undertaking.

You'll still be travelling a lot alone. However, you are used to it by now and we know that it's not a big deal for you anymore to live in foreign lands.

You understand now why being photographer fits you like a glove. That will be your cover up—so nobody will be suspicious of your comings and goings. Financially, everything will be taken care of, your needs will be met wherever you will be. We must add that many more benefits will be drawn from it; you will be energized by your work and more aware at an earthly level of what you do and why. Last thing, you will go through a big ordeal once again but please, take courage and patience, you will understand that life and death are the same thing. Sadness will disappear quickly in your heart and one day, you will be reunited with those you loved.

You have passed the test with us. We believe that your training is done. We would like to give you more information about her but we cannot.

As you know, there is a negative vibration trying to amplify its power on planet earth. The Chosen One has a tremendous work to accomplish by freeing the world from damaging energy that knows it has terminated its assignment but does not want to leave. It is addicted to its new power. However, if it goes on; it will bring chaos on this earth and consequently to the rest of the Universe. It needs to be stopped right now.

We are simply observers of different worlds and try to understand the reasons why some are working better than the other ones.

Coming back to this negative vibration now, be aware—that dark force will try everything to get rid of that chosen being. Therefore, you will have to intervene sometimes as a NEUTRALIZER until she will be fully awaked of her powerful influence.

You have received that gift a long time ago. We hope that you get it! Each time you deny it you just make it harder on you. You neutralize the negative force in people: by just thinking about it, you are able to stop the vibration to work. You are still afraid of these prevailing abilities you possess but with the experience, you will understand that these violent human beings are doomed to this—fetal position—until they die. What will happen to them after life is not your business or ours. You have been practising your art of neutralizing long enough—twice in real life and the rest in your dreams. YOU ARE READY FOR YOUR ASSIGNMENT.

Therefore, we repeat: first, you find Her and second, you protect Her until She will be ready to operate. Before letting you go in the world, we want you to know that we have loved you very much since the first day of your birth. It has been a delight for us to watch you playing with life—moreover, we have enjoyed your sense of humour and your unique way of looking at life.

Kara, here is the last guideline from us: the next destination is Tibet. Accept the news and read again this letter. By the way, you have no choice—free will is not an option for you anymore. At this very moment, it is taken away from you until you get the job done. IT IS NOT UP TO YOU OR TO US ANYMORE. When you are perplexed about which way to go, think about the Pure Loving Energy, it will put you on the right path again and send you the right people.

Love, the Upper Midnight Circle.

Kara read the letter three more times, and then looked at Mitsou, which was sleeping like an angel. I would love to be a cat at this very moment just relaxing in the reality of life, she thought.

Suddenly, she began to cry like a baby, the emotion was too strong. A few minutes later, she heard a voice inside, "Let it be Kara." She recognized that voice—it was her own. And it got louder. She could not stop it anymore. In a way, she was relieved to know why those horrible events in her life took place.

But then, she asked herself, "Why Tibet? Is there something to do with Kevin? What the hell is going on here?" Trembling, she went to lie down on the couch and drew a blanket on her.

Later on, to change the emotional state she was in, she started doing the inventory of all pictures she had in her studio—rearranging them in a new category, compilation and selection. She put all the ones about nature together, and then the ones of people face close-ups, family pictures, architectural pictures and so on. She ended with the ones she called poetry pictures. It could be any objects or things—candles, mirrors, fruits, old furniture—they all possessed that magic light and shadows that the camera lenses had reached at that moment.

When she finished it, she looked around satisfied. The cat sitting on her desk, observed her with a royal attitude of detachment. However, when she met her eyes, Kara sensed without effort what the cat was thinking—it was weird. Hey Kara, isn't it your birthday today? Indulge yourself! It is time to take care of me, me, me...so I can take care of you...Got it!

Kara called her gently. Mitsou jumped on Kara's lap. She admired her big green eyes and soft fur. "Do you know Mitsou that I have missed you a lot when I was away. But—you were lucky to have the Andrews looking after you," she said. She played with the cat until they both got exhausted.

She went to lie down on her bed and read another time the blue letter. She began daydreaming about the meaning of it all. Then, she rested her mind by taking a quick nap. As soon as she opened her eyes, questions gushed out rapidly in her head. Who is she? How old is she? Where is she? What is her name, nationality? What part of the world is she living in? The questions went on and on.

Then in a flash, she remembered. Kevin and she had talked about a little girl on that famous New Year's Eve. She thought aloud, "Oh, yes, I do recall now having seen a little girl sitting in a yoga lotus position.

Her hands joined as if she was praying, her eyes wide open. She had a big smile on her face. It could be her."

She closed her eyes trying to picture her again. A few minutes later, she said aloud, "she appears to be Caucasian, brown hair and brown eyes. She wears a red top, a black skirt with little red flowers. It looks like she is sitting in a meadow close to a forest edge. She notices my presence..." Then, the image blurred away.

In the evening, Kara put some soft music on and tried to relax. She thought about Kevin and Tibet. <u>Why do they want me to go there? What's going on there? And I don't know why he has not called yet. Oh, God! Protect Kevin and Jerry in whatever they do and wherever they are.</u>

The following days, she didn't feel like doing anything. In fact, she got so tired she could not get out of bed. She could not even read. No energy left. It was beyond her understanding. However, on the seventh day, she started feeling better.

#

That late morning, Kara sat on the terrace and watched for a while the birds chirping in the backyard. <u>The garden seems to be bigger and nicer every year,</u> she thought. She breathed deeply. She could smell in the air the combined fragrances of flowers, vegetables, fruits and trees—the lawn freshly mowed added to the pleasure of just being there. Kara appreciated that exquisite lightness while savouring the words, <u>home sweet home.</u> Mitsou shared that moment of bliss with her while having an eye on her and the other one on the birds.

Mr. Andrew seeing Kara outside joined her and asked, "Do you like the renovation I made on the terrace of your apartment?"

"I'm really pleased with it," she answered. "I like the new half cover you have built—I can sit longer in the shade without having to move. Even if it rains, I can still enjoy the terrace. By the way, thank you so much for the roses you have planted all around the terrace and the plants alongside the wall. It looks just great! Well, you have made a very good job, Mr. Andrew," she added.

Mrs. Andrew got out of the house. Kara immediately invited both of them to sit down around the table. They talked about the renovation they had done on the propriety that year. Kara offered them something to drink, she was glad to have time to chat with them. She came back with an ice tea for Mrs. Andrew and lemonade for her husband. She gently suggested to the couple that it was a good occasion for them to contemplate their artwork. They both laughed at her comment. But Kara said seriously, "You know that you can win any contests about gardening. I'm not kidding here, you can compete with any landscaper designer, nursery expert or great experienced gardener that do it for a living."

Kara smiled and continued. "You both have the green thumb. The landscape at the front and the back of the house is something unique, original and beautiful. No wonder why I don't want to move from here. You will have to drag me out of this place..."

The more she went on, the more the Andrews laughed. Mrs. Andrew finally succeeded to place two words together and acknowledged. "Kara, we really miss you when you're away. Don't worry—we will never get rid of you. The reason is—you are too popular, too well known in town to let you go. We will keep you until you get fed up of cohabiting with two old creatures like us. Mr. Andrew followed up right away. "I've always wanted to ask you that. You are so successful at what you do...why have you chosen to stay here all those years. I know that you can afford a bigger apartment or even buy a condo or a house in the city."

Kara thought about the question for a few seconds. Her face beamed. "Nothing like home sweet home...It's funny you ask me that because I was repeating that expression to myself this morning. Okay, you want to know—well, this place is my anchor, my shrine...I feel good here...so there's no price for it," she answered. "In addition, it smells good all around. Each time I sit down, I see a paradise garden. Believe me—all I need is here. All the birds that visit your little houses in the trees would tell you the same thing than me. Why looking for something I already have. So I just enjoy it." She paused and took Mitsou in her arms. "You take care of the cat and my apartment when I'm away. You pick up my mail, water my plants. And I feel secure here. I know that I can count on you for anything. However—if you want to increase my rent; feel free to do so. Your rate will be mine..."

Mr. Andrew interrupted her. "Stop right there Kara. You have already paid us in double for the past two years. That's more than enough, and if you're happy to live here—it's just all right with us. We're very glad to have you as tenant."

"All right," she replied.

"Have you had some news from Kevin and his whereabouts in Tibet?" Mrs. Andrew asked.

At the mention of Kevin's name, Kara's body contracted a little. "Kevin has faxed me two weeks ago from Lhasa—he said he had a good time. However, he pointed out that the next step would be more challenging and longer. Chinese administrative people made them fill out lots of papers. Apparently, the trekking permits needed, to allow them to do so have been just a hassle from day one. Since that, I've had no news, nothing."

Kara became wistful. "I must say that I'm worried though, because Kevin and his friend Jerry had decided not to bring any communication tools with them. Keep it simple was their motto before leaving. However, on the fax sent, he also mentioned that they had to change guides on the premises and finding the right ones was an exploit by itself. Well, I hope they still have a good time up there."

"It's sometimes difficult to communicate with the outside world once you are in Tibet," Mrs. Andrew said.

"Do you know that forty years ago, my wife and I went there?" her husband added.

Surprised, Kara said, "You did!"

Mr. Andrew proudly responded, "Well...it was a short stay because we had so many problems at the border. Nevertheless, we had stayed in Lhasa for a week. I still have all the maps and the itinerary of that trip."

Mrs. Andrew continued where her husband left it. "That year, we had visited China, India, Pakistan, Afghanistan, Nepal and that's right..." She looked tenderly at her husband. "We had finished by the roof of the world, Tibet. I just have good memories of that wonderful trip." She paused trying to recollect her past, and then she smiled. "We were young, healthy and stupid. We felt like aliens from Mars on that journey. Everything seemed so different out there. We did travel a lot before but those countries were totally another world to us..."

Mr. Andrew let his wife rave about those good days without interrupting.

"That was the first time in my life that I felt so adventurous," she admitted. "A few misfortunes did happen along the way but we improvised quickly, and we survived. Once we were robbed with knife under chin—that one happened in India. In Afghanistan, we trekked in a very isolated area...and we got lost. But we miraculously found our way out after two days of starving and a few drops of water left. We met people who fed us and we came back to life. Then to finish it, we spent time in jail in Kathmandu, Nepal. Well, one night but still...They had apparently mistaken us for another foreign couple who had done something fraudulent but I could not remember what it was, anyway..."

"It was quite an experience," Mr. Andrew acknowledged with sparkling eyes. He looked affectionately at his wife. "After that, everything came back to normal, thanks God. We were a little shaken at the time but it was short. You see, forty years ago, we were feeling like teenagers in a forbidden place. Therefore, after that, we dusted ourselves off and went back to the business of life, which was to see more countries and things we could in a year. We did actually pretty well. Isn't it, Mrs Andrew?"

"You got it right, my friend," she answered.

Stupefied by what she just heard, Kara stayed silent for a few seconds. Then, she smiled. "I didn't know you were such wild things forty years ago! I cannot believe that you had actually gone through all those horrible events but now...it seems almost amusing. Let me tell you that you are my kind of people. You're my heroes," She rose up her glass and said, "This deserves a toast."

They all cheered up with their glasses.

Still in a good spirit, Mr. Andrew said, "We were born wild, I must confess."

His wife chuckling at his remark, continued. "Believe it or not Kara; it's the first time we brought it on the table...about that year and the trip. At that time, we promised each other never to mention those events to our family or friends lest they would try to dissuade us about travelling. Well...that trip made us stronger."

Her husband with a thumb up, said, "You got it right, baby!"

Kara cracked up laughing hilariously. They joined her.

Mrs. Andrew ended up by adding, "It's good to talk about those foolish things we did. It's not very dangerous anymore. I guess that sharing with you keeps us young inside."

Mr. Andrew got up, concluding, "We thought that we could handle anything but in fact, we were just dumb crazy, we still are but in a more gentle way." He kissed his wife on the cheek and lightly said, "The crazy one was rather this lady but I was so in love with that woman—I was ready to follow her when necessary and to lead when appropriate. I call it mad love."

Mrs. Andrew smiled. She got up and put her arm around her husband waist. "I must say that it was an extraordinary period of life for both of us. Well, it was nice to let you know that we were once young too but now I'm feeling a little tired just thinking about that. Time to go home and have some rest. Thank you for the ice tea and your good company. See you later."

They walked home holding hands. It's just wonderful to witness people who actually love each other after all those years of partnership. They are the rare wild birds of the jungle, Kara thought.

She went in and came back with a magazine. After reading some articles, she put it on the table. Then her eyes followed the cat running after a bee. At that moment, the sunlight and shadows emerging from the trees appeared so perfect in the garden—Kara thought it would make excellent shots. She went to get the camera she had bought in Paris. I will enlarge one of the best pictures, find a nice frame and gave it to them for Thanksgiving Day, she thought.

The day after, she received unexpectedly a call from her friend Jason. They had not seen each other for ages. He was in town. "I took a chance with your old phone number—wow! You are still there," he said. After talking a few minutes, he asked her if she would be interested to join him at a bar that was close from her place.

Kara accepted with pleasure. "I would be there in twenty minutes. Don't move. It's such a joy to hear from you. Bye."

Entering the bar, Kara looked around but could not see Jason yet. After getting accustomed to the dim light, she scrutinized the tables. She hardly recognized him sitting in a corner of the counter. Jason had changed a lot—the Greek Apollo had transformed himself in something that Kara first did not like. He had gained a lot of weight, had long hair and a beard. In addition, he wore glasses too big for him.

Jason hugged Kara and kissed her on both cheeks. He knew what Kara was thinking. He immediately said, "Great seeing you Kara. You look good. Don't look at me like that...I'm not a monster yet..."

He had a forcing smile. She realized that he was not anymore the Jason she once knew.

He ordered her a drink. They both stayed silent for a while not knowing what to say. Kara started talking. Jason listened quietly. He seemed to be more in tune. He then asked her about her family and what they were doing.

Kara made it short. She then asked him, "What are you doing yourself? Where are you living? What's going on in your life? To be frank with you, you don't look like the guy I once knew."

Jason confessed that he had been depressed for the past three years. "It has begun very slowly after the traumatic event—you know what I'm talking about. At first, I could cope with it and then, that stupid disease must have decided to keep me company."

"Sorry Jason," Kara said.

"Don't. I have tried everything to come back to life. I've met the best psychiatrists but nothing improved—forget and forgive the past is still too painful to do, I guess."

Kara nodded and let him continued.

He repeated himself. "Before being in that miserable state, work was the only remedy to my sadness and I kept going until the day—I had a deep breakdown. After it, I became so fed up of everything—I knew my condition was serious."

Kara touched his hand and then gently, his cheek.

"All I need, in fact is taking a break of myself." He looked at her. "You think I look bad now, you haven't seen me last year. I'm much better now because—I have a reason to live. I moved back in town a month ago. I had an offer to work as a basketball coach with trouble kids, teenagers. You know that I always liked sport. That could be the break I need...I'll see to it," Jason said.

"Well...for a big career change, it is. But you know better than I do what you need. Tell me everything...We both know that after that horrible nightmare, we haven't done much to support each other afterwards. Please, go on, Jason."

A little relieved, he resumed. "I'll make it short Kara. No need for a shrink or medication anymore to ease my sadness or just going through the day. The reason I'm gone a take the coaching job is to release myself of myself...I already feel better since I have come back to town. I've seen my family and friends who still lived here. Then today, I see you; I'm so glad I made that phone call. I missed you Kara and of course, Cloe and Kate..."

"I missed them too Jason. We had such a good friendship together—I never had it after that."

After those confessions, Jason said, "Okay, that's your turn now."

"Well, everything's fine with me. I love what I do. I'm still in the photography business." She smiled. "I didn't give up my dream. I make a decent living at it. I have a comfortable life and one more thing—I'm in love with a handsome adventurer."

"I'm happy for you."

She hesitated; then, decided to go for it. "I was as depressed as you for a while. Remember, we did see each other but with the years, we lost touch. Then one day, I had that job where I began traveling a lot everywhere in the world...I do think that is the reason why I kept my sanity. In other words, that job saved my life. Therefore, this new job offer could be a good thing for you, Jason."

With a big smile, she admitted, "That guy I'm in love with—his name is Kevin Conte by the way—well, he has certainly played a role in my recovery. Everything has started with him and I hope will finish with him. Do you know what he is doing at this very moment?"

"No, I don't but I have the feeling I will soon..." he answered. He laughed.

Kara seeing him laughing for the first time felt encouraged to continue. "My man is a crazy nut. He's now trekking somewhere in the Himalayas with a friend."

After it, she talked about the kind of relationship she had with Kevin along the years.

Jason listened with interest. Then he said, "Good for you my sweet heart. You deserve to have it nice. I know that life had not been easy for you either. However, what I admire about you is your resiliency. Once again, it's so good to see you. I was afraid that after all those years of not seeing each other; things would have changed—you know, been cold between us today. I'm glad it did not. I mean, you're still the Kara I know, the unpretentious one. That Kevin of you is lucky to have you in his life."

Kara smiled. She protested. "Stop it! You always had this tendency to put me on a pedestal. I'm very lucky to have you and Kevin in my life, all right!"

They had another drink and then, left. Kara gave him a lift to his dad's house. Before getting off, Kara made him promise to stay in touch with her no matter what happened with the job or else. He kissed her on the cheek, gave her his phone number and said good-bye.

Back home, Kara first checked the messages on the answering machine. She then went to the dark room and started developing some pictures. After that, she sat in the studio and thought about what Jason have said earlier in the afternoon. She closed her eyes and murmured, "Kate, Cloe, I love you—and seeing Jason today makes me realize how much I miss you. I wish you well wherever you are my friends." Right after saying that, Kate and Cloe appeared before in her mind. They wore large light rainbow dresses. It seems like they were floating around in that white space.

They both smiled at her.

"I love you too, Kara," Cloe whispered.

"We miss Jason and you but don't feel sorry for us— it's so pleasant to be in that dimension." Kate added.

Cloe almost chanting, declared, "Life is pretty good up here. You will see one day. Kara, we have manifested our presence in order to let you know that you will start being very busy in a few days. You have taken enough rest—you are ready to go. And Jason is in good hands now, let him be."

Kate continued. She sounded very serious. "Listen carefully, something is about to happen. We cannot tell you what it is. Just keep in mind that help will be on its way when you feel discouraged in your endeavour or don't know anymore why you are doing that. In these moments, just close your eyes and think about the way your cousin and we have died. If it's not enough, then keep thinking about all women who suffered and still suffer the non-stop everyday violence. Then you will see that your power will rise at its top and therefore, allow you to face the most commanding adversary."

Cloe backed up the advice. "Kara, practice doing it."

Kara responded plainly, "Practice what! I implore you to tell me more..."

On that, Cloe and Kate disappeared in the nowhere of her consciousness leaving Kara one more time in the darkness of the unknown.

Before sleeping that night, she cleared off her head. She relaxed first her mind and body, and then proceeded to get crystal-clear with the people involved in her life that day. "Are they helping me or are they knocking me down?" she asked herself. After answering that question the more fairly she could—she began releasing all the people involved in the circumstances and wished them well. Then, she affirmed that the universe and planet earth would take care of the rest. Just before slumbering, she thought, I'll know when it's time to reactivate that powerful fetal touch.

The morning after, she developed some more photos in her tiny darkroom. After two hours, she took a break and sat on the couch. Mitsou approached her gently wanting to be cajoled. Kara picked up the cat and kissed her. They stayed there a long time in the silence of the place. They both knew they had better taste that quiet and peaceful time when it passed.

Something in the air was on its way to announce trouble waters and put an end on a calm season of life. Yet, Kara could sense an inner strength, gradually installing itself in her body cells—the history would rewrite itself.

#

That day, she was in an anxious mood. She had a strong urge to go see her two brothers and wives. She needed to feel their healthy presence—she also thought that it could be the last time she would see them.

While driving to Dave's house, she thought about Michelle and Nancy and how great women they were. On one occasion, she recalled that Michelle was visiting her family and friends in France at the same time that she was working there. Michelle called her and insisted on spending time together. She brought Kara to special and unique places in the countryside. They enjoyed having these three days together. Michelle also introduced Kara to her eccentric parents. The father was a sculptor and mother, a painter; both making a decent living of their art. They had settled in the countryside and renovated an old French stone house with their own hands. They lived there with some chickens, sheep and abandoned dogs found on the deserted road leading to their estate. Both very relaxed and warm, they invited her to stay a few days before going back to work. Michelle told her to decline knowing that a few days meant a week or two to them.

Michelle was quite the opposite of her parents—very disciplined, organized and business oriented. She also hated cooking or creating things. But what Michelle retained of her parents was her authenticity.

Michelle, Steve and Kara arrived at the same time in the driveway. After greeting them at the door, Dave invited them to sit in the living room. He mumbled he had not been allowed to enter the kitchen since the morning because Nancy and Candice had been busy cooking all day to prepare something supposedly special. Thirty minutes later, Kara attracted by the wonderful smell could not resist anymore—she went to the kitchen. She kissed Nancy and Candice.

"What's happening here?" Kara asked.

They let her know how glad they were to have succeeded to make a gastronomic menu right on time. Soon after, Michelle, Dave and Steve joined them in the Cordon Bleu culinary area. Nancy wearing a big chef hat on her head and white towel on her left hand said, "Follow the chef in the dining room, please."

The flower arrangement on the dining table and the disposition of colourful flatware plates and dishes were amazingly beautiful. Lit candles warmed the atmosphere—Bach music was playing in the background. Candice invited the guests to sit assigning them a chair.

She poured wine in fine glasses while the chef Nancy brought the first service on a wheeling table. Before serving them, Nancy went to her chair. Standing up, she took her glass of wine and had a sip. She then saluted them. "Candice and I have talked for a long time about preparing a real gastronomy menu one day. Years went by and we never had an occasion to do so. This week, everything turned out to be perfect. Candice showed up yesterday, Kara told us she was coming last night, Michelle and Steve had no plans for the weekend and Dave offered himself to do the cleaning of the house two days ago. Therefore, last night, Candice and

I went through all the little and fancy steps. And today, Candice and I did make it. It's a lot of work but the results are very good." She rose her glass and added, "Michelle and Kara know very well the French gastronomy, and they will be my critics tonight; they will let me know if it really tastes as good as it sounds. Please Candice, would you give them the menu."

Candice presented it to the guests, and Nancy began to read aloud. "As appetizers and main dish, you have two choices: Snail 'Cargolade' with garlic cream or poultry medallion with a mix of vegetable jelly followed by fish, Pike mousse with crayfish or frog legs with parsley butter. The other option is Crusty, 'Andouillette' with spices or Beef filet with pepper sauce. Then, the cheese I have selected is Roquefort. Of course, the dessert will be a surprise. Wines selected to accompany this menu are Beaujolais, Chablis and Champagne.

Nancy's eyes sparkled when looking at Kara. She concluded, "I just want to say that I'm so happy to have you Kara at this table with us. You always are on the go and I don't know if we will have another chance to be reunited the six of us together. Okay before getting too emotional..." She paused and stuttered, "Everyone, enjoy your meal."

They all cheered up and clapped.

Nancy and Candice had effectively succeeded to create a series of magic moments that night—they served their guests as if they were kings and queens. Everything was just perfect and delicious. Michelle, Kara, Dave and Steve applauded at each service and congratulated the chef and her assistant for their tremendous and wonderful work.

It was a fantastic evening—eating, drinking, laughing and talking. Dave and Steve wanting to show their appreciation cleared away the dishes and even cleaned up the kitchen while Nancy, Candice, Michelle and Kara had champagne in the living room.

Kara slept over at Dave's house. The first one to get up in the morning, she checked if she had a call from Kevin at home. Nothing, just business calls. She went to the grocery store. When Dave and Nancy got up around ten o'clock, a wonderful brunch was waiting for them. She spent another night over and left in the early morning.

At home, she checked all the new phone messages; she returned some of them. Having a look at her watch, she thought, Kevin, why don't you call? I worry about you. She called Jerry's wife. "Hello Jennifer, it's Kara. Have you heard from Jerry and Kevin lately?"

With an anxious voice, Jennifer answered. "No, I haven't. Obviously, you have not either. Kara, I...I'm telling that I'm getting paranoid! I've started being in that state three weeks ago. Something awful must have happened..."

"Jennifer, relax!" Kara said. "Listen, they know what they are doing. They must have some sort of communication problems up there."

Jennifer got upset and riposted, "Kara, I just wanted to remind you that they are supposed to get back in four days according to their plans and schedule, and we have had no news at all."

Kara sighed. "I understand you. You're right," she replied. "I'm getting worried myself. I hope they will give us signs of life before leaving Tibet. I called Kevin's secretary in London two days ago—she did not have any news either. So, as soon as we get some news, we called each other right away, all right Jennifer."

"All right Kara. However, I would prefer if we call each other every day from now on."

Kara agreed and hung up the phone.

Her hand was still on the phone receiver when it rang. She quickly lifted it up and answered feverishly. It was Kevin's friend, Don Robert.

He was still talking when Kara dropped the receiver on the table—her shaking body was crying and screaming at the soul of Kevin, "You cannot do it to me...You cannot..."

She fell unconscious on the floor.

Thirty minutes later, Don arrived at Kara's front door. He buzzed. No answer. He knocked loudly. No answer. He went to the nearest window trying to look in for her presence but could not see anything. He decided to go to the backyard. Luckily, he saw Mrs. Andrew opening the door. He walked up rapidly toward her, introduced himself and explained quickly the reason he was there.

Mrs. Andrew called her husband and told him to bring Kara's apartment key. They went directly to the backdoor and Mrs. Andrew opened it.

Kara was still lying lifeless on the kitchen floor. Don tried to reanimate her without success. So Mrs. Andrew put a cold cloth on her forehead. Her hands seemed to move a little. She finally opened her eyes and looked around. She appeared confused and surprised to see Don and the Andrews in the kitchen. As soon as she saw the phone, it hit her again, Kevin was dead.

Don asked Kara if she needed any medical attention. Sitting on the floor, she shook her head. She got up. Still trembling, she murmured, "Can I have a glass of water?"

Mrs. Andrew brought her some. Kara sat on the chair and drank the whole glass.

After it, she looked at Don. "Is it true, Don?" she asked.

"I'm afraid so," he answered. "The Canadian Embassy called me an hour ago to let me know that the

Chinese military police had found two frozen bodies on a trekking trail near Rongbuk village." He paused. "The bodies found correspond to Kevin and Jerry profiles. They were the last foreigners seen in that area. Apparently, they froze to death. Cause unknown...Were they lost? Were they robbed? I asked the embassy agent. He told me that the police had not finished their report yet. He called me first because your telephone was busy and he asked me if I could get in touch with you..."

At that moment, the phone rang. Kara reached it and answered. That was Jennifer—she had just received the bad news. They both cried over the phone without saying a word. After the emotional outburst, Kara tried to articulate something. "Jennifer, we have to be sure it's them."

CHAPTER ELEVEN

IN DOUBT

Kara and Jennifer made together the arrangements for the funeral—Kevin and Jerry were both buried in London.

Kara stayed with Jennifer for a while. Kevin's friends and Jerry's family helped them go through the paperwork and supported them all the way. As for them, they heavily relied on each other for comfort; releasing a little at a time shredded emotions of painful memories.

A few weeks later, the notary called Kara and Don Robert to let them know about Kevin's will.

Kevin's parents were dead and he had no brother and sister. Therefore, he had left to Don Robert a big part of his fortune; the rest went to Kara which was a considerable amount of money. She could have retired right there if she wanted and not being worried about money for the rest of her life.

Going out of the attorney's office, Kara invited Don to have a drink somewhere. He agreed that they needed one. In the bar, Don looked perturbed. He admitted, "I did not expect to receive such an amount of money. I'm very uncomfortable with that."

Kara looked right in his eyes. "Don't. You deserve it. You were not only his best friend but also his family," she said. "I'm glad that you have it. To me, it's fair and I won't talk about that anymore. You see, money is not a big issue to me."

Don stared at her. She reaffirmed again. "I will never resent you for having it."

That was it. She then changed quickly the subject. She told him she was determined to go to Tibet in order to know what exactly happened over there.

Don Robert said, "I know that you want to go there by yourself but..."

"Thanks Don but I can do it without you," Kara replied firmly.

I know...I know you can but I want to go there with you. Kevin was my best friend too...I want to know what went wrong. Kara, I'm following you..."

After listening to him quietly, she nodded. Next, she ordered another drink. "Make it two," she said to the waiter.

During the week, Kara, Don and Jennifer gathered all the map duplicates left behind at both homes. Depressed and worn out, Jennifer declined the offer to go to Tibet with them. However, she warned them that she wanted to know every step they would take, every move they would make.

Kara and Don assured her they would call every day. It seemed to calm her nerves for a while.

#

Don slept most of the time on the plane for Asia—Kara did not mind at all. It gave her the opportunity to think about what she was going to do up there. She thought about the letter. Next destination: Tibet, she reminded herself. In her head, she tried to focus on the word Tibet. Nothing came up...she could not let it happen. A feeling of rage took place—then, more rage. She started raving over, my Kevin is dead—it looks like they used him as part of my f...job. Clenching her teeth, her mind shifted in a 180-degree consciousness. Upper

Midnight Circle—why are you doing this to me? Do you think I will take all that shit without rebelling? I got news for you! That's right! I'm going to get the bastards who did it to Kevin and Jerry and that's all. The earth guardian-savior-angel can find her way without me. Who do you think I am? Unbreakable! I've been broken in thousand pieces since my cousin died. Do you get it or do I have to kill myself to stop that nonsense?

Tears of anger and indignation began to pour heavily on her face. She did not want to wake up Don or disturbed the passengers around. She wiped them off, rapidly got up and went to the washroom. In that little cubicle, she sat on the toilet cover and madly let herself cry until the tears dried up. Bitterness inhabited all the space. She got up and washed her face. She looked harshly at her reflection in the mirror. She despised it. She then looked down. I will do it but first let me get these beasts.

Don was still dozing when she came back to her seat—she glanced at the window. Through the plane porthole, the sky was infinitely blue. Don woke up at that instant and said stupidly, "Nothing new under the sun."

She stayed silent. Then, she reached for her bag and took a tourist booklet on Tibet and started reading it. Don excused himself and left his seat to go to the washroom.

Kara was not done yet with her old image—the wound in her soul was too deep. And without her soul, she could not operate. Nothing new under the sun, she repeated silently. Abruptly, she put a hand on her mouth—she wanted to scream so loudly, so the sky would know for sure she was just not upset—she was f...mad...mad at that crazy world, mad at herself for having accepted something bigger than she could chew.

She ranted and raved at some vague entity telling it that the universe took her for granted. And it was laughing at her at that very moment—why—because it gave her some powers she could only use after terrible things happened, always too late to save lives. What good that could be!

After recalling what the voices had revealed to her in the past, she swore again. That made her feel better and then, she asked herself, <u>what is the f...reason I chose to live on this earth in the first place?</u>

When she saw Don coming in the aisle, she rapidly moved to his seat trying to make him believe she was napping. He sat and looked at her. Not wanting to disturb her, he got his small bag and began to check the maps.

Kara continued her inner conversation. She repeated the question many times—no answer came, and her energy depleted. Finally, the sleep deprivation caught her and she slumbered. When the flight attendant saw her, she put a small pillow on her lap.

She dreamt about Kevin. His smiling face let her know he was fine—he implored her to keep the little faith she had left, alive. "We will be together one day my beloved Kara. You know, you are still lovely to me even when you are mad." He laughed and his face faded in the mist.

Don and Kara went immediately to the consulate before going to the hotel. The government official appointed to the case came down the hall. He introduced himself, shook their hands and announced that he would meet them later in the evening. "Forgive me but something urgent had just came up," he simply said. He wrote down the hotel address, phone number and let them know that he would bring with him all the documents he had in his possession. He excused himself and went up rapidly to his office.

That night, the consulate agent came in Don's room at eight o'clock. He gave them names of the people who found Kevin and Jerry. He pointed out that he was not supposed to tell them but he felt that it was his duty to do so. "Don't mention it," he added. He tried to answer the many questions that Kara and Don asked but often failed due to the lack of information he had received. Before leaving, he said, "My staff and I did the best we could under those circumstances. Your next best help will be the police report—they are still investigating these cases. They will certainly disclose with you what they know."

First thing in the morning, they made an appointment with the police inspector. His English was very good. He asked them to show him the maps and the itinerary. After examining them carefully, he updated the maps with what he knew, particularly during the last seven days before their deaths.

After that, he invited them to follow him in another room where two other Chinese officers were busy profiling their cases. They all sat down at a long table— Kara and Don on one side, the two officers on the other one, and the inspector at the end of the table. He introduced them to the two agents. "My men have worked hard to try to find out through the information they had and the forms filled by Kevin Conte and Jerry Brown what could have happened to them from the beginning of their journey to the day they died."

He nodded at one of them. The officer began to talk. The inspector did the translation.

"First, the autopsy revealed that Kevin Conte had the left shoulder dislocated. It could have occurred on the slippery trail while trekking or he might have fallen while fighting with someone...You see, we are open to any possibilities at this point in the investigation. As to Jerry Brown, he had been found with a broken neck a mile away from Kevin's body—this one had bruises all over his body. The soldiers did not find any papers on them, no equipment left around, nothing. Both bodies were frozen. The soldiers looked around but did not find a single thing or tracks, again...nothing."

The inspector looked at Kara and then at Don. "However, we don't think it is a trekking accident. They had probably been mugged by road thieves, bandits. Their numbers have increased these past years but—they usually don't kill people—I mean, they usually stole whatever they could and left their victims alive. But in that case, the thieves had probably fought very hard with Kevin Conte and Jerry Brown before getting what they wanted or it could be for another reason. It's all speculation at that moment...We hope we will discover soon what really happened out there." He paused.

He listened attentively to the other officer before continuing the translation from Chinese to English.

"Here is his theory: these men whoever they are knew what they were doing. They hoped that the whole scene would look like a hand to hand fight between trekkers. They must have left some papers on them and equipment on the site. However, other travelers or criminals going that way could have taken it away after the crime not saying a word lest it could incriminate them."

The inspector checked his files papers, he then observed, "The autopsy also reveals that their deaths dated back approximately two days before being found..."

Kara interrupted him. "Can I have a duplicate of the autopsy, please?"

He looked a little annoyed. "Yes you can but you will need to fill out a form before reading it."

"Thank you," she simply said.

The inspector went on with the investigation report. "We had questioned the people who had found them and those who were involved with them in the past weeks. We have checked their alibis. Unfortunately, nothing significant appeared in order to bring some light on the case. The last two guides who had been with them at Rongbuk were two Sherpas. Monks from Rongbuk Monastery spoke highly of them." He paused before indicating to them, "Well, it's hard to believe that they were involved in that crime but we never know."

The inspector got up. Kara and Don followed him in his office. They talked for another hour. Then, Kara and Don returned to their hotel. After having a shower, Kara got dressed and left a message for Don at the clerk office. She needed to get some fresh air.

While walking and looking around, she thought, I feel like a fish out of water here. Lhasa was so unique and different. Quickly, she checked her belt. She sighed. She thought she had forgotten her camera. No, it was firmly attached to the belt—an automatic gesture, a second nature to her.

She walked at random, fascinated by the people, their clothes and the everyday life in the city. At the first tea house, she stopped and went in. The owner brought a teapot and a cup—he put it on the table. Smiling, he said, "Tourist...tourist..."

She just nodded.

Satisfied of her short answer, the old man showed again his rotten teeth and poured some tea in her cup. He went back to the counter and then served another client.

Kara took out of her bag a paper and pen. She began doodling, thinking—robbery seemed to be the only motive. Money, passports would be a good enough reason for culprits to murder them. While drinking slowly her tea, she became more determined than ever—she came all the way there for a reason too. She would not leave until she got the bad guys. Therefore, the only way for her to know who and where the suckers of energy were, was to find out whom...Obviously, she could not ask the investigators if they had found people in the area sucking their thumbs in a fetal position.

Her thoughts came back on what the inspector said before they left. He recognized they had no suspects yet. On the other hand, he declared they would pursue the investigation until they found the guilty ones. To her, he just wanted to reassure them in order to get rid of them—he had no intention whatsoever to go any further after they left the country. Kara had done her homework before leaving. The truth was they had no budget for longer investigation. She knew that the inspector could not do more than that—it was not his fault if the Chinese government did not want to spend any more money. Nevertheless, the authorities in place needed to save face by saying they were taking that case very seriously. Kara would take them at their words.

She decided to retrace Kevin and Jerry's path from Rongbuk Monastery to where the crime happened. Don could follow her or go back to Canada—that was up to him. She had to see for herself who those suckers were and how they handled that position. So she would be able to close the file of her heart once and for all. Then, she would go looking for that special being. But first, she had to stop at the police station.

Back to the hotel, she went directly to Don's room. She let him know what she had in mind. Not very happy to hear that, Don tried to discourage her about going to Rongbuk Monastery. She retorted she would go there anyway with or without him. Her stubbornness won over Don's arguments. Kara even convinced him to go back home. She told him she had already made all the arrangements with the police. The inspector had agreed to send her with two other police officers—they were supposed to drive there anyway.

When he heard that, Don mumbled something between his teeth.

"I have to take this opportunity," Kara said. "You know that I need to do it for myself. Don, I'm sure you understand why I insist so much about going there?"

Don gave up. "If this trip makes you feel better, then do it," he replied. "But I want you to know that I don't feel comfortable to leave you alone even if you go there with two cops."

"Look at me. I'm old enough to know what to do, and nobody is waiting for me at home," she said. "Please go home Don."

Resigned, Don said, "All right. I'll call Jennifer in London to give her that last news and then, I'll change my flight ticket."

In the morning, Don went with Kara to the police headquarter. He made sure she was still okay about going there. They said good-bye to each other and both left for different directions. There she was, leaving with those Chinese soldiers instead of two police officers. Kara did not mind at all—they were better equipped and would not be on her back all the time. It also meant more freedom to check out who appeared atrophied in the small population she would be meeting on her way to or in Rongbuk.

Taken aback by the majestic view of Tibet, she forgot for a moment who she was and let the mountains seduce her on the way to hell.

The day after, sitting at the back of the Land Rover, she read about Rongbuk Gompa and the monastery located in the sky at 5030 m—built sometime in the early part of the twentieth century; it was considered at that time to be the highest monastery in the world. Rongbuk Valley was also known as "the sanctuary of birds" and many other marvels. The inhabitants were not allowed to kill any animals in the area.

The soldier sitting in the front passenger seat turned his head. He saw that Kara was reading about their destination. As he could speak English, he told her about what the first British climbers found out when they arrived at Rongbuk in 1921. "The animals in the valley were extraordinarily tame. Wild blue sheep would come down to the monastery, not afraid of people. The scene continued to delight climbers and trekkers in the area for many years after..." He paused. "Unfortunately, things and events had changed over time..." The soldier ended the story abruptly as if he had already said too much to a white woman who had come there to make trouble.

Kara did not say anything. She knew his reason for not going any further. She had read everything she could on Rongbuk. People and animals had lost their freedom at the same time that they razed the monastery in the 1960's. Those orders came from the Red Guards; however, she could not bring that up to him. She stayed silent and looked at him as if she appreciated the effort he took for talking to her. Kara would finish the story herself—the inhabitants and monks began to rebuild the monastery in the late 1980's. A dozen monk and thirty or so nuns lived at that time at Rongbuk Gompa...She closed the book and for no apparent reason, she suddenly fell asleep with the book on her lap. Her dreams became saturated with a brownish background.

Approaching the area in the afternoon, Kara woke up and checked right away where they were. She could see more clearly the village surrounding the monastery. The soldier speaking English pointed to her with his finger.

"Further up the valley is a nunnery and there are some cave retreats scattered around the hilltops."

When they arrived, some nuns were outside talking to each other. As soon as Kara got off the Land Rover, she went directly to them and asked if someone could speak English. One of them came up to her. Kara let her know she wanted to spend two nights there. The nun simply nodded. Kara walked back to the Land Rover and told the soldiers they could get her in two days. They agreed and informed Kara they would contact her before it if they had new information concerning the investigation. She thanked them and picked up her backpack. After that, she followed the nun and paid for two nights. In return, she got an outhouse, two hot water thermoses and two extra blankets. In broken English, the nun let her know that they had no electricity and the night could be very cold. She also informed Kara that after seven o'clock, it would be impossible to get something.

As soon as she heard that, Kara told her she was hungry and asked if she could eat something before going to the room. The nun plainly said, "Be in the kitchen at five o'clock, you will eat what we eat— nothing less, nothing more".

After checking the outhouse, she put her backpack and the blankets on something that looked like a bed. Then she went out and walked around the monastery. Indeed, the view from there was breathtaking, Kara felt a little dizzy about being at such a high elevation but fortunately, she knew she would be all right the day after. She stayed there for a while contemplating the splendour of that place close to the roof of the world.

Around five o'clock, the starved Kara entered the monastery kitchen. One of the nuns gave her a bowl of rice and something else she could not recognize at first sight. The nun looked so stern that Kara just said,

"Thank you." She went to the nearest table where five nuns were eating. She asked them if she could sit there and one of them just showed the empty chair with her finger. She knew that the meal was considered 'sacred'. She ate in silence. She could not figure out what was in the bowl but she was so hungry that it seemed good enough to fill up her empty stomach.

After the meal, everyone started talking. She took the opportunity to show to the nun sitting next to her a picture of Kevin. She asked her if she knew the man. The nun shook her head and sighed. Then Kara showed it to the rest of the table. With great gestures, nuns made her understand that nobody in the kitchen spoke English. With the help of her Tibetan dictionary, she learned that only three persons spoke English in the whole monastery: the Head Lama, the old nun who received her in the afternoon and a young monk. She finally understood through their signs that she could not see them that night. She got up and helped the nuns with the dishes. Through the open window, she could see some pilgrims accompanied by their lamas talking outside with monks. Then, she turned her attention to the kitchen atmosphere. It was alive. Nuns were laughing. It sounded like a magical crystal clear chorus. Kara joined them laughing without knowing the reason. Her heart sadness lightened for a short moment. It's surprising to see how happy they seem to be without any artificial means to alter their egos, she thought. I can clearly hear the resonance of their hearts. I really feel better. It's hard to believe. That joyful sound might be contagious around here.

Suddenly, a young man ran into the kitchen. He spotted the strange woman among the nuns and came to her. Without wasting time, he asked Kara many questions, "Where do you come from? How long do you think you will be staying in Rongbuk? Why did you choose to stay here on your own for two nights?"

Kara only answered the first question.

"What brings you up here?" the young monk asked. "Because the Head Lama wants to know."

Kara smiled. Aware of what she might say could play for or against her, she said, "I have a good reason for being here. I would really appreciate to see the Head Lama as soon as possible and talked to him about that. Would it be possible to see him tonight?"

The young monk answered quickly, "Tomorrow will be better. I will let you know first thing in the morning at breakfast. See you tomorrow, madam."

He left the kitchen as fast as he came in. The nuns had finished their work there and were ready to go to their rooms. Kara went out for another walk.

In the outhouse, she prepared the bed and then, some clothes for the early morning.

She had brought candles with her and lit them up. All the cracks on the walls made the little room look surreal. The silence was complete. She lay down thinking about Kevin and Jerry that had slept in that monastery, maybe even in that room. She imagined them having a good time, then the good time changing into a nightmare. And darkness closed in on them, she thought.

The pain and sadness came back again. I miss you so much Kevin. She cried for a long time.

She woke up early in the morning, got dressed and went out immediately. She walked around. When the sun started rising, she stood up there looking at that wonderful event.

Shortly after, she heard a noise—she turned around and saw an old nun sitting on a porch. She was breaking some branches and putting them aside. Her face was deeply wrinkled. However, something infinitely beautiful emanated from her face and gestures—she was focusing only on what she was doing. Kara assumed she was preparing the morning tea.

She continued to watch the woman and looked at her clothes—the woman wore two brown overlapping robes, a brown felt hat and brown suede boots. It reminded her of something but she could not quite figure out what.

Then, the nun picked up pieces of branches and threw them in a kind of old bucket upside down with a hole at the top to feed the fire. Then, she put back an old rusty kettle on the center of that strange burning container. The nun continued to ignore Kara's presence—she seemed to concentrate completely on the act of feeding the fire. When the task ended, she lifted up her head, looked around and made a sign to Kara to approach.

Kara could not hear anything but crackling fire. Singing birds went mute at the same time that the nun waved at her. There were only the sun, the fire and the two of them invited to that sacred moment. Kara walked slowly toward her.

The nun put the last piece of wood in the container. At that very moment, Kara had the first insight—it happened like an electrical shock in her head. She did remember the woman. That one had been in one of her dreams—a long time ago. She even recalled the year it took place. The Redwood Forest, she thought.

Everything came back to her, the brown color of the building, the brown clothes; she stayed there astonished in front of the déjà vu woman and monastery. She could also remember the voice saying, "You will survive this tragedy as you did before. Don't blame yourself for it."

Closer, Kara repeated aloud, "This is not a dream; simply a different reality."

As soon as she said it, the woman looked intensely at Kara. Her eyes were so dark that Kara instinctively put her attention to the middle of her forehead.

The nun began chuckling and in flawless English said, "You have passed the test Kara. You have looked at where the real power lies. You have done it without thinking for the first time in your life. From now on, you will stop thinking before making every move. Life will be much easier on you and more enjoyable to you."

She stopped, looked at the fire again and continued. "There are many voices in your head. Don't fight them. Make them work for you instead of against you." She paused. "A way to do it—manage them by being the Voice. You are strong enough to do it now."

Kara stared at the nun. She wondered if that could be true.

After looking around again, the nun asked Kara to sit close to her on the porch. In a lower voice, she said, "Nobody knows that I speak English around here, not even the Head Lama. They all think that I can't read or write. That's all right. That's the way it was, is and will be. You see, I've been waiting for you all my life. The hope that day will come sustained me in my everyday tasks."

The nun touched her arm and said, "We don't have too much time to spend together...the night I spoke to you...I am not the one who made it happen. I had the same vision than you that night and I do remember..." She talked about Cloe and Kate for a while. She paused. "That was then," she added. "But now, you are here to do justice to Kevin and Jerry. Well, you come to the right place—they were here. They died a few days after. I would tell you more about that in a moment. You are also wondering why I know about your friends and you. Well, let me put it this way, I have good spiritual connections too."

She took Kara's hand and rubbed it. She gently said, "I know you are very upset by Kevin's death. He was the love of your life and no one but you can soothe your heart ache. Your distress is deep but..." She looked for words and finally told her, "Kara, believe that you fairness principle is at work here. You'll see by yourself; what I mean..." And she told her what she knew.

They both stayed silent for a while contemplating the scenery. Then, the old nun signalled, "Okay Kara, we have not too much time left. The fact that I speak English is our secret..." Her hand seemed to warm up Kara's spirit. "You're not only here for dealing with the death of your loved ones. There is a deeper purpose behind that. I have a message for you. I have known it since the age of ten. The One you will be looking for is a little girl living in the middle of blue waters. She is part of the tradition where children are considered Kings of the earth. She is ten years old, had brown hair and brown eyes. You have seen her many times in your visions and at first, you thought she was Caucasian. Well, you're half-right—she is Métis. As you already know, your job is to find her, then protect her and let her be until she can fly on her own. She will change the world forever." The nun laughed. "Of course, for the better—she will enlighten humankind...okay now...I remind you that you will be in charge of her security and that means being at her side until they will tell you to let her go. Then, you will be able to go back to your life the way it was before."

Kara looked suspicious about that.

"I assure you that you will be free of doing whatever you like after the mission is accomplished."

The nun got up and went down the porch. Stepping back a little, she said, "Let me have a good look at you—I'm so happy to see you and feel you. Your light inside is so intense. As the fire, you have the power to warm, feed and destroy. However, yours is slightly different—it's burning to rekindle the joy that strives at that moment to resurface through the turmoil of your soul."

Kara thought about the nuns' laugh in the kitchen the day before. That was pure joy but she doubted she would have that some day. She got up and stepped down. The nun pushed her gently on the back. She smiled with all the four upper teeth she had left. She emphasized with her hand, "Go girl! Go to your destiny."

The sun had disappeared to give place to the mist. Through the light fog, they heard voices. Nuns were coming to have their early morning tea. Quickly, the old nun gave her a cup of tea and murmured, "Good bye, my loved one."

Kara thanked the woman for the tea. She knew she would not see her again. She kissed her quickly on the cheek. On her way back to the outhouse, she felt amazingly calm. I am on the right path, she thought. After it, she had breakfast in the monastery kitchen and waited for the young monk to show up.

He appeared in the door looking for her, He walked up to her. "The Head Lama is ready to see you. Have you had breakfast yet?"

She nodded. She followed him to the Head Lama room.

As she went in, all the monks and the one that brought her there disappeared by the back door—Kara was alone with the Tibetan priest.

He greeted her. They introduced each other. Then, he invited her to sit down on one of the cushion on the ground. He observed Kara for a while without talking. Then, he asked, "What brings the honour of your visit to this monastery, madam?"

"I have come to Tibet to know what exactly happened to my fiancé Kevin Conte and his friend Jerry Brown," she answered straightforwardly."

The priest nodded.

"I was informed that they were trekking in this area before being killed by road thieves. In Lhasa, the police officers in charge of the investigation have told me that they had spent a few days here with some Sherpas. Now...I would like to know if they talked to you or any of the monks and if so what did they say? I also want to know if my fiancé and friend mentioned anything unusual like they were afraid or suspicious of someone. I mean—did they look fearful for their lives? Anything would be appreciated, particularly coming from you?"

The Head Lama raised his hand. "Forgive me madam but I must stop you right here because I will tell you the same thing that I told the police officers and you already know it. However, I just want to clarify something here before going any further. These two guides that the police mentioned are not from the region."

He perceived her eagerness for any piece of truth. "Would you like to meet the two men that accompanied them for a few weeks before the tragedy occurred? He asked.

Kara acknowledged with her eyes.

The Tibetan priest called the young monk. "Go get the Sherpas," he told him.

As they arrived, the Head Lama said, "Madam, you can ask them anything you want." Looking at the young monk, he added, "He will translate it to you."

"Thank you," Kara said.

"Hi," said the two Sherpas. One of them told her that he could understand English but had a hard time to speak it.

The young monk explained to them the reason she was there—their faces changed dramatically. Then the Head Lama talked to them. A few minutes later, he signalled with his hand that they were ready to answer her questions.

Kara went ahead with it. They tried to answer the best they could. Their responses sounded genuine—she knew in her heart that they spoke the truth. On the other hand, they looked fearful of something...but what? They are probably afraid of being accused if the police could not find the culprits, she thought.

She made them repeat the whole story again and began writing down the important points—Kevin and Jerry slept only one night at the monastery—the young monk added, "In the same outhouse than yours." She had goose bumps while hearing it but did not let it interfere with what they were saying—she paid attention to their stories instead.

There it went: Kevin and Jerry trekked with the two guides for two weeks before being killed. At the monastery, they left the guides know they were not sure about what they were going to do. The Sherpas contract ended up there. However, they were open to the opportunity to be hired again.

The day after, in the early morning, Kevin and Jerry went to the village. They came back in the afternoon and paid the Sherpas. After giving them extra money, they explained that they really wanted to know that area well, so they needed to be with people from the place. They had just met people in the village that were ready to take them to some places never seen before. They specified that they had little time left before returning home and were still thirsty for some excitement.

The Sherpas asked them their names. As they never heard of them before, they warned Kevin and Jerry to be cautious.

One of the Sherpas concluded, "They were having a good time. They thought the good luck was on their sides. Then, we heard about their deaths..."

The young monk finished the story. "After their deaths, the two Sherpas and the Head Lama tried to know more about those three so-called guides but none in the village seemed to be acquainted with them."

The Head Lama explained to Kara that the villagers were very reticent to give information after the tragic event, lest that it would bring bad luck to the village. Therefore, they chose to stay silent. "They asked me to pray for them in order to get rid of the curse hovering over the area," he said.

Kara knew that the police had tried to get better results from the villagers while investigating the area but failed poorly at extracting any elements of information.

The Tibetan priest informed Kara that the two guides would be leaving the day after for Nepal. "If you have any other questions, this is your last chance to do so," he added.

The two Sherpas looked anxiously at her.

They just want to be done with it and go home, Kara thought. "It's all right," she said. In fact, she wished the same thing for herself—closing forever the file of death.

She took their hands and thanked them for their time. The two guides immediately went out.

"I'm going to have a walk to the village," she said to the Head Lama.

He nodded. Then, he told her, "This monk will accompany you to the village."

The young monk seemed very pleased with the proposition.

Kara went to the outhouse. She touched the walls slowly in memory of Kevin and Jerry. After it, she picked up a light coat, a hat and a small backpack. She closed the door and put her sunglasses on.

The young monk was waiting for her at the central entrance. As soon as she showed up, he looked at her tourist disguise and simply smiled with compassion.

Kara smiled back. She put her hand on his shoulder and said, "Thanks for being with me today. I think it's time to tell me your name young man."

"You can call me Doya, it's my birth name," he answered enthusiastically.

They walked to the village that surrounded the monastery. It was not very far away. Doya told her he had to do some errands. And he asked her if she would be all right on her own for a short time.

Kara nodded.

He showed her a tea house. "We will meet each other there. Okay?"

She quickly said, "I now realize that the village is not very big. I will find easily my way around. So, don't wait for me—I will walk back to the monastery without problem."

He pointed out that the Head Lama would not like it. So to put the young man at ease, she showed him a green gate. "Come meet me there at five o'clock. Okay?"

He reluctantly agreed. And they both went on their way.

Kara had something else in mind than just walking around. She knew that if the guides were still hidden there, she would know it. On the way, she asked a villager where the market was. Amused by her clothes, the middle-aged man first commented, "You tourist."

"Yes, I am," she said. "Where is the market?" And she began gesticulating about food.

Finally, the man understood. He pointed his finger at the wanted direction.

While going toward the place, she became aware that more and more children were gathering around her, touching her clothes and asking money, all at the same time. They kept laughing and screaming until Kara stopped abruptly.

She got her camera out of her backpack and raised it in the air. Very loudly, she said, "Get off my back!"

The children stared at the camera and stayed silent for a moment. But they went mad again. Kara saw a big rock beside a fountain; she walked to it and climbed it.

On her pedestal, she shouted, "Stop!" She put back slowly the camera inside the backpack.

All the children stopped yelling. They seemed suddenly cheerless.

She stayed up there patiently, thinking about what she would do next. A few minutes later, she began to mimic them. Then she made them understand with a sweeping gesture that she was ready to give them a second chance. She got out her camera again.

Some passer-by villagers stopped and watched with amusement the command she used on children. Before jumping on the ground, she added, "Okay, that's better now." Then she decided to mime to them what she wanted from them in exchange for their pictures.

The children all laughed at the way she did it. Nevertheless, they obeyed to all her gestures. She took pictures of them in groups and then individually. One of the villagers approached and asked her in English if she could photograph him. He explained that his mother was very sick and lived far away from there. Therefore, she would appreciate having a picture of her son by her bedside.

Kara agreed with pleasure. She then asked him for the village address. After writing it, she said, "Please, let the children know they would receive their pictures by mail." They were all happy to hear the good news.

"Can you translate too to them? Children, I was very pleased to do it for you but if you want your pictures, you will leave me alone from now on."

After he translated it, the children looked at each other, made some comments, giggled and ran away.

The calm came back. The man asked Kara if he could help her with something. At that moment, she got an idea. "As a matter of fact, you might be able to help me. I have come here in order to find the best guides of the region. Do you know someone who does that in this area?" She explained to him that she was preparing a tour for a group of people, and she wanted to know what the village could offer as resources and equipment.

The man pointed out that the army had a base camp not far away—it could supply the expedition and transport people and material. She nodded as if she seemed very interested by what she heard.

But then she shrugged her shoulders. "Thanks but— what I need and want—let's say...having soldiers as guides are not something I have been looking for..."she said. "You see, I would rather choose Tibetans, the ones who know the region well. I must say that the clients I represent are ready to pay more if they have the right people." Then, she mentioned the amount of money involved in the whole project.

"Thanks anyway," she said, faking her disappointment. She turned back and started walking toward the market. She had a last look at him. She saw his face changing when he understood that a lot of money would be spent in that expedition.

He went after her and while walking together, he said nervously, "I know some people who could help you. Please follow me."

On the way, he indicated, "These guides know the region well."

Kara could see a grin on his face when he turned on his right. They took a small alley.

"Please answer my curiosity?" he asked. "I'm wondering why they choose a woman to prepare and organize this expedition or tour; well...I just want to warn you that men here are not used to deal with women that try to be men."

"Do you want to help me or not?" Kara firmly said.

"Okay, okay."

She could feel the heat inside. But she had to shut up—otherwise, he would be suspicious. The man looked openly at her body while walking. She could not stand it—she gave him a hard stare. However, she stopped it; she was too close to the truth.

"It's not far," he told her.

On a casual tone, she said, "You know this is not a scientific expedition. These people just want to have a good time. They are not climbers but trekkers. Some of them are photographers like me; others just want to enjoy the splendour of the Himalayas. They have no desire whatsoever to climb the Everest.

The man just nodded. He turned on his left and went in a very narrow alley. He stopped at the first door and knocked three times.

A big bald man opened the door. Kara thought that he didn't look like being in a good mood.

In Tibetan, the villager explained to him what the matter was. With a look of annoyance, the bald man said he was out of business, and he knew nobody who would be willing to do that kind of expedition. Then, the other man asked him if he could talk to him alone inside. The big man let him inside and closed loudly the door on Kara.

She could hear the big man talking vociferously to the other in Tibetan. So she assumed he was telling him she was a liar and certainly not here for hiring people.

She was not far away from the reality of their exchange. He was informing the villager that the two foreigners found dead on the road had a link with that woman. And he warned him that it was too risky to let her know more than she did. He opened the door, pushed rudely the villager out, had a last glance at Kara and shut the door vigorously.

Still shocked by that revelation, the villager stared at Kara. "I can help you no more. I think you're here for another reason," he said nervously.

She recognized that she had to be straightforward if she wanted him to cooperate with her one more time. She asked him very calmly, "Does the name Kevin Conte ring a bell to you?"

He became pale. "So it's true. You came here to make trouble," he replied. The police had already questioned and investigated the whole village. Nobody had nothing to do with it—I think you'd better go back to your country—It's the only advice I can give you because..."

On that, he ran away without finishing his sentence. Kara realized, I'll have the villagers on my back soon if I keep questioning them.

"So now, what am I going to do?" she asked herself aloud. She started walking at random. Suddenly, she had a big hunch about going to the village outskirts. She changed her direction and walked out of the village. She stopped at the top of the hill and sat down. She opened a bottle of water and looked at the peaceful landscape.

Down the hill, she saw a young boy in the meadow. Probably a young shepherd watching his sheep, she thought.

As soon as the child became aware of her presence, he ran up the hill with curiosity. However, while approaching, he stopped and kept his distance.

Kara smiled. She said, "Hello."

He looked very shy. He smiled a little.

She took off her sunglasses. The boy seemed surprised—he stared at her face.

He was a handsome young boy around nine or ten years old. His hair was like those people from Jamaica, long twisted curl—his clothes, very colourful. He began to walk slowly to her. Then, he sat down not too far.

"What's your name?" Kara asked.

With broken English, he said candidly, "My name—Chosang. What—your name?"

Kara was surprised that he could speak English a little. "My name is Kara," she answered. "Where did you learn to speak English?" she asked him slowly.

"From my dad...he died last year."

Kara said gently, "I'm sorry to hear that."

A strange thought came to her, <u>I don't know why but if I had a son, I would like him to be just like this boy. He seemed such a genuine child—you can see it in his pure brown eyes.</u>

The boy moved closer to her without saying anything. He then touched her hand and murmured, "I know why you are here...I can help you with that."

Perplexed, she stared at him. Her mind opened up—she had met him in one of her nightly trips.

"I feel like I already know you, little boy," she whispered.

The child nodded. He then admitted. "I dream too of you." He immediately got up, took her hand. "Come with me."

They walked down the hill and followed a path along the meadow until they reached an old house.

"Grandmother's house," he said. "Wait outside. I...I talk to grandmother first."

He went in the house and came back with her. They both stayed on the porch. The old woman looked upset.

However, she started talking. He then began to translate to Kara what his grandmother was telling him.

First, Kara did not understand a word. She told him to go slower. He rephrased it.

"My grandmother...hid three men...in the shack behind the house...two weeks now. Know them from another place when they were young. At that time, they were okay...but now they are bad, bad men...She took care of them when they arrived because...because they are sons of her best friend when young...But these men are road thieves...and a terrible thing happened to them. My grandmother now believes there is a curse on her house and the village."

After paying attention to every word the boy said, Kara made him repeat it. His grandmother started shaking. The boy stopped talking. A heavy silence covered the air. The only thing they could hear was their own breathing and heart beats. The woman murmured something to the boy's ear. He nodded.

"Come with me. I will show you," he said sadly.

They went to the back of the house. An old shack stood there, and behind it, was another. They walked to the last one. When the boy opened the door, a horrible smell came out. She glimpsed inside with a hand on her mouth. She could not see anything until Chosang pointed with his finger where they were. A few minutes later, she got used to the dark and distinguished on the ground three men curling in a fetal position.

She observed, "They do not seem very alive."

The young boy answered. "They all died yesterday. My grandmother could not do anything for them anymore."

She assessed the situation rapidly and asked the child to leave her alone for a while. He refused.

She said loudly, "Just go!"

He left in disgust.

She put a handkerchief on her mouth and went in. Twenty minutes later, she had a last look at the three men and concluded silently, <u>mission accomplished.</u> She closed the door and joined the boy and his grandmother. The old woman looked petrified with fear when she saw Kara approaching; she stepped down and fell on her knees. She began praying the sky, crying her heart out. Chosang went behind and put both hands on her shoulders. His eyes met Kara's. "Now justice is done Kara. Please, forgive us," he said gravely.

"No need to be forgiven, you have done the right thing," she replied. "Your grandmother and you had followed your heart and showed compassion to those who refused it...Okay...I will ask the Head Lama tonight to take care of the corpses. I really don't want the police or army to be involved with it. Translate it to your grandmother."

The old woman looked relieved. Chosang came up to Kara and put his hand on her cheek. She put her arms around him and kissed him on both cheeks. Then she helped the woman to get up and walked with her to the porch. After it, she talked to the boy alone. He then went sitting on the porch and repeated it in Tibetan to the woman what she just said. "I don't want you to be in trouble. I did not come here to do harm or hurt you in any ways..."

To make them feel better, she stood at the front of the house and raised her hand. "I declare that the curse over your house and the village is lifted forever. As soon as they will remove the bodies, you will enjoy your life the way it was before and will forget quickly that event. My work is done here. I will return home in two days."

The boy whispered the words to his grandmother.

Chosang walked back with Kara to the meadow. His sheep were waiting for him. Kara got out the camera and took many snapshots of him with his sheep. She really loved that child. Before leaving, she hugged the child a last time and wished him well.

The weeping Chosang admitted, "In my dreams, I first thought...you spiritual energy wanted to punish us. Now, I know...you goddess and wish us well. Thank you. I love you."

"I love you too with all my heart little boy. But as you can see, I'm just a human being like you, nothing more."

She went up the hill, turned and waved to him a last time.

The young monk was waiting at the green gate. He smiled largely as he saw Kara coming. She checked her watch. <u>Perfect timing,</u> she thought. It was exactly five o'clock.

#

Kara flew to London before returning to Vancouver. Jennifer wanted to know everything. Carefully, Kara chose her words before making up a story about the police investigation and the so-called villagers' revenge over the three road thieves. Jennifer listened to it while holding her breath.

Kara ended up saying, "Well, they did not get away with it; they died. I can personally confirm that they were the culprits." She got up and reached her purse— then, gave to Jennifer Jerry's watch.

"I found it in one of the thieves' pocket," she said.

Jennifer put the watch in both hands and rubbed it as she wanted to make Jerry reappear before her. Powerless, she began crying, opened her hand and let it fall on the floor.

Kara waited a few minutes before saying, "The Head Lama and the villagers are deeply sorry about our losses. They hope that you and I can forgive them, so they can move forward with their lives."

Jennifer reached Kara's hand. "At least, justice is done for our dear ones."

Then, she asked Kara to go with her to the church where Jerry and Kevin's funeral had been held. In the church, they both lit up two candles and prayed for their lovers and for all the people who were involved in the tragedy. Then, Kara lit up another candle for Tibet and its people sufferings.

Kara spent the whole month with Jennifer. At the end, they both admitted that they had enough to feel sorry for themselves. The mourning process was not over yet but...Kara had to go back to British Columbia. The search for the girl would begin soon.

At home, the first thing she did was rereading the blue book and letters. After it, she took her journal and revised all her dreams, visions and encounters. Then, she made a flow chart. After doing it, she recalled the old nun's wise words; it just validated what she saw on the graphic representation. While reworking the chart, she thought, she is supposed to be found in the middle of blue waters, well!! it means in the middle of nowhere—where the child is considered the king...legends, myths or truth. She raised her arms and implored to whomever, "What do you mean by that? Give me more info, please. I cannot go through all the seas of the earth with just that as tips."

She began walking in the apartment thinking obsessively about that nowhere. Mitsou the cat, regarding it as another departure, started following her like a dog. Kara observed the cat. She stopped her neurosis. Mitsou was afraid to be left alone again. She picked up the cat and comforted her. Purring, purring was the cat—she felt guilty of not knowing what to do with her. I will go to a nowhere land in a very short time with no way of knowing when I will be back. She caressed the cat and whispered to her ears, "You will be ok with the Andrews. I'm sure they will take good care of you."

With her big round eyes, the cat stopped purring and looked at her. Kara could feel intuitively what Mitsou thought, I got it. I cannot follow you. I'm less energetic than before. I'm too old for chasing the dragon. And actually, I preferred my cosy life. The Andrews are good to me and I have good cat neighbours. It will be all right my friend.

Then, the cat went back to her purring. With a smile, Kara thought, I don't know if I have too much imagination or just want to feel good but... She laughed.

That little break appeared to be beneficial—she got an idea. She went to her desk, looked behind and picked up a rolled world map. After unrolling it, she stuck it on the wall. She sat down before it and checked oceans and seas carefully while saying to herself, "Well, well, well, the middle of blue waters represents to me an island somewhere in the ocean." Looking first at the Pacific Ocean, she shouted, "There are thousands and thousands of islands. Where do I start?"

After chewing her thoughts on the map for half an hour, she went out to buy a big Earth globe in a specialized geographic store. She also bought some books about different islands in the Pacific and Atlantic Oceans and other seas. At home, she put the Earth globe and all the stuff on the kitchen table and began working. Another hour went by without making any significant progress—she went to get a beer in the fridge. She sat back and opened randomly one of the books. When she looked at the picture on the page—the image hit her like a brick. She screamed and then, mumbled, "How could I miss it? Oh, my God! It was so obvious! I'm brainless."

It took her back in the past—around eleven years old, she had read a book on Tahiti. She had been strongly impressed to learn that the Tahitian people treated children as kings...My memory is getting sharper; I remember exactly my thoughts...that's the way it should be on this earth, the child is king, and when he grows up, he treats in the same manner the younger ones. At the end, everyone becomes a king or a queen of life. Wow!

She continued where she had left; in transmitting the same philosophy to their children, the parents and caretakers understood that the result would bring a more balanced society. She paused. Marleen was on her mind. She began idealizing the magic island. The child abuser would have a tough time under these circumstances. He would probably be put out of the picture at the first offend. But, I'm pretty sure that they have a small number of these bastards...given the fact that these islanders have a loving and happy childhood themselves. In their wisdom, they must know how to deal with those who exhibit a deviant behaviour. They receive help or send away immediately. That would be a good pattern for us...

She then came back to children's kingdom. The child would receive early in his life many gifts as self-esteem, confidence and love. What a nice dream! What a good model of society for the rest of the world to embrace! I wonder if they are still doing it.

By then, Kara was almost sure that it meant Tahiti. The day after, she bought everything she could find on it. She read all day trying to find out what island she would go first. She went to bed early, exhausted. Before sleeping, she asked the Universe to let her know if Tahiti was the right place to look for the One.

That night, she dreamt she was flying over the Pacific Ocean. She knew that it was the Pacific because she flew over Easter Island—she recognized the big statues. First, she hovered around them and then twirled on one of them. Kara grasped part of the statue's message. The Big Head told her, "You are going in the right direction..."

Glad to hear the good news, she was ready to fly back. However, the wind got stronger and pushed her back. The wind stopped, and she swiftly felt drawn by the statues. And then, she froze in the air. They communicated to her that they would not let her go until she listened completely to what they had to reveal to her. Having no choice, she accepted and graciously landed at the statue foot that first talked to her.

At first, she felt intimidated when looking at the huge statue size. However, she was not frightened at all by the gigantic head facing her fragile body. After all, they were allies. She sat down and listened.

The Big Head immediately began speaking. "She does not know she is the One, her parents either. You will have to be very careful at your first encounter with this little girl—not to scare her. The Universe or Loving Energy if you like is preparing her coming in the world. Now, what is important for you to know is as soon as you will be alone with the One, you will use the key word MITI-FETIA=PO, which means in English SEA AND STARS=NIGHT. It will then set off her memory of the Big Plan concerning the planet Earth." The statue paused.

It then suggested strongly to Kara to write everything down as soon as she woke up.

The statue went on. "Her first name is Namui Mata—it means the Eye. All we know about her parents is her mother is French, his father is Tahitian. They are both loving parents. They do not belong to any religion; however, they do believe in the human wisdom. To us, it is the best beginning you can give a child. Life tries to understand itself—therefore, the process becomes easier when it is not distorted by preconceived systems of beliefs or worship around God or other deities."

Kara could hear the rest of the statues giggling. The Big Head said, "We know what we are talking about. Men carved us from volcanic rock and erected us for a specific purpose. They lined us up on raised platforms as giant guardians of the world. They thought we would cast a powerful spell on evil deities and therefore, protect them forever. That was the reason our creators put us here in the first place. Unfortunately, they denied the law of nature by cutting trees on the island. So, by lack of wisdom, these people died of malnutrition, disease and hopelessness. A few of their children survived to tell the story."

A heavy silence enveloped the statue. Kara waited.

Finally, it continued. "But us...after that, we became useless. We could not take it any longer; therefore, we decided that it was time to get a life on our own—we made a vow to serve life the best we knew: we, Big Heads, would wait for the One who would set up the beginning of a new era...Namui Mata is the One. The Loving Energy let us know that she will arrive on a Sunday. In fact, the same Sunday the explorer the Dutch Admiral, Jacob Roggeveen put his foot on land in 1722. So it will be on Easter Sunday.

The statue lightened up. "What is good about the history of Easter Island is everything makes sense in the long run." It vibrated a good laugh and the rest of the statues expressed amusement. They murmured to Kara, "We may look austere but indeed, we have a good sense of humour."

The spoken statue explained to Kara why they had been delighted that the island received the new name of Easter. "As you know, the word Easter has many pagan customs associated with it; therefore, it is not simply a religious story. To us, Easter means the Goddess of Spring and Dawn. We thank the Anglo-Saxons for historically connecting us to that version of Vernal Equinox. Okay...to us, the symbol Easter means new Life, a coming back into use, a celebration of the spring, the renewal of nature itself. Moreover, ten years ago on Easter Sunday, we have felt at the daybreak the wind coming from the East. It brought us the good news. Then later on during the day, we have seen our destiny written in the sky in blue and white. The message was: she is here on planet earth. Right after it, we began smelling her divine nature and tasting her earthly flavour. And with the time, we learned that we could see her more in the dawn when the stars and the sea create a new vision of the day. Since we have known that you would be dropping by our place, we can see her now more clearly."

The Big Head stopped talking; however, Kara felt it had not finished yet. She did not move and stayed quiet.

It then continued. "Until now, we were the voices unheard. You have changed it by flying over us tonight. Kara, the main thing you need to know is you are on the right path from now on. You will come back physically with the One to visit us. Know that we are the teachers that have been chosen to guide the One through her journey. Go back to sleep now. See you tomorrow for the completion of the message. Good night, my friend."

First thing in the morning, Kara wrote down everything she had heard. The night after, Kara flew again over Easter Island. The Big Head greeted her, and without wasting time, continued where it had left. "The teaching will start with us. Protecting the One is your work. However, don't worry about that too much—you will not need any weapons to defend her. You already get the power within you. You can easily neutralize the enemy. Nevertheless, you need to have something more because you will be the Eye until she will be ready to play that role. Therefore, we want you to know that you have just received new skills. Vigilance and watchfulness will be inseparable with your neutralizing effect on people. It will not be easy at the beginning; you will get tired quickly. After all, you are just a human being!"

"Of course, I'm not made of stone," she ironically riposted.

The statue sighed and went on. "All right. Get some rest when tired but keep going..." It paused.

It then added, "We also want you to know that Namui Mata and you will be laughed at and ridiculed by many men on the planet. Don't let these morons stop you—Namui Mata's work is too important. Encourage her, get her up when she is down and let her be free to speak up her mind even when it is dangerous to do so. She will have to dare a lot in order to confront people and the Establishment as you say in your country. In fact, she will have to shake up many numbing soles, particularly women. Many of them do not know which way to go—stay silent about their uncomfortable past or speak up of their unacceptable future.

The Big Head stopped and talked to the other statues. Kara waited patiently. Before going back to sleep, put your thoughts together. Know that we have longed for Namui Mata and you before you had even existed on this plan. You are welcome to visit us in your dreams, anytime...Tomorrow morning, you will know what needs to be done. Please, do remember the key word MITI FETIA (SEA AND STARS) because you will use it to communicate on a larger scale many times in the future. Good night Kara."

CHAPTER TWELVE

BLUE WATERS

Kara woke up muttering MITI FETIA. After rubbing her eyes, she looked around. Good! I'm in my bed—in my room. Mitsou started meowing. Kara got up fast; she felt a little dizzy, so she sat back. It went away; relieved, she slowly walked and said aloud, "Happy to walk on the floor instead of flying around. I guess I'll need more flying and landing lessons in my nocturnal escapades if I don't want to crash during the day. What would Big Head think of me, little head?"

She fed the cat, made some coffee and had breakfast. She put on some soft music and took a book on Tahiti on the table. The more she read, the more she was convinced that French Polynesia was the right place to look for the child. She devoured the book in no more than two hours. After that, she got dressed and went out. She came back at the end of the afternoon with a ticket for Papeete, Tahiti in her pocket.

Three days before going for the great adventure, she called her family, then Don Robert and Jennifer. She let them know that she had been offered a big project—and that one would take a long time to be realized. She emphasized on the fact that she did not know when she would be back. So she informed them not to try to contact her because she would be on the road most of the time—she would be in touch with them when possible. To her, that was time to say goodbye.

Family and friends were not surprised at all—they knew Kara could not stay at the same place for too long. Her family was pleased to hear it. To them, Kara was ready to move on with her life.

After the last phone call, she said aloud, "Now I'm back to business."

In the afternoon, she bought a new camera and many films. Then, she shipped the rest of her equipment to Papeete. If she wanted to be taken seriously by Tahitians, she had to look professional. With all that camera equipment, they too would assume she was on a big project.

On the last day, she relaxed all afternoon with Mitsou on her knees. She had to make a decision about her. She called the Andrews. They invited her to come up right away. When Kara appeared at the door with the cat in her arms, Mrs. Andrew insisted that she had dinner with them.

While eating, she calmly let them know that she would leave for Tahiti the day after.

"On the road again," Mr. Andrew said.

"Yeah...it must be in my blood." Kara laughed. "I was offered a big project in Tahiti. However, the reason I came here is about the cat..."

"Don't worry about that; you know that we will take care of Mitsou," Mrs. Andrew said.

"I know you will," Kara replied. "The only problem is I expect to be away for a long, long time. I thought about bringing her to Tahiti but the truth is she is too old. I think the best for the cat is to stay in the same environment. Now...it's up to you," Kara said.

The Andrews both said at the same time, "Yes."

Mr. Andrew added, "I'm so used to this cat; she's part of the family to me. What about you, Mrs. Andrew?"

She smiled at her husband. "The cat likes us and we like her. There's no problem; we will adopt her. She'll be just fine with us."

"Thank you so much," Kara gladly said.

"Why are you going to Tahiti and for how long?" Mr. Andrew asked.

Kara simply repeated the same thing she told the others.

"That's good," Mr. Andrew said. Then, on a mocking tone, he continued in broken French, "Comment...is...votre...Tahitian...or...Français, mademoiselle.

Kara giggled. She answered in a flawless French, "Mon français est assez bien. Je vais apprendre le tahitien sur place. Et vous, madame Andrew, comment est votre français?"

"My French is simply rusty," she answered. "However, I do remember a song in French." She took her glass of red wine and started singing an old song in French that she had learned by rote when she was a child.

They all cheered up.

After the meal, Kara went down to her apartment and came back. She gave the Andrews a cheque and told them, "That would pay for the medical care of the cat if there's any need; and for the food. And the rest is for the apartment. Hope it is ok with you."

Then she gave them another envelope full of cash. "That should take care of the rest."

"It's too much. You are too generous," Mr. Andrew said.

"Take it, please. It's easy to be generous when you deal with other generous people," she replied.

She wrote down a phone number. "This number is for emergency only," she said. Just before opening the door, she added, "Oh, yes. I forgot to tell you it may sometimes happen that my brothers stay in the apartment when they are in town for business."

"No problem Kara. They are welcomed," Mrs. Andrew replied.

In the morning, she woke up with the blue envelope opened on her heart. She felt rested and in a good mood. Ready for Papeete, she thought.

Mrs. Andrew came down to help her close everything in the apartment. With the cat in her hand, she said to Kara, "Don't call a taxi. We will drive you to the airport." And she went up.

#

From the Faaa airport, Kara took a cab which drove her to the Kon Tiki hotel. On the way, she turned down the window and inhaled deeply the sweet air—a mix of flowers fragrance and sea scent. She thought about the travel agent that sold her the ticket, she was right. I'm pleased to be on the most glamorous tropical island. For a short moment, her body experienced a kind of nirvana—an indescribable bliss. A soft voice inside let her know, welcome to the pearl of the Pacific Kara, Mystery and joy will be part of your present and future. Embrace it with a passionate eye."

And so she did—seduced by everything her eyes could take. Downtown, the streets fully alive were swarming with people, running children, bikes, cars, and trucks, and colourful buses.

The view from her room gave on the sea—she immediately went to the balcony and gazed at the horizon. After a while, her body began screaming. She realized she did not eat for the past twelve hours. On the plane, she had no appetite and refused to eat anything that could jeopardize her stomach. It's time to get to know the Tahitian cooking.

Instead of going to the hotel dining room, she went out. She walked on the Boulevard Pomaré and stopped at the first restaurant. It had a nice terrace—the menu was interesting and the smell coming from the kitchen terribly inviting. She could not resist anymore. While eating, she thought, I spoil myself. Everything is mouth-watering and delicious. Thank you Papeete. She thanked the waiter and let him know that she was very pleased and satisfied with the Tahitian cooking.

After that elaborate lunch, she had a little walk. Wandering around, she ended up at the waterfront where several rows of worldwide yachts, powerboats, rusty freighters, big tankers and interisland schooners were stowed. She sat on a bench and watched for a while busy men discharging their copra cargos.

Later on, while strolling on the wide crowded boulevard, she met a man she swore to herself having seen before in her life. She turned back to have a better look at him but by magic, he was already gone. She continued walking. Where and when could I have met him before? After a while, she gave up. Well, I guess— I have travelled too much and met too many people in my life.

It was getting hot and the traffic heavier. Time to go back to the hotel, she thought. On her way, people seemed to disappear in the streets. She checked the time. It was right after noon. She smiled reminding herself about the customs and habits of Tahiti. People go home, have a big lunch with wine, then had a nap. That's the way to go, Papeete. Minutes later, she followed the custom—she went to her room and relaxed.

An hour later, she checked the pamphlets, info and maps of different islands. However, it didn't help her know what to do or where to start. Then, she considered, first thing, where is Namui Mata living? On Papeete, Moorea, Raiatea Hahaa or Bora Bora. She took the phone book and checked all the Matas. There was no Mata last name, only first name. She was disappointed. It meant that she would have to search seriously everywhere, starting by Papeete and then, the other islands. I'm determined to comb every square on foot if necessary; however, I wish that it would be the last resort.

She went sitting on the balcony with a map of Papeete in her hands and started to look at it. However, a few minutes later, by lack of concentration, she gave up. Her mind was focusing instead on the man's face seen earlier.

She closed her eyes, relaxed deeply and visualized his face. She then let the first thing come to her. The scene came back in slow motion. That was the man she had met once in a bar restaurant in LA—a big man with a large neck and shoulders. Oh! Yes. I remember vividly now the grin on his repulsive face and his warning. He tried to frighten me. That man will do anything to abort my mission in Tahiti. He is evil and dangerous. He will try to kill the little girl as soon as I find her. This is very bad news. I should prepare a good plan in case of attack.

She lay down on the bed and visualized the girl seen in her past dreams. She put the child in a situation where the man was about to approach her. At that moment, she automatically neutralized the man in her mind by seeing him sucking his thumb in a fetal position.

After meditating on it for a while, she ordered her subconscious to be aware of Namui Mata and the situation. If he touches her—you start operating right at that moment.

She opened her eyes. Without a doubt, she knew her subconscious got it. She did remember having touched the man in the back of the bar. That horrible man would not get away with it.

Later on, she went to the city tourism office. She took some pamphlets on boat schedules for different islands. After it, she walked along the dock to the Quai des Goelettes. She stopped. <u>What am I doing here? Okay, it's time to follow my guts,</u> she thought. She looked around and saw opposite the boarding dock the thatched-covered House of Shells.

It was the place where Polynesian women displayed and sold their shell handicrafts. On the premises, she bought two pairs of earrings, a bracelet and a little souvenir—that made the vendors friendlier. So she took the opportunity to ask them in French if the name Namui Mata was a common name in Papeete. They all laughed. Four of them raised their hands—they told her that was their first name.

"I see that it's a very popular name. May I ask you if you know any ten years old girl named Namui Mata?"

They all nodded. One of them asked her why.

Kara made up a story. Then she said. "It's important that I find this child. Unfortunately, I don't know her last name."

The same woman asked, "Does she live in Papeete?"

Kara answered positively.

So the woman gave her the name and address of an elementary school. "You could start by this school. It's a good way to find out," she said.

Kara took the note and thanked her—she promised she would start right there. Hope was in her hand as she walked back to the hotel.

Her hotel was a tall building with a restaurant on the top and two bars at the entrance. She first went to the empty bar. It was quiet—however, thirty minutes later, a navy crowd mixed with tourists invaded it. A handsome navy officer sat next to Kara at the bar. He tried to engage the conversation. She did not want to be rude, so she excused herself and left rapidly the bar. Flirting was not on the menu for that day.

In her room, she prepared a list of all elementary schools in Papeete with their addresses and phone numbers. While looking at it, she thought, I'd better prepare myself before acting on it—they would be suspicious if I don't have a good or plausible reason to present to them. However, the fact that she is Métis can facilitate the search. She tried to make up a story for the school director and teachers.

The best thing to do before meeting them is checking the children coming to school in the morning and then going home in the afternoon. I will recognize the child immediately and—follow her to where she lived, she thought.

She went out and rented a car. After it, she checked the city map and pointed out with a pen the elementary schools.

For four days, Kara played the photographer—the only role she knew how to act well. Near the school, she took pictures around. Then, she sat in her car and looked closely at the parents accompanying their children to school, and the children getting off the school buses.

She did the same scenario at different schools without a single result. On the fifth day, a little discouraged, she came back to the first school. I've seen so many children—I don't know if I can recognize her—they all looked the same to me—maybe she's living on another island, she thought. Okay, now it's time to meet the director.

She got out of her car to do just that when suddenly her eyes followed an elegant woman walking to the school gate. It was the recess. Children were playing outside. The woman waved to a child. "Namui Mata," she called her. That did revive Kara's interest.

She looked at the little girl running toward the woman. With the help of the camera zoom, she examined her face from a distance. There, she became thrilled. "That's her," she exclaimed, adding, "I'm sure!" She then began doubting her eyes. It's too good to be true; I'd better check it out more closely and carefully.

The woman and the child walked down the street. Kara followed them slowly with her car. Two blocks after, she parked quickly in the street. She then tracked them on foot. They turned right and took a street named Charles de Gaulle, and then rue Marechal Foch. They turned left and ended up in the middle of the block. It was the market place.

There Kara saw the woman ordering meat, seafood and vegetables. However, she did not bring anything with her except flowers she bought along the way. The little girl seemed very happy to be with that person. They did not look alike—however, the way the child behaved; Kara was pretty sure that it was her mother.

All along the way, the market people greeted them, and the woman and child smiled back to them. They seemed to be well known, Kara thought. After it, they walked down two more blocks and then entered a restaurant.

Kara wrote down quickly the name and had a brief look inside through the window. The woman went immediately behind the counter bar and opened the cash register. Then, the child and she went to the kitchen at the back.

Kara assumed that she was the owner.

She checked the menu on the front door and the opening hours; it was open from 8 am to 10 pm. Tomorrow is Saturday—no school. I'll come back tomorrow to have breakfast; I might see her again. The menu was interesting—a combination of French and

Tahitian cuisine. Excited, she repeated to herself, "It's too good to be true. Well, go for it! You have nothing to lose anyway."

Just before leaving, she went to the back alley and walked by the kitchen door. Luckily, it was open. Kara could hear the little girl laughing heartily. Someone was talking to her in French but Kara could not see who that was. <u>I'll know more about them tomorrow. I got my reward for today.</u>

She went back to the car and drove around Papeete. Light-hearted and elated by the luck she had that afternoon, she thanked the Universe for helping her. After admiring the many beautiful sceneries of Papeete, she drove back to the hotel.

In the evening, she felt again an overwhelming joy going through her mind and body. "I might float in the air at any moment," she said while laughing. That sensation lasted a long time. When the good feeling passed, she went to the pool for an energetic swim to finish the day on an even note.

In the morning, she woke up with a big smile on her face. <u>I'm already excited by the day and the discovery of the Lovely One.</u> That name came naturally to Kara. She would often use it later on.

She arrived at the restaurant in the first opening hour. She did not see the little girl but fortunately, she saw the woman. That one came to the door with the menu in her hand and gently invited Kara to follow her. She led her to a table. A few minutes later, a young Tahitian woman took the order. Kara slowly ate her breakfast. She faked reading the newspaper while listening carefully to the conversation the French woman had with the waiter behind the counter.

At the same moment she was ordering another coffee, she saw a handsome Tahitian man coming in. He went directly behind the counter and kissed the

French woman on the cheek. They exchanged a few words and then, he went to the kitchen. Kara thought, he could be the father's child. The Big Head had told me that the father is Tahitian and the mother French.

It reenergized her. She thought that all she had to do then was to find out where she lived. Having something in mind, she finished her coffee, got up and went to the cash register. Chance smiled to her once again—she heard the French woman telling the server that she had to go home—and would be back in the afternoon.

Once outside, Kara crossed the street and waited for the woman on the corner hoping she would get out by the front door. Ten minutes later, to her relief, the woman walked out. She went down a few blocks before stopping at a door gate—she opened it and entered. The door was left open. Kara waited a few minutes. Then, she walked to the gate and had a glance inside. The view was magnificent. For a short moment, she peered at the stylish house. It was surrounded by a beautiful garden covered of shrubs, groves and at least ten different kinds of colourful flowers. The wide-open French window doors gave the house an air of breathing freely through the big plants and flowers placed on the front terrace.

Then, she saw the French woman going to the left of the house where a mid-aged woman was busy cutting flowers. They talked together. They seem to enjoy each other—Kara could hear them laughing. She kept watching the scene while taking a step forward. Her eyes caught sight of a little girl sitting on the lawn at the opposite corner. She was in a yoga position, her hands joined together—she had an adorable smile on her face. Being the exact representation of the first dream she had about her; Kara froze there, almost in trance.

It took her quite a while to realize that there was another person observing the little girl not far away.

Then, she saw the French woman going toward that person. After exchanging a few words, they both watched the child moving to a new position. I guess she must be the yoga teacher, she thought.

She was right. Soon after, the teacher sat next to the child and showed her a movement. The girl imitated it right away. The French woman clapped her hands and the teacher got up. The little girl stayed there without moving. But after a while, she turned her head and looked intensely at her. Kara tried to back off but could not—the little girl's eyes had paralyzed her body.

Then Kara saw the French woman and the yoga teacher coming to the garden door. Still there with her mouth wide open and the camera in her hands, she tried forcefully to put herself together.

Surprised, they both looked at her. However, the French woman recognized Kara. She smiled. "Can I help you?" she asked.

Kara could not articulate a word. The teacher helped the situation by saying goodbye to the woman. It gave her time to thaw out.

Her mind came up rapidly with something plausible. "What a coincidence!" Kara said in French. "Oh...let me introduce myself. My name is Kara Lewis." She reached the woman's hand and shook it. Showing the camera, she added, "As you can see, I am a photographer. I—I am on vacation but I am also working on a kind of project. It's my first time in Tahiti and surely not the last."

The French woman appreciated her effort to speak French. She smiled warmly. "Are you lost?" she asked.

"Yes and no. The door was open...and I could not resist having a look at this beautiful garden and house. As I stepped in, I saw this little girl in a yoga position among the plants and flowers. Well...well, I thought that it would make a wonderful picture."

The woman seemed flattered by her comment. "The client is always right," she replied wittily.

She invited Kara to come in and they walked around the garden. Still in the same position, the little girl kept an eye on her. When Kara met her eyes, the child smiled widely.

The French woman introduced herself, "My name is Elise Rodier. I was born in France. I have been here for the past twenty years. My husband and I opened this restaurant five years ago and we enjoyed it very much since that. May I ask you where you are from?"

"I am from British Columbia, Canada but I have been working all over the world for so many years that I don't know anymore where my real home is," she answered.

"Interesting," the woman replied. "Come meet my daughter."

"Her name is Namui Mata," Elise said. As you can see, she takes her yoga lessons very seriously." She laughed. "She has started it last year. She enjoyed it a lot. Namui Mata, this is Kara Lewis—she is photographer. She is on vacation in Tahiti. I met her in the restaurant this morning. As she walking around, she recognized me. Then she saw you. She would like to take a picture of you. Would you like it?"

Glad to hear it, the little girl nodded.

Kara asked her, "Can I take some pictures of you in this position?"

"All right...fine with me," Namui Mata said.

Kara took several snapshots of her alone and then, with her mother. She could not fully realize what was happening to her but accepted it gratefully. The more she looked at the child through the lens, the more she felt calm. Everything seemed so heavenly right for the first time in her life.

A short while after, Kara said, "I think I had enough shots. Thank you Namui Mata. Elise, would you like me to take pictures of your house and later on, maybe...your restaurant facade?"

Her professionalism and interest impressed the French woman. However, she took it lightly. "I don't think my house is so spectacular, neither my restaurant."

Kara insisted. "It is worth it." She enthusiastically added, "You know as well as me that charm and taste are priceless. The way you have put things together generates beauty. For instance, the landscaping is in perfect harmony with the house. The restaurant also possesses some cachet—the building is very inviting. I believe that the French accent mixed with the Tahitian touch give the interior an air of serenity." She paused. "That must be the magic of Tahiti: the art of transforming things in a surreal way," she ended up.

"Well, I am happy to hear it," Elise said. "You almost convinced me...Go ahead, photographer. I hope the pictures will be as good as your words."

"All right then," Kara replied.

She walked around and began photographing the house, then the terrace, then the garden. Elise and Namui Mata watched her doing that for a while. Afterwards, they went in the house.

Ten minutes later, Elise came out on the terrace. Checking her watch, she said, "Enough work! You are on vacation—remember! Come in, it is getting hot. Have a drink while I help my daughter get dressed."

Kara accepted. She followed Elise in the house.

"Please, sit here; I'll be right back," Elise said.

The mid-aged woman that Kara saw earlier in the garden came in the living room and greeted her. She served her a drink. "It is made from five different fruits. I hope you'll like it madam," she said.

After tasting it, Kara replied quickly, "This is excellent, thank you."

They talked casually while the woman watered the plants. She was very nice. Kara liked her right away.

"Please, call me Kara. What's your name?"

"Everyone around here calls me Madame Toti."

The Tahitian woman looked at her camera. A little embarrassed, she said, "I saw you taking pictures. Would you mind...I mean...can you take a picture of me at the back of the house?"

Kara accepted with pleasure and there they went.

They walked through the first floor of the house and arrived at a large open door which gave access to a huge open covered kitchen in the middle of another garden. They went down a few steps. The effect was amazing; Kara admired it while walking around. She stopped and breathed deeply—her nostrils receiving freely the smell of different herbs and spices.

Madame Toti took her a little farther. "I have planted here different sorts of flowers," she said. And pointing with her fingers, "These are Tiares; the floral symbol of Polynesia. Those are vanilla orchid flowers and some other varieties of Hibiscus."

"Wonderful! Wow! You even have fruit trees among these huge plants? Kara said.

Madame Toti nodded.

They came back to the open kitchen. While taking the last picture, Kara declared. "Astonishing! To me, this the kitchen of paradise? I know that it is my first visit in Tahiti but I feel like I'm already showered by beauty and simplicity and...I did not even have to get out of town. It is divine!" Kara really meant it.

She heard the little girl giggling at her comment from the second floor's window. Kara looked up at her and smiled.

At that moment, Kara knew that a cosmic connection had been made. She said to her, "Miti-Fetia."

The little girl smiled back at Kara. And then, she began singing with a melodious voice the word Miti-Fetia on different rhythms.

Kara just stared at her.

Madame Toti started dancing. She said to Kara, "Celebrating life is our way of living...Here and now..." After having expressed herself, she noticed, "I did not know you could articulate some Polynesian words. Islanders love it when tourists make this effort."

"Unfortunately, I know only a few words," Kara admitted. "I want to learn more of your language." Then, she changed the subject quickly.

Elise and Namui Mata appeared in the back door. Madame Toti gave them a drink and she also poured one for her. They all sat around the wooden table and talked casually. The atmosphere was light and harmonious. Kara's heart was celebrating the first encounter with the Lovely One.

However, after an hour, she knew she had better leave. She didn't want to abuse their hospitality and sabotage her mission. But before it, she had to find quickly a reason to come back.

She did remember that Elise asked her earlier in the conversation where she stayed and how long she intended to be in Tahiti.

While getting up, Kara said, "I had better go. Thank you so much for everything."

"Are you going to your hotel the Kon Tiki? Elise asked.

"Yes I am. However, I think I'll look for a quieter place to stay this week. It's noisy with the traffic downtown...I'm thinking about renting an apartment in Papeete. You see, I want to start this photographic project as soon as possible. I don't know yet how long it will take me to realize it...and I have to see the rest of the islands too...But it will be easier if I have an apartment in Papeete. So I can come back to the administrative center and complete my work here."

She picked up her camera on the table. "It was very nice meeting you. Well, thank you again for your hospitality and kindness," she added. "Last thing, I'm wondering if you can tell me where the best quiet area to live in Papeete is. Do you have any advice to give me?" The truth is I really don't know anybody here."

Namui Mata who had stared at Kara for the whole hour, promptly said, "But you know us now!"

Kara laughed. "That's a very good start to know you, indeed," she acknowledged.

Elise suggested, "Before doing anything on your own, let me see what I can do for you. I know people who might have the right place for you. However, I just want to let you know that everything is very expensive around here—but you must be aware of it by now."

Kara agreed. "Oh! Yes I do. Nevertheless, the price is not a problem—I can afford it. All I want is a nice and comfortable place where I'll feel at ease to live and work at the same time."

Kara wrote down the hotel phone number at the back of her business card and gave it to Elise.

On the way to the front door, Elise added, "I'm a very curious person. Can you tell what kind of project you are on?"

Kara invented something. "Well...it's about creating a book on the magic of Tahiti. I hope I will find the right pictures for describing it with texts, poems etc." She cut it short. "I have many other ideas too: like discovering through pictures the essence of Tahiti and writing about its home style and design. So I could sell it to different magazines as a freelancer. You see..."

Satisfied to learn that it was in fact a big project, Elise read again her business card. Namui Mata ran to the door and told Kara in one breath, "Now I remember! I have known you for many years—I have always had a good time in your presence."

Shocked, Kara laughed nervously. "Good for you," she said.

Elise immediately asked her daughter, "What are you talking about? It's the first time you meet this person today."

"I am sure mom. I have seen her many times in my dreams," she said candidly. "Remember when I was a little girl...I used to play with an invisible friend. Sometimes, you asked me to describe the person who played with me. It was her; I just know."

Kara kept smiling but felt very uncomfortable.

Elise smiled. She explained calmly to Kara. "The philosophy of the island is based on the respect of dreams and reality as being one big reality. One cannot live without the other. Namui Mata learned it early from his father and Madame Toti. However..." She looked at Namui Mata and gently suggested, "The person in your dreams could have looked like Kara but you see it ends there for me, my darling. Ask Kara?"

Kara said softly, "I would have loved to play with you but you see; I have been so busy in my life...so when I go to sleep and wake up in the morning, I rarely remember my dreams. Sorry!"

The little girl remained silent for a few seconds. "All right mom. I won't talk about that anymore." And immediately after it, she added with a big smile on her face, "No need to do so because she is here now!"

Elise kissed her on both cheeks. "Go play, little naughty girl!" she said.

Kara thought that Namui Mata possessed charm, wit and grace, and she gave the impression she could get away with anything.

She gave her a pat on the back. "See you, Namui Mata."

Before leaving, she shook Elise's hand. "I will bring the pictures as soon as they will be ready." At the gate, she waived at Namui Mata and Madame Toti.

On her way back to the hotel, Kara felt as if she didn't touch the ground. That was an extraordinary day to her.

However, in her hotel room, she relaxed a little and kneeled down. She joined her hands together, "I want to thank you Universe for the divine encounter...Now, I declare to whoever is in charge that the big Adventure is on and will keep rolling."

In the evening, she ordered a copious meal and some champagne. She brought it on the balcony and savoured her first victory. She said to herself, "I have found the pearl within the pearl of the Pacific."

She looked at the sea and stars and began chanting slowly Miti-Fetia. Her heart resonated contentment and deep appreciation for being on that enchanting island. The light wind brought her the smell of Hibiscus, Frangipaniers and Tiares; she let her senses welcomed gently these wonderful aromas.

#

Kara had been in Tahiti for the past six months. She had moved in an apartment, which was only three blocks away from Namui Mata. Day after day, she began to know more Namui Mata and her parents. Her father was a great man. His name was Mari Po. She highly respected his wisdom; he had a way to say, "Be always proud to be a human being." He seemed to do just that in whatever he was doing or undertaking. To him, being human was a game to play. The pleasure he got from it was enough to give him energy and determination of action. He was indifferent to the words—winning or losing. Kara's philosophy of life approached his closely. He was also an excellent dancer. During the dance fests, Mari Po, Namui Mata and Madame Toti introduced Kara to Tahitians songs and dances. She admired Polynesians people's way of living and their voluptuous morality. Those who had faith were religious enough to assist the mass on Sunday. However, the expression "repent sinners" was not acknowledged like a noble cause to pursue.

Another great thing she appreciated was she was welcome wherever she went. Of course, playing the professional photographer was one of the reasons—people felt flattered to have their pictures taken. The other reason was she often went out with the caretaker, Madame Toti and the little girl. Islanders got used to it and accepted her like one of them.

Namui Mata's parents observed that their daughter was getting closer to Kara; however, they didn't get upset. They confessed to her that they were so busy with the resto and other professional responsibilities that they felt guilty sometimes of not having enough time to consecrate to their daughter.

Mari Po let her know, "We are lucky to have Madame Toti and you in our lives."

Elise seemed a little more reticent.

One evening after closing the restaurant, Elise talked to Kara about Namui Mata. "After all, we have chosen her to be part of our lives. I hope I will have more time soon to spend with her..."

"Namui Mata doesn't look too traumatized with the matter," Kara said. "I personally think that each moment you spend with her, you really give her a good quality time. Madame Toti is a good caretaker. I wouldn't worry about it too much if I were you."

"Thank you Kara. You see...we have another five years of money struggling before being financially free. But if everything goes according to the plan, we will have enough money in the bank to retire whenever we feel like to...we have bought a house in France three years ago. I want Namui Mata to go to school in France in order to give her a chance to have a better future.

Kara smiled inside when she heard it. Are you kidding yourself? Namui Mata's future is already encrypted in her present. The world will embrace her soon.

"Would you like a glass of white wine?" Elise asked her.

She needed to talk to someone and Kara was there.

"All right," Kara said.

She began to unveil Namui Mata's past. "I have always wanted to have a child but I couldn't have one on my own. That was eight years ago. Mari Po and I were looking for adopting one when the miracle...But first, let me tell you what happened before it. We thought it would be nice if the child happened to be Métis—my husband being Polynesian and me, European. So it appeared to be the perfect match. However, we knew it would be difficult to find such a child."

Elise took a sip and continued. "We were right; it was difficult. Always the same story...we were overwhelmed by paperwork, consumed energy and time and yet, no result. That went on and on for months. It became almost unbearable to me. I began being depressed. Mari Po tried to encourage me but...even his best shot did not work anymore."

She got up, went behind the bar and lit a cigarette. She came back with an ashtray and put it on the table.

"One morning, Madame Toti pulled me out of bed. She dragged me out of the house for an early walk. We were passing the hospital when I noticed at the building side door a large brown box with a light white blanket covering it. At that very moment, we heard a child crying and we both rushed to see if it was coming from the box. What a surprise! It was the most beautiful child I ever saw in my life." She stopped.

Kara saw tears coming down her eyes. She gave her a tissue and waited.

"I took her in my arms, and then Madame Toti and I ran into the hospital. Soon after, doctors, nurses and staff surrounded this little marvel. Doctors examined her immediately. Nurses told us to go sit in the waiting room. I felt anxious and excited when one of the doctors came to inform us about the child. He told us that she was about two years old, very healthy for a little girl left at the hospital doorsteps. He added that he believed that she was half-Native, half-Caucasian. Then, he asked us to follow him because he needed our help to make the report for the police. A nurse checking the brown box, found a note; she read it aloud, "Here is the baby the mother earth was waiting for. The person who has found the child will take care of her as long as it is required. She will let go of her as soon as the Big Heads prepare her for the beginning of the new era."

Elise offered another glass of wine to Kara. She continued. "I remember hearing one of the doctors saying to his colleague. "The mother who left this child must be a very disturbed person." The other one replied, "Let the police take care of the case."

Elise reached her purse. She took out a paper. "I have kept the note," she said. She gave it to Kara.

Kara read the note twice to make sure she was not dreaming. That paper was as real as Elise was there.

She put it on the table. They both stayed there staring at the old paper.

Kara broke the silence. "So the police, the doctors, the hospital staff or you didn't have any clues about the mother? I mean, nobody came forth for the missing child after all those years."

"That's right," Elise replied. "The mother could have been remorseful and come back to the hospital for her child but she never did."

Kara asked, "What happened next?"

"Let me explain first that around here; it is very rare that you hear about a mother asking to have her child back. You see, every woman is almost the mother of every child in Tahiti. The family is deeply based on the community. Therefore, it is not seen as a transgression or a sin or whatever if someone can take better care of the child."

Kara said, "I'm following you but what about the note?"

"The hospital staff, Madame Toti and I thought that it was probably a young and confused woman that wanted to make sense about giving up and abandoning her child to strangers. I must say that we did not pay too much attention to the note—we were too busy focusing on the beautiful child. Everyone adored her from day one. To make a long story short, the doctors helped my husband and I with the adoption process, and after it, everything went fast. Namui Mata stayed at the hospital for a month under supervision. The police put an end to the investigation and simply closed the case file. The governmental agency agreed to let us keep the child if in the following two years, nobody asked for her. I was so happy the day I brought her home—my life changed completely."

Elise laughed. "Madame Toti likes to remind us, "At last you have received fully what you have been asking

God for..." However, Mari Po and I thank our lucky star instead."

Elise looked down at the paper. She acknowledged, "In the first two years, Mari Po and I were afraid that someone would come and get the child back but nobody came. Therefore, she was our little girl for good after it. What a relief it was! We love her so much. She is just a joy to be around—smiling, laughing, and radiating her light around everything she touches. She has been a blessing to us ever since."

She picked up the paper. "But I must admit this note bothers me sometimes, particularly when I see the way Namui Mata focuses on people, animals and nature. I can tell you she doesn't look at things the same way we do." She stopped. She was lost in her thoughts.

She came back to herself and changed lightly the subject. "I remember having read an old book about Tahiti when I was young living in France. The author wrote that the Polynesian people could not hold their attention on things for too long."

She smiled.

"Now, I'm sure this writer was a pretentious moron. They do pay attention but it must be in harmony with their frame of mind or body—if not, forget about it. I have learned that lesson from Mari Po. They still know how to live in accord with nature and do remember the power of all senses not just the power of mind. Therefore, there is no wonder that we look so stressed out to them. The Polynesian people will not tell you what to do—instead, they will let you be. Nowadays, it's almost a forgotten virtue." Then she came back to her daughter.

Kara listened to her with interest. Elise had repressed her thoughts about Namui Mata for too long, and Kara needed to catch up with the little girl's story.

Back home, Kara jotted down on a paper sheet the most important things about the conversation she had with Elise. She recognized that Namui Mata could not have found better parents then Elise and Mari Po. She loved them and they loved her back. In addition, Madame Toti was a good companion and caretaker; she taught Namui Mata many things about the Polynesian culture and customs. She introduced her to the vegetal realm. At four years old, Namui Mata could name every plant, tree, flower, fruit and vegetable on the island. She also enjoyed to go fishing with Mari Po's family. According to what Elise said, anyone exposed to her seemed to be spiritually attracted to her joie de vivre. Moreover, she got along very well with other children. Elise gave her a solid French education basis—Namui Mata could be extremely polite and gracious but could also be goofy in funny situations. She was a very curious child always in search of new discoveries. Finally, she combined very well the gift of two different cultures in a unique way. Kara understood that her work from the moment on would be to gain Elise and Mari Po's trust; she had to be patient.

#

Kara had already been there for a year. She often visited her new friends. One evening, Elise and Mari Po asked her if she would be interested to give conversational English lessons to Namui Mata.

"Our daughter seemed gifted for foreign languages," Mari Po said.

"I noticed it," Kara replied.

"I'd like her to start slowly with English as soon as school finished," Elise added.

Kara took the opportunity right away. At last, she would be alone with her.

"How is your project going?" Mari Po asked.

She talked casually about it without emphasizing too much. "It's going the way I expected, slowly but surely," she said. "I still enjoy very much living in Tahiti," she added.

Weeks after weeks, Kara continued to establish a trust with them. However, in order to keep doing it, she would have to reveal certain facts about her past. It was time to be more tangible. For that reason, she invited Jennifer to come visit the islands. She introduced her to them. They seemed very glad to know she had a life with friends before. Jennifer stayed there for two months. They visited the first month the islands of Tubai, Moorea, Huanine, Raiatea and Bora Bora. And the second month, they went to Maupiti, Manihi, Ranriroa and ended up with the mysterious Marquesas Islands. They enjoyed a lot of their time together. Kara was happy to see that Jennifer had made peace with the past. She looked healthy and in good spirits.

When Jennifer left, Kara went back to her so-called photographic project. While waiting for Namui Mata to finish school, she took hundreds of pictures of the closest islands. She even began to write about Tahiti and its treasures.

That night, reading what she had written, she started laughing. She said to herself, "Gosh! That would need more thinking and polishing, mademoiselle. My English skills are rusty since I've been speaking only in French and Tahitian." The weeks after, she read many good books in English to fill up the gap.

Finally, the school was over, and Kara had the first English conversation with her pupil. At the beginning, she went to her home and then, she did it most of the time while doing something with her. Namui Mata was a fast learner—she could absorb a lot effortlessly. Her parents were very proud of their little prodigy—

nevertheless, they never put her on a pedestal. Kara appreciated it.

Each day, they did a different activity. One day, it could be visiting the Museum of Discovery—another day, picnicking in a park or just having a walk. However, Kara was always cautious—she often checked around her. Deep inside, she knew that in order for the bad boys to operate, the two of them had to be together alone. These men could be anywhere but nothing had happened so far, so she felt good about it.

#

Namui Mata made so much progress in English that she almost alarmed Kara; therefore she began to slow down a little. However, the girl wanted more. Things were going too fast for Kara. Namui Mata was growing up rapidly. The little girl was then twelve years old.

That morning, on the beach, they were walking slowly while talking in English. After watching the surfers for a while, they went on walking until they reached a little bay. Kara made sure no one was around. Then she got two bottles of juice from her bag and gave one to Namui Mata. They sat on the sand and just relaxed in that pleasant setting.

Waves were rolling a few feet away and a light breeze was coming from the bluish green ocean. Everything was perfect.

"It's a wonderful place. Isn't it?" Namui Mata said.

"Yes, it is."

Her eyes watching the horizon, Namui Mata continued in French. "I know why you are here and befriend my parents and madame Toti."

Kara remained calm. "Good if you do, it will be easier for me."

However, after having said that, Kara felt a little uneasy because she did not know where to begin. And suddenly, flashes of blood, dead bodies and fetal positions ran through her mind.

The young girl understood that something was going on—she could hear Kara's heartbeat going faster even through the crashing waves. She got up, walked in the water and came back. She sat before Kara and took her hands.

She looked directly in her eyes and slowly said in English, "Don't worry; I'm not upset by your presence on the island. You see, I like you a lot...but...I'm just sad at the thought that I'll have to leave this paradise, the people I love in order to mark my place in the world."

Kara did not say a word. She only recognized that the young girl was now fully aware of her destiny.

Namui Mata broke the silence. "It is time to teach me everything you know. You have six years ahead of you to prepare me. I know that you're my guide and protector. And I'm very happy that they did choose you to be with me."

Kara's big dark eyes nodded. Then, she smiled and hugged Namui Mata. In that peaceful place, they let the time and space be still for a while.

Then Kara took Namui Mata to her apartment. In the kitchen, she made a punch with fruit juices and sherbet. She served it in the living room where the blue book on the table was waiting.

They sat on the couch and Kara opened the book and took the letter.

"Let me introduce you to the blue book and the blue letter," Kara said, smiling. "I have already translated the book into French. Once you have read it, you'll begin studying it in English. You're getting better in English and I swear to you that by the end of this year, this language will have no secret for you anymore. Your learning process is amazing—I believe that you'll be able to decipher the meaning of this book. Why? Because this book was written and intended to you. The unknown author has condensed in these pages the last five thousand years of wisdom of priestesses, prophetesses, poetesses, philosophers and women writers." She paused. "I must confess that after all these years of reading the blue book, I, sometimes, don't get the full meaning of it but...you probably will."

#

Namui Mata was then seventeen years old—she was becoming a beautiful young woman.

One night, the Big Head from Easter Island reached Kara in her dream. He let her know that she had that last year left for taking care of unfinished business. She knew what it meant.

"We will protect her during your absence," he said.

#

Back to BC, Kara went directly to her father's house; he had been seriously ill for the past six months. Unfortunately, he died one day after she arrived. After the funeral, she stayed with her brothers for a while.

On the last weekend, just before going back to Vancouver, her brother Dave asked her, "Why did you choose a so far getaway to live for God's sake? You don't like us anymore."

She laughed at his question.

Then she reassured him, "I want you to know that I did not run away from the family. I just chose to live there because I love it. That's all. And...and it didn't actually change anything; I was always on the road before."

Then, her older brother Steve said, "I'm sure that you like Tahiti but...I think...what Dave wants to know is how come you have never invited us up there...and why don't you come visit us more often?"

"Come on! Guys. You know that you're always in my heart. My project is not finished yet...and...every month, I live on a different island. So, it's difficult to invite you up there..."

She kissed her brothers on the cheeks.

"We miss you sister. That's all," Dave said.

Steve smiled. "You were never family-oriented anyway," he said. "But I understand what you try to say."

Kara looked at Nancy and Michelle and then at her brothers. "You're both little whiners!"

Nancy laughed, "Do you know what they really miss? she said to Kara.

"No I don't,"

Nancy looked at Michelle. "These brats miss teasing you," Michelle said. "You know the way you had fun in those earlier years trying to get the best and worst of one another."

"I know...I know they cannot get enough of my sense of humour," Kara admitted.

And at the delight of Nancy and Michelle, the game of taking each other up and down began. That was exquisitely funny.

#

Nothing had changed in her old apartment. On the terrace, she observed that the Andrews' garden was smaller, and with fewer flowers. Mrs. Andrew welcomed her with open arms.

"I'm glad to see you. We heard about your father Kara. All my sympathy," she said.

"Thanks."

Seeing that Kara was looking around, Mrs. Andrew told her, "Mitsou the cat has gone too for a better world." She stressed on the fact that she had been a healthy cat until the end.

Kara was sad but she expected it.

While having a coffee with them in their living room, the Andrews informed her that the house was for sale. They wanted to buy a condominium for retired people.

Mr. Andrew explained. "You see, the facilities and services on the premises will help us achieve a better quality of life." Turning his head toward his wife, he went on. "We are still alert but my wife and I know that we have a few years left before the grand journey. So Kara, I'm afraid that you have to make a decision about your apartment."

"I understand very well your concern," she replied. "I hope you'll be happy in your new place. Well...it's a good timing because I came here to sort out things I don't need anymore."

That week, Kara got rid of lots of things. She packed the rest and shipped it to Tahiti. The apartment looked empty after that. I'm glad I did it, I feel better now, she thought.

The last evening before her leaving, Mrs. Andrew came in the apartment with a cane in one hand and a bottle of white wine in the other. She sat down at the kitchen table and said, "You know how much I like you my darling. Now, get two old glasses and sit with me. I want to know everything about your life on the islands."

The morning after, Kara said goodbye to her little shrine and locked the door. After giving the keys to the

Andrews, she wished them the best. And with a lot of love, she kissed and hugged them for the last time.

The first thing she did when going back to Tahiti was buying a house. She believed that it would be easier for both of them to have a "pied a terre" on planet earth—a place to replenish when the goings get tough and find their bearings for the next move.

After that purchase, she started renting places—two to five years in advance—at different locations around the planet. It was not difficult to find the right places—she was so wealthy. Moreover, the good contacts she had made in the past as a freelance photographer helped her a lot. She often thought about Kevin and her financial freedom. "Well, Kevin. I hope you did not die for nothing," She reminded the Universe that those sacrifices were nonsense. "Too many had died for the cause and we haven't started yet." But in spite of her bitterness, a deeper feeling was pushing her to keep going on no matter what.

The day she fully realized the importance of the mission, she began to feel better at all levels. The Danish woman, the Tibetan nun and the Big Head had told her that before—Namui Mata would change the world.

Kara's difficulty was how she would help her do it.

It did not take long before Kara witnessed the tremendous power Namui Mata was exerting on people. Welcome with open arms everywhere on the islands—her intelligence, wisdom, wit and "love of life" mesmerized people. Marquesas Islanders deeply believed that she had a healing power on them, and by word of mouth, Namui Mata became known as the One who can.

The young woman played well that role—the one who can. She had perfected the art of dealing with just that moment and nothing else counted. People in

Papeete could sometimes see her meditating under a tree near the beach in a remote location. She could stay there for hours without moving a finger. Her peaceful composure impressed passer-by and excited their religious curiosity.

Most of the people on the islands were Protestants or Catholics. The only religious Tahitian book was still the bible translated by King Pomaré 11. With the years, Kara had noticed that some of them respected better the Christian moral teachings when mixing them with their ancestor divinity, the Atua. Although, they no longer sanctified Tiki statues, they still had several persistent superstitions like fear of evil spirits named Tupapaus which inhabited the dark. For that reason, Namui Mata mystified the elderly—she puzzled their faith without doing anything.

Kara did not question the significant relation that Namui Mata had over her people. In some way, they were like her. Kara viewed Polynesian people as very open, benevolent, not greedy or jealous. And curiously, they rarely blasphemed. She admired their freedom of thinking and great wisdom. Although believers, most of them did not consider physical love as a source of sin, their instinctive free sexual nature did not permit it.

While Namui Mata was studying philosophy at the university, Kara spent more time with her parents. She was patiently preparing the field. Mari Po could talk for hours about his version of French Polynesia history. He enjoyed saying the same story over and over while changing words from time to time. He would begin his story the same way. "We all know that Chevalier de Bougainville landed here in 1768 but that didn't give him the right to...Mari Po would never finish his sentence. And then, he would continue. "At the beginning, all the Europeans and missionary groups who set eye on Polynesian islands tried to change my people. English, Spanish, Portuguese and French people used force to break our spirits. We didn't like it. France took charge of Tahiti by establishing a protectorate under the reign of Queen Pomaré V. She finally gave the country to France in 1880..." And then, he would conclude on the same line, "We may speak French but no matter how hard they tried to change us—they never succeeded to tame us."

That night, Madame Toti was there. She backed him up. "My grand-mother used to say—poor little white people, they put so much effort on trying to make people think their way that they have lost their way to get in touch with themselves." She smiled. Her eyes still in the past, she continued, "Each time, my grandmother was not in agreement with white people, she would sing in Tahitian, "Don't waste your time with us...we know better...""

Kara observed Elise listening to them. She seemed not to mind at all; she knew better too.

However, she teased her husband. "French people got you anyway. They have succeeded to make you love one of them," she said.

"I had no choice, you have stolen my heart at the first minute I saw you, "Mari Po replied tenderly.

It was getting late. So on that, Madame Toti and Kara left the lovers alone. On their way out, they saw Namui Mata sitting on the front terrace. She was deeply absorbed in her book; Kara had a quick look over. She smiled. They young woman was reading a book on astronomy.

Before sleeping that night, she recalled the Big Head's words about Namui Mata's parents. It was right. They did not belong to any church. To them, it was impossible to know if God existed and therefore, they did not practice any creeds. However, they were highly respected by the believers in the community for their integrity. Nevertheless, she wondered how the spiritual Namui Mata dealt with it after all those years.

#

After getting used to see Namui Mata meditating on the beach on weekends; sometimes, elderly people would approach her and ask if she believed in God.

"I believe in myself and in the Universal Nature before me," Namui Mata would candidly answer.

If they insisted, she would smile and stay silent. Each time, it worked. Satisfied by her short answer and behaviour, they would walk away.

#

After succeeding to master the English language in a record time, Namui Mata began speaking fluently five other languages—Japanese, Spanish, Italian, Arabic and Russian. That same year, she received a master's degree in philosophy and then, attended for her own pleasure different courses—the best teachers of the world gave her privately classes in biology, mathematics, astronomy, anthropology and theology.

Kara paid them to teach on the premises. She did not to have to break a leg in order to convince them that they had to live in Papeete for a while. Most of them admitted that it was the best offer they ever had in their life—wages were great and life, exquisite in Papeete. Moreover, teaching to such a talented student was a reward in itself. They were all amazed that she could absorb so easily enormous amount of data while understanding deeply the meaning and interrelations of all those different dimensions of knowledge.

At the beginning, Elise and Mari Po felt uncomfortable with all these people around them.

However, Kara persuaded them that Namui Mata was an exceptional gifted person.

"Encouraging your daughter is the best thing you can do for her," she told them.

They both recognized her obvious talent. However, they were concerned about not being able to support her financially with her education.

Kara finally let it out. "Well, there is something about me that you don't know. I am a wealthy woman and..."

Mari Po responded, "It doesn't mean that you're obligated to us..."

"No but if you allow me, I would like to spend some of my money on a genius as Namui Mata. You have helped me a lot since I've been here and it's time now to demonstrate my appreciation. Sponsoring your daughter's education would be my way of gratitude toward you. I deeply believe that Namui Mata could go very far in life. Please...please let me help you financially."

They seemed relieved to hear that; however, they indicated that they needed to talk about that with their daughter first. The week after, they gave the okay to Kara saying that Namui Mata, almost an adult would decide what would be the best for her.

#

Her eighteenth birthday was approaching, and her parents decided to celebrate it big. There were two reasons: first, it happened to be at the same time than July festivities; second, Mari Po's family liked to highlight the eighteenth year—it was an old family tradition.

Kara liked those festivities. She compared the July Fete to the Rio Carnival in Brazil—on a smaller scale but still...The big party would last for three consecutive weeks. Year after year, Kara continually enjoyed that national celebration. She often thought that Polynesians knew how to have fun. Some of them would usually dance until dawn while others set stands for eating, drinking and for some temporary gambling. They always made sure that there was a lot of amusement for children and entertainment for grown-ups. Outriggers canoes races attracted by itself half Papeete population. Javelin throwing contests were also very popular—fans would cheer up until they almost lost their voices. But the bigger attraction that would bring together natives from every part of Polynesia was certainly dancing and singing. Tahitians were never tired of that.

Kara was daydreaming about that on the couch when she heard somebody knocking at the door.

She got up quickly and opened the door. That was Madame Toti appearing in all her splendour, all gloriously dressed up.

"Are you in shape, mademoiselle?" she asked. She didn't let time to Kara to answer and entered the house. "You know that this year celebration is a big one for you." Clapping her hands quickly, she added, "All right! Please, show me all the dances you have learned since you have been here."

Kara froze.

"By the way, Namui Mata and my nieces are dancing too; they are rehearsing at that very moment at my brother's house backyard. I'm here to pick you up before you decide to hide somewhere. All right! Come with me."

"But let me..."

"No time for that. Come on exotic dancer, follow me."

Kara laughed. She knew she could not do anything against Madame Toti's determination to make her dance at the July festivities. Grabbing a bag on her way, she responded, "I know that you like it when I make a fool of myself." And they left the house.

Madame Toti walked in the streets as if she was at the head of a commando. She brought up other dancers along the way. In front of her brother's house, she turned around and stopped the group with her hand.

"Okay Kara. Recite all the dance names and what they all are about." It sounded like an order to Kara.

Kara sighed. "Okay. The first one is Otea and it is a ballet that looks like a war dance. The second one is Aparima; it's a sitting position dance, which the dancers do in a languorous way. The other one is called Hivanau; it's a circle. Paoa is a satirical dance accompanied by drumbeats and hand claps. Tamure or Ori Tahiti is a dance where men scissor their legs and women shake their behinds. Well, something like that...That's all I remembered, Madam Toti."

The other dancers applauded Kara.

Madame Toti stopped them abruptly with her hand. "Well; that's not bad for a foreigner but now you have to prove us that you can dance..." And succeeding to keep a straight face, she added, "Of course, you do remember that you have to perform one of these dances tonight for Namui Mata's party." She told the rest of dancers, "You may join the others in the backyard, I will come back later."

She then took Kara by the arm and brought her in the alley. Then she said, "What about Paoa? Show me what you've got."

After that traumatic experience, they joined Elise and Mari Po on the beach. Those ones were busy to put the last touch before Namui Mata's arrival. They really wanted to surprise their daughter by giving the party one day before her birthday.

"What do you have in mind for tomorrow?" Madame Toti asked them.

With a smile, they let her know that it could be a very long birthday party. Then they went back to work. They were everywhere making sure that everything was under control. Some of their friends and Mari Po's family members were decorating the place while others were preparing the low stage for singers and dancers. The rest of them were helping with the food. Musicians were already there practicing on the side.

Looking at what was going on, Madame Toti's mood seemed to shift; she began to dance. While shaking her body, she sang to Kara, "Tonight, half of Papeete will be here to see you perform. Are you ready?"

"What's wrong with you?" Kara replied, anxious. "Don't you understand that you make me nervous just at the thought of it? You have seen me dancing. You know that I cannot do better...I...I don't have your sense of rhythm. And...and to answer your questions; yes! I'm ready. Satisfied!"

At that moment, Madame Toti recognized that she went too far about teasing Kara. Smiling, she tried to correct her naughty remarks. She put her arm on Kara's shoulder and gently apologized, "Sorry my dear Kara, just the act of willingly dancing will be very appreciated by my people. They all will respect that nice gesture..."

Kara knew that Madame Toti just wanted that day to be a success. She replied, "Okay, you've got me by the heart again. I promise...I will do my best tonight."

With the festivities in town, Mari Po and Elise anticipated to receive more people. Elise told him, "I don't know if there will be enough food for everyone." Then she suggested, "I think we'd better order some more food from the restaurant's kitchen. You know, many curious newcomers will be attracted by the party."

"Good thinking," he replied. He went talking to his brother.

Everywhere on the beach, something was happening. Vahines and Mahous wearing their costumes were rehearsing their acts with the musicians. In another corner, singers were rehearsing too. A huge underground hot stone oven was right in the middle of that amazing playground—the meat was cooking slowly there—on the top, piles of bananas leaves covered it. They had dug a big hole the day before and prepared the meat. Cooks in charge checked from time to time how that astonishing natural oven was doing.

A few hours later, Elise and Mari Po, then more relaxed, sat with their friends and had a good time. Kara spent her time walking and talking to people around. Laughing and rejoicing were the order of the day. Again she thought, these people really know how to celebrate.

Mari Po sent Madame Toti to get Namui Mata and her nieces.

Thirty minutes later, Namui Mata showed up with the rest of the troop. At her view, everything stopped— the music, the dances, the laughing voices, and the chatter. A little upset by the sudden silence, she asked her parents, "What's going on here? Someone died?"

Mari Po laughing put his arm around her and said loudly, "Not at all, we are celebrating life here. You birthday is tomorrow...but...your mother and I have decided to start the celebration today. Of course, that will continue until tomorrow. Happy Birthday! My loved one."

Elise gave the sign to bring the cake—she turned around and kissed her daughter. Then she began singing followed by the others, "Bonne Fête Namui Mata..."

Four Mahous brought a huge cake place on a large tray. Eighteen candles oblivious of the wind were lit up. Elise gave her a pat on the back and suggested, "Time to make a wish."

Namui Mata closed her eyes and silently informed the Loving Energy, "I'm ready. Be your love and strength with me, here and now and forever."

The cake was so big that she walked around and then, decided to blow the candles one by one. She did it graciously while people cheered her up.

Mari Po could not stop repeating to his friends. "That's my girl! Isn't she beautiful?"

Observing the scene, Kara thought, no need to say it. She could feel people's affection for her. In fact, what people liked about her was her originality, uniqueness and simplicity.

After the blowing ritual, Mari Po's mother improvised in Polynesian a little song. "There is just one like Namui Mata on this earth and we are very happy she is among us. Happy Birthday, my dear one...Everyone, cheer up!"

Clapping in their hands, they repeated the refrain.

Namui Mata let them finish the song but just as they were going to start over again, she raised her hand. She said to all of them, "Thank you, thank you and thank you! It is a very nice surprise. I really appreciate it." She kissed her parents and those who were around.

After that, Mari Po signalled to her that the surprise was not over yet. He invited her to sit down. Some friends brought a low table and placed it before her. Then the guests formed a line-up and one by one, they gave her a gift and left it on the table.

The last one to come was Kara. She kissed Namui Mata on both cheeks and put a little green stone in her hands. She whispered to her ears, "This little rock will give you power and energy when you feel low or just want to give up. However, I don't think you need that today." She smiled. "Happy Birthday Namui Mata."

Touched by her gift, she replied in a low voice, "Thank you Kara for your big help and emotional support. Thank you for being my mentor, my guide and my friend. Today is really a wonderful day to be alive."

Mari Po raised his hand. He shouted to the musicians, "Let the party begin." And what a party it was.

On the beach, people slowly began to sing and dance, and then eat and drink. After that, they started all over again. Later on, Kara performed with other women their dance. Madame Toti's sister watched with joy Kara and her nieces dancing like pros. Impressed by Kara, she went right after the show to see her. She declared enthusiastically, "From now on, you are part of the family. Thank you for your nice effort today."

Kara pointed her finger at Madame Toti and said, "Well, thank your sister. She demanded a lot from me but I..."

Madame Toti cut her, "But the end result was worth it."

They all laughed.

Then she joyfully stated to Kara. "It's not over yet, mademoiselle. Next year, you will have to learn other dances."

Kara riposted, "No way...I comply this year with the torture. And next year, just forget me!"

At midnight, people gathered and formed a big circle around the low stage. The professional dancers and fire performers took their places in the middle of it. The revellers were just happy to sit down after all the good food and alcohol consumed that night. In a relaxed position, they watched with respect those performers that had practiced all year round for those three weeks of festivities.

After the third dance, Kara went for a walk on the beach away from the crowd. From the crescent moon and stars' light, she could perceive in the dark a little black shadow coming toward her. "What the heck is that?" she said to herself. Getting closer, she realized that it was a cat. Surprised, she asked the cat, "What are you doing here little cat? Is the smell of food attracting you? Are you hungry?"

The cat approached, turned around her legs and then, sat on its behind looking up at her. Kara found it funny. She sat on the sand and stroked the cat. While caressing her, she felt bizarre. The cat mewed twice, stopped and did it again. Then, Kara telepathically read the cat's mind.

Rapidly, the cat communicated, "Listen Kara, no time to waste. You've got to go back right away and sat next to Namui Mata. Her life is in danger...quick...run Kara...run...run..."

Kara ran as fast as she could. She found her way through the sitting crowd and sat down on the ground next to Namui Mata. Her eyes looking everywhere, she mumbled to the girl, "Watch out! Someone is here to kill you..."

Then looking at the stage, she saw right in the middle of the dancers a strange face. Although disguised in a Mahou costume, she recognized him right away. That was the same man encountered in the bar in LA and in the street of Papeete. He was coming fast toward Namui Mata with a knife in his hand. Kara had just time to grab the girl and rolled with her on the ground.

Suddenly, the cat coming from nowhere jumped on the man's face scratching it forcefully. The feline left as fast as it arrived. The man stood there unsteady for a few seconds—blood was coming down his cheek. He then put a hand on his left eye and kept walking toward

Namui Mata with the knife pointing to her. When Mari Po understood what was going on, he just bounced behind him and got his neck while other friends grabbed the rest of the body. They laid him down on the stage.

The music stopped. The dancers ran away. Mari Po asked Kara and her daughter if they were okay.

They nodded while getting up.

Elise ran to her daughter and hugged her. Everyone got up, still shocked by what happened. As soon as Madame Toti learned that someone had tried to kill Namui Mata, she walked around and told everyone, "The party is over. It's time to go home now."

After the place cleared up, Namui Mata's parents nervously thanked Kara. Ten minutes later, Mari Po alone with Kara said, "I asked everyone sitting close to you what happened. They all told me they did not see anything unusual until the cat jumped on the man and then, they saw you rolling with my daughter. What have you seen?"

"The same thing than them." she said, "However, he was coming up directly toward us...so..."

He listened to her while lost in his own thoughts, and then he said, "Talking about the cat, nobody can find it now. People are still looking around for him. The whole thing is so strange. Why would someone want to kill my daughter? Well...Kara, thank you for having been there."

Kara just said, "The most important thing is your daughter is alive. None was wounded but that sick man. By the way, don't thank me—you're the one who stopped the man after all."

Namui Mata joined them. She kissed her father and then Kara. "You're both my heroes tonight. Thanks infinitely," she said.

Then the police arrived on the premises.

An hour later, Mari Po's family accompanied them to their home while Madame Toti's brother and nieces drove Kara home. Getting off the car, she waved to them and waited until she could not see the car anymore. She needed to decompress. She went for a walk.

In the streets, people were celebrating. She stopped for a while to watch some musicians performing and then headed back home.

She took a bottle of water in the fridge and sat on the backyard terrace. Breathing deeply the fresh air, she realized how lucky and well-protected Namui Mata and she had been since the first encounter. I'm just the watcher, she thought. On the side of her left eye, she saw a shadow moving. She turned slowly her head. In the corner of the terrace, behind a big plant was a half-hidden cat.

The cat came out and transmitted to her mind, "Let me introduce myself. My name is Venusa. You already know me. Once, you were with your friends on vacation on the Pacific coast, and you wrote in the sand with a stick my name in big letters. Your friends asked you why you wrote it and you said, "I don't know; I just like the name." The cat jumped on her lap and said, "Here I am."

Kara asked, "Are you real or you're just the product of my imagination."

"I am as real as your imagination. By the way, I know that your cat had passed away last year; you have made the right choice by leaving Mitsou with the Andrews. She died with dignity. I know it because I was her spiritual feline guide."

Kara said softly, "Thank you for letting me know and for having saved the situation tonight.

"You're welcome. We usually provide protection when you're not around her but tonight...it was special.

Gradually, Namui Mata will have the ability to defend herself—she's getting stronger and stronger every day. Nevertheless, she still needs you. She has to learn a lot before being completely ready for the task." The cat paused. After purring a few seconds, she went on. "Kara, you have done a good job tonight."

"Well, I rather believe that I have done a poor job. However, I'm grateful that you were there."

Venusa said, "You're too hard on yourself; nothing had happened since you've known the One. However, they tried tonight their first serious move on her. They are now very aware that she's getting more powerful and they will try again to kill her and you. We will assist you the best we could. The man you saw tonight is called the liquidator. He will be replaced soon by others. Just be on the lookout. I have to go now. My best to you Kara."

The cat disappeared behind the plant. A few seconds later, Kara went looking but Venusa was not there anymore.

Late in the morning, she walked to Namui Mata's home. When that one saw her coming from her bedroom window, she went down the gate. Kara kissed her on the cheek and said, "You know, the man who tried to attack you last night. Well...I can tell you just one thing—justice was done this morning at dawn."

"What do you mean justice was done?" Namui Mata asked.

"You'll see it with your own eyes what I mean."

Namui Mata opened the garden door for Kara. As she closed it, two men arrived at the gate. They introduced themselves.

One of the detectives asked her, "Are you Namui Mata?"

"Yes I am."

"We would like to talk to your parents and you," he informed her.

The other detective looked at Kara. "Are you the one who rolled over on the ground with the girl?"

"Yes I am. How can I help you?"

"We need to confirm certain things with you as witness in order to write the report," the same detective said."

"All right," Kara replied.

Namui Mata invited the detectives to sit down in the living room and went to get her parents in the backyard. Elise and Mari Po greeted them and sat down. One officer read aloud the statement he had in his hand. Mari Po visibly upset could not wait any longer, he asked, "What do you know about this man and why did he want to kill my daughter?"

"I'm afraid we will never know it," the detective answered. "We found him early this morning in his cell unable to talk, walk or move. Police officers did not find any identity papers on him when they arrested him last night. His wallet contained a few bills, nothing to lead us somewhere. Therefore, what we'll do is putting his picture in the newspapers tomorrow. Then, our agents will go around town with his photo asking hotel, motel owners and staff if they recognize him. Early this morning, we have checked with the airport and other police departments on the islands but nothing so far."

He stopped speaking. The other officer wearing big rings under his eyes, continued. "When he arrived last night at the police station, I tried to interrogate him but he did not say a word. Then, out of the blue, he started to have convulsions. So we put him back in his cell."

"Have you done something to him? It is bizarre that he cannot move anymore," Elise commented.

"That's the point madam; we haven't done anything to him other than bringing him to the clinic for his eye.

Then, we have just asked him firmly some questions. We have not maltreated him in anyway. However, this morning we found him in his cell in an awkward position." He stopped, looked at his report and continued, "Two of our doctors have examined the man and tested his blood and urine. After checking the test in our lab, they could not find anything wrong in order to explain his sudden paralysis. They assume that he was already physically and mentally ill when he tried to kill your daughter. After reading the report, the forensic scientist of our department went as far as saying that his metabolism must have been triggered to change radically when the cat jumped on his face, and later on paralyzed the whole body."

The other officer carefully looking at Namui Mata asked her, "Do you know this man?"

"Not at all," she quickly said.

"Have you been watched or followed in the past?"

Namui Mata firmly said, "No I haven't. I would have been aware of it because my parents and I know almost everyone in town. His face did not ring a bell. I guess he must be a foreigner."

The same officer turned his eyes on Kara and asked her the same thing. She answered negatively. Then he demanded that she described in details what she did before and after she saw the man coming toward them. After it, they turned their attention on Elise and Mari Po, and kept asking them questions. Thirty minutes later, one of the officers looked at his watch—they both got up and let them know that they would keep in touch. Mari Po accompanied them at the gate.

He came back in the house, dismayed by the whole story. He sat down and tried to make sense of it. Elise, Namui Mata and Kara were at the back having a coffee. After a while, he got up and went joining them.

In attempting to hide his distress, he said to his daughter, "Today is a new day. Today is your birthday and Papeete is still celebrating. Why not join friends and talk about our good fortune instead of feeling sorry for ourselves."

Namui Mata smiled. She got up and hugged her father. "Dad, you're so right," she said. "I'm still alive and all the people I love too. Today especially, I feel like rejoicing, let us join the party." She put her hand on Kara's shoulder. "What about you?"

"That's a good day for it," she said. "What I like about Polynesian people is their way of putting light on dark days," and looking at Elise, she continued, "And what I like about French people is they agree with that one hundred percent."

With tears in her eyes, Elise laughed at Kara's comment. She concluded looking at her husband, "Kara is right. That is one of the reasons I have married you. You show me the way to live fully in the moment." She got up, kissed her husband and daughter. Then she glanced at the blue sky and shouted, "Indeed, it's a good day to celebrate"

The following week, Namui Mata went to Kara's house every day. They both agreed they should go see the liquidator in prison to start the procedure of exorcising themselves from him. Kara knew that as soon as Namui Mata would visualize the mental process of neutralizing she would be able to do the same.

And there it went. After seeing twice the vegetable man, Namui Mata became herself another neutralizer.

After it, they spent their days walking on the beach. One morning, Namui Mata, satisfied that nobody was watching or walking by, raised her right hand before the ocean and stated, "I declare to myself and to the Universe that from now on, everyone that uses their power unfairly, violently and forcefully on others by mental or physical means will be severely damaged. If I or other neutralizers witness individuals who use bloody methods to attain their ends, they will be put out of order immediately. That is and will be the cosmic principle for those who believe in a better world."

She took Kara's hand and said, "We have to make sure it will be applied this time on earth."

Kara nodded.

On that, they kept walking without saying a word.

At the end of the month, Namui Mata communicated to Kara, "It's now time for me to go to my destiny. But first, I have to explain to my parents the reason why they will not often see me."

Kara agreed. "When are you going to tell them?"

"The sooner, the better. Come with me Kara but let me do the talking. I'm almost certain that my father knows it in his heart. Just the way he looks at me tells a lot. It will be more difficult with my mother but I know something about her life that could help free both of us."

She paused. Then she said, "My mother has a secret...she has never revealed to anyone what happened to her in her teenage years in France. She has lived with that secretive pain ever since. My mother had been violently raped one night in an alley when she was fifteen years old by two men in their thirties. She saw people in the street walking by but none stopped to help her. They were afraid to confront them because those two men were well known to be part of the little mafia in town. Scared to be killed, they simply walked away. After the two men were done, they kicked my mother all over her body until she felt unconscious. Many hours later, she came back to herself. Her body was hurting everywhere but she managed to get up on her own and started to walk. Her whole body shook all the way home. She invented a story to her parents and...lived after that like nothing happened that night."

On that, Namui Mata and Kara left the house.

On the way, Kara said, "What a horrible story. But now...I understand why she had been so depressed before having you in her life. One night, she talked to me about the years your father and she tried to adopt a child. She confessed to have a hard time coping with life at that period. Well, I believe that you will find the right words to soften her pain and her past..."

Namui Mata nodded and then said, "I'll take her alone to talk about that. I'm sure she will be very upset but...greatly relieved...and she'll realize that I'm more than her daughter."

"Something else might help you convince her to let you go," Kara suggested. "One night, she showed me a note that she still keeps in her purse." She then told her the whole story.

At first, Elise and Mari Po dealt with difficulty about Namui Mata's decision to leave Papeete. They thought she was too young and the whole thing just foolish. They demanded that she gave more information.

She was careful enough to tell them just what they needed to know about her new life. Of course, they cried, supplicated and implored her not to take that path. Kara left early that night without saying a word. It was not the right time for her to talk—they were too emotional.

After days of begging and talking, they understood that their daughter would not change her mind. Namui Mata was gentle in the way she communicated with them but stayed firm all the way.

One night, Namui Mata called Kara. "Come. It's the right time."

As soon as she arrived, Namui Mata brought her to the living room. She said to her parents, "Kara has something important to tell you."

First, Mari Po looked at Kara with distrust. "Are you the one who puts all these weird ideas in my daughter's head?" he asked. "I noticed that since you've been around, Namui Mata is not anymore the one we used to know. What have you done to her?"

He kept asking questions but she did not answer any of them. Instead, she waited for him to come down. Elise, sitting next to him, was strangely distant and silent.

After carefully listening to Mari Po's recriminations, Kara calmly said, "I knew that your daughter was going to take this path the first time I saw her...I'm sorry for all the pain that it may cause you but Namui Mata has been placed on earth to do a job that no one else can do...I'll be accompanying her in all her travelling the first years until she will let me know to let her go on her own, and that day, I will comply."

After an interminable moment of silence, Elise began crying. Mari Po looked at her. He wiped her tears with his hand.

"Me too...I have something important to tell you," she succeeded to say. She took his hand. "I have kept to myself a secret all those years. Nobody knew about it but Namui Mata told me what it was this morning."

Mari Po stared at Elise. "Are we in a kind of soap opera or what?" he shouted. "Can you tell me what the hell is going on here before I lose my mind?"

Elise looked so upset that he stopped yelling and gave her his handkerchief. He articulated slowly, "Elise, if you have something to say. Please, say it."

She revealed to him what happened when she was fifteen years old...the rape, the shame, the pain and hurt. Mari Po became lividly disturbed—his eyes widening in surprise while listening. However, he let her finish the account.

At the end, she added, "I tried hard to convince myself that bad memories belong to the past and would stay in the past. However, I was fooling myself because I never forgave myself for not having been strong enough to fight back after that..."

Mari Po put his finger on her lips. He then embraced her. They both cried.

After consoling each other, Mari Po ignoring Kara, told Namui Mata that Elise and he needed to be alone. Going up the stairs, he turned back and added, "Namui Mata, I would appreciate if you stay here. I need to talk to you later."

"I will dad. Take your time."

He nodded and joined up Elise.

"I believe I'd better go," Kara said.

"I prefer you to stay," she replied. "You see even if my mother does not completely accept the idea of my leaving—she knows what to say to my father. In fact, she is the only one who can actually find the right words to explain the situation. She will show him the note they found when they discovered me. My father is a great man, he will understand. Sorry Kara if my father had been cold to you. He will come to his senses soon. Come and have lemonade with me in the backyard."

An hour later, Elise and Mari Po came down. They joined them to the outside kitchen.

He was the first to talk. "Kara, I'm sorry if I've been impolite to you but I thought that you were trying to steal our daughter from us. Having said that, I now want to talk about the spiritual quest my daughter desires to undertake. Elise and I are not believers of any religions but we do believe in the goodness in people and the kindness towards others. My wife showed me the note she kept away from me. I already knew that my daughter was an exceptional human being. However, I don't quite get what she is supposed to do. Saving human beings from their fears of being human! Is that the quest?"

Namui Mata suggested that she might want to respond to it. "Dad, I already knew that I had a kind of mission to accomplish very early in life."

She reminded him of her childhood's dreams—Kara was part of it all along. She finally made clear to him. "I have accepted it a long time ago."

Mari Po thought about it for a while. "Has the man that tried to kill you on your birthday had something to do with that?"

Namui Mata looked at Kara—she could not lie to her father. Kara answered for her, "It was a random act of insanity. That's all."

He then concluded, "If that's the way you choose to live your life. You are free to go; you have my blessings."

Still a little shaken by the emotions of the day, Elise said, "I knew from the beginning that Namui Mata was a special child—the way she had been found—the way she acted and behaved towards others. She has given us a lot of joy. Mari Po and I are grateful of it. I realize that my daughter has been lent to us for a given time and now it's time to let her go. Of course, I'm sad but..." And taking Namui Mata's hand, she added, "But we will not interfere in whatever she decides to do from now on." She kissed her daughter and whispered, "I'll just ask you to give us some news and visit us sometimes."

Namui Mata hugged her mother and kissed her father. She told them, "Yes, I will keep in touch with your dear ones. I've been so lucky to have you as parents. I love you and will always love you with all my heart."

Patiently, Kara waited. When she felt that they had completely accepted that she would leave them soon, she said, "Your daughter was born to lead, and she will lead."

She then began communicating firmly what would be expected from them. Before leaving the house, she made them swear they would not reveal to anybody what they had learned about Namui Mata.

After she left, Elise and Mari Po observed to her daughter that Kara was not anymore the easy outgoing photographer she tried to make them believe. In fact, they noticed that she had a very strong and powerful personality.

Namui Mata just commented, "You are quite right. She is very solid, indeed."

Before sleeping that night, Elise admitted to Mari Po, "It's a good thing that they chose Kara as protector of Namui Mata. Even if she has lied to us all those years, I trust that she will take good care of our daughter. Have you felt that force emanating from her when she started speaking to us?"

Mari Po answered, "At first, she surprised me by the tone of her voice but then, I saw the fire in her. She now sounds authentic to me, and I think we can trust her. Moreover, she is in charge of our daughter for the moment...but I still feel that the whole thing is strange... but we will see. Do you know what?"

He embraced his wife and whispered, "Tonight, I feel like praying for the first time of my life."

Elise smiled. "May be...we could start with the loving Universe!" she said.

CHAPTER THIRTEEN

THE BIG HEADS

Early in the morning, Namui Mata and Kara boarded the boat that was going to take them to Easter Island. On the deck, Namui Mata kept waving to her parents and Madame Toti. When the boat began to sail away, she wiped a little tear. "Bye-bye Tahiti, little pearl of Pacific. It feels so strange to leave the islands," she said almost to herself.

"Don't worry. We have other treasures to see," Kara replied.

When the island looked like a little speck, they went down to the cabin. Namui Mata lay down on her bed and opened a book on Easter Island. "Kara, you must know as I do that Easter Island's inhabitants called it with reason—the Navel of the World—Te Pito-o-Te-Henua," she said. "Do you know why?"

In a very good mood, Kara could not help herself. "I think I do. The statues scattered all over the island became "big heads" when they started to look too much at their navels."

"What are you talking about?"

Kara laughed. "I thought you knew the expression "contemplating your navel". All right; it has nothing to do with Easter Island but...well, I thought it was a good one. Okay...it means that you will start losing touch with the rest of the world if you focus too much on yourself...like...looking at your navel...got it!"

Namui chuckled. "Very funny. Indeed, it's a good one," she said.

#

They approached the tiny volcanic island on Easter Sunday exactly as the Big Heads had told Kara in her waking dreams. And of course, it matched with the arrival of the Dutch Admiral Roggeveen. But what the heck! After all, Namui Mata is also rewriting history, Kara thought.

The big sailing ship moved slowly towards the island. On the deck, a few passengers and they looked at that mysterious island with interest and wonder.

At that moment, Kara let her know about her dreams, "I flew more than once over the island. The first night, one of the big stone statues talked to me about the One..."

Namui Mata listened carefully but did not comment at all. Instead, she just fixed a point on the island and stayed focused on it while Kara kept talking.

When Kara stopped, she looked at her. She seemed in a trance state. Not wanting to disturb her, she went down to the cabin and picked up what was left on the desk. I am glad I will be physically there this time. I am wondering if the Big Heads will want talking to me again in a real time frame, she thought.

The ship was getting closer and closer. They began enjoying the scenery. With her binoculars, Namui Mata looked at the sight of the statues. "What a display it is!" she happily said. "Hundreds of giants, tight-lipped basalt statues litter the island." She was delighted. "I'm so happy to see these marvels with my own eyes. I read so many books about it. The experts must be right when they say this small island and its strange statues present to the world one of the most fascinating archaeological riddles of all time."

Still in a good mood, Kara suggested, "It would be nice if you could solve that one."

Namui Mata gently pushed her. "Dream on, Kara. You're good at it."

"Sarcasm! That's all it is. What about getting the luggage ready?"

"All right...all right."

With their entire luggage hanging on them, they were ready to get off. Both tired and anxious, they started laughing for no reason on the passenger bridge. That was good—it helped release the tension between them, the sea and the volcanic rock.

There was no safe harbour. Therefore, the ship had to anchor out. A small boat ferried in them to the port of Hanga Roa.

They sat on a bench and waited for the small van that would bring them to the place they had reserved before leaving Tahiti.

To pass the time, Namui Mata said, "Remind me of your little Easter Island history, please."

"In English that time." Kara took an old teacher voice, and began, "The first European to stumble across this speck in the Pacific Ocean was the Dutch Admiral Jacob Roggeveen. You mentioned his name before, remember. Anyway, he and his crew landed and spent a day ashore on Easter Sunday in 1772, and guess what! Today is...Coming back to my story, the Admiral christened the island for the occasion. Later on, the renowned English navigator Captain James Cook landed in 1774 after a journey through the Society Islands, Tonga and New Zealand. The two sea explorers both described in their journals what they saw but it seemed that they could not comprehend what was going on...These days, scientists that try to explain what happened to this place believe that the population of Easter Island had simply outgrown its resources. The food supply diminished, and then after the forest felling, the soil started to erode. Without wood for making canoes, they could not escape the island. Consequently, the hard times brought the tribes to turn on one another in destructive wars—they toppled and broke the giant statues—and cannibalism became common. However, some archeologists say that cannibalism was not for ritual, it was only for surviving." She paused.

What took place here could happen everywhere else," Namui Mata said. "It certainly gives us a good picture in miniature of the Earth's own future. The human race consumes the planet's limited resources, as if there were no tomorrows. Generations and generations will suffer in order to repair the damage done."

The van arrived. It took them to the small township of Hanga Roa where most of Easter Island population lived. After getting off on the main street, Namui Mata, amused, indicated to Kara with her hand, "The good thing about this place is I cannot get lost."

"Well, I'm happy they did not turn that town into a big tourist attraction," Kara replied. "It's refreshing to feel the real thing. Don't you think?"

"You're right."

They had chosen to stay in one of the small residenciales. After being led to their rooms, they rested a couple of hours. After it, they paid a visit to the Moais on foot.

On the premises, they checked carefully the six-meter high statues (20 feet). Their distinctive heavy foreheads, pointed chins and elongated ears were something to ponder over. They sat there for a long time meditating on the past, present and future of their adventure.

On the way back to the residenciales, Kara admitted that she was happy to walk on solid ground. Namui Mata nodded. However, she didn't have any problem with her steadiness. The owner greeted them warmly at the door. As soon as they finished their meals, they went to their rooms. It did not take long before Kara fell asleep. As for the young Namui Mata, she read a few chapters of the blue book at candles light before joining the dream world.

The day after, right after breakfast, they prepared some food and water. Then, they walked out town. After two hours, they stopped and checked the map.

Looking around, Namui Mata saw six horses. She pointed them with her finger, "What do you think?"

Kara nodded first but after a second look, she said, "They really look like they are on the verge of starvation."

Namui Mata agreed. But then, she said, "That's why we will choose two of them." She walked to the farm.

Kara did not argue and followed her. At a distance, she saw a man working outside. "Okay, let me do the talking and make the deal here," Kara said. "Just rescue me if he looks like he does not understand a word of my Spanish. All right."

"Go ahead," Namui Mata replied.

The man greeted them with a short nod.

"Can you understand English?" Kara asked.

He said, "Yes." Then, he asked her combining English and Spanish what she wanted.

With her finger, she pointed the horses. "We would be interested to take two of them in five days for the whole week."

The man smiled. "Okay, good..." he said right away.

He ran to his old pickup, grabbed something in it and came back. He then showed her an old paper with rates on it and gave her a price. Without wasting time, the man asked them which one they would choose. Namui Mata walked toward the horses in the field. She chose a brown one and white one. Kara still with the man, acknowledged it with her hand.

She took some money from her wallet and put it in his right hand. The man smiled largely and began to count it. Kara approached him—she was as tall as him—her face almost in his face, she said in Spanish with a severe look, "Make sure they will be fed properly today, tomorrow and the day after."

Surprised, he stepped back. Kara started counting money in her hands before him. The islander stepped back farther that time. After putting the money in his pocket, he walked around for a few minutes. He stopped. He took out the money and gave it back to Kara. Slowly, he explained why the horses were such in a bad condition, then added that he could not feed his family either in the moment. He sounded genuine and broken. Kara thought that like his horses, he looked pretty skinny himself. But when she saw his wife and children coming out of the house...she fully understood.

Kara decided to have a little talk with her friend. But while walking to the field, she got an idea. She turned and walked back. She asked the man if they had a veterinarian on the island. He answered positively. She called Namui Mata who was still checking the horses.

She took her aside and explained what she had in mind. Namui Mata smiled largely. "What a great idea. But you know...you can do whatever you feel like...it is your money after all. You don't need me to validate your decision." And then, she looked at the little family." These people really need to eat and these horses required a medical attention today!"

"You're right. Come with me," Kara said. "If he doesn't understand what I'm talking about, just help me."

The man invited them to sit on the house's gallery with his wife and three children. When Namui Mata sat, she noticed immediately that the woman had a tattoo on her right forearm. Then, a strange thing happened. The children surrounded her and sat by her side. The mother told them to be nice. A few minutes later, all the horses loose in the field came very close and all looked at Namui Mata.

Kara observing the scene thought, these poor little beasts are waiting for an answer. This is so weird.

The man and his wife, impressed by it, started laughing nervously. Namui Mata smiled at the parents and the children without saying a word.

Kara finally made an arrangement with the islander. "I will buy two horses—the horses will stay here. If you take good care of them, I will continue to give money each time I come here during the year." Looking at the rest of the horses, she added, "I buy two but I will rent the others. So I will pay for their care too. Do you understand?"

His wife understood everything. She quickly explained every detail to him. The man glad to hear it, rapidly nodded.

Before closing the deal, she added, "And with the years, you and I will decide if we go on with the agreement or cancel it."

With tears in his eyes, he looked at his wife and children. He stood up and shook her hand. "It's a fair deal," he said. Then he asked her in Spanish, "It's very nice of you that you want to buy two horses but why do you want to pay for the care of the rest too."

"I told you before...we are doing an important research here, and we don't know how long it's going to take. We'll have to come back sometimes on the island with other people. So we need someone we can trust with the horses. And because you will help us with the horses, we want to help you too...okay."

The islander was convinced that the two women were some kind of scientists. He stopped questioning them—he was just happy to be able to feed his family and animals.

#

After being properly fed, the horses got better quickly under the vet's supervision. Namui Mata visited them every day. Each time, she touched them—she whispered something to their ears.

One morning, the farmer's wife came to her in the field. "You talk to animals...why?" she asked.

Namui Mata put her finger on the tattoo of her right forearm. "Ask your tattoo? She said.

The woman's face whitened. She took Namui Mata's hand and put it on her cheek. She began to cry. "I now understand. They were waiting for you...the Moais..."

"It's our secret now," Namui Mata murmured to her ear.

She could feel the woman's heart beating hard. "What's your name?"

"Sotoro and my husband is Lorenzo...So you're the one—my children knew it before me." Then she put Namui Mata's hand on her tattoo and pressed it down a little.

Her body started trembling. She closed her eyes. Inside, she reached another dimension. When she opened her eyes, she said to Sotoro, "Thanks infinitely. I know that I can trust you."

#

Very early that morning, Kara and Namui Mata went to visit again the enigmatic megaliths. They examined closely the strange inscription known as Rongo Rongo writing or script which was on small wooden boards. The script contained one hundred and twenty different figures based on the birdman or what seemed to be human forms.

After reading all the information available on the premises, Kara commented. "They say that these wooden boards could be read alternatively from left to right then right to left. Well, I don't get it ...it's too bad that none of the surviving islanders knows how to read them. Apparently, the only one who could understand them—he was a priest—died after the Peruvian slave raids in 1862. Russian and German experts tried to decipher the script but had so far no success at all."

Namui Mata pondering on the meaning of those scriptures, replied, "I had no idea of what this is about but I like to contemplate the idea that it will be deciphered one day."

"I hope I will still be alive that day," Kara said.

The day after, they went to the farm. Lorenzo, his wife and children welcomed them warmly. Namui Mata made an attempt at speaking the Rapanui language. "Iorna...good morning..."

The man joyously asked, "Pehe Korua? How are you?"

"Just great," Kara said.

"Maururu...thank you," Namui added. She succeeded to say something else but after a while, she gave up. "I'm afraid that is all I know in Rapanui."

The children said together, "Good. We will help you speak Rapanui."

Lorenzo went to get the horses. Namui Mata immediately walked to the white one. She looked at Kara. "I have to make sure the legend is still alive," she joked.

In a vain manner, Kara walked gravely toward the brown horse. Ruffling her hair, she replied, "I don't mind. I like the brown one...it goes with my hair colour."

Everything was ready...the camping equipment, food, water and a medical kit. Lorenzo displayed all the saddles he got in the barn. They chose the ones that seemed more comfortable for long hours of riding.

Lorenzo asked them if they needed him as guide. They let him know that they would be fine on their own for the first day. They had just a few sites to visit. However, they indicated to him they would probably require his services later on the field.

Sotoro, Lorenzo and children smiled when they mounted the horses. It was quite a spectacle. A few minutes after, they watched them riding away. They could hear the two women laughing hilariously at each other.

The first site was Ahu Tahai. They got off the horses before reaching it. Five Statues were slanted in row on their Ahu facing the interior. They walked around admiring those marvels. They sat and had a light lunch. A book in her hands, Namui Mata read aloud. "The living conditions on the tiny Easter Island became increasingly difficult. As the island was still crowded, some people turned to carving as a way to direct energy and labour. They believed that it could also transmit power to the living family chief—prosperity in peacetime, success in wars..."

Lying down on the ground with her backpack under her head, Kara kept listening to Namui Mata. In her mind, she imagined those people in their everyday lives.

An hour later, they rode to the next site.

At the end of the afternoon, they found out that it took longer than thought to ride between sites. So they decided to return to the farm before reaching Ahu Vinapu.

Surprised to see them so soon, Lorenzo asked them if they had had any problems. Kara shrugged her shoulders and dismounted the horse. "I think we will need more food, water and...someone to accompany us from now on," she said.

His wife ran to him and said rapidly in Rapanui, "Let me do this. I know the island as well as you. It will be a good change for me. The children will be alright with you. And since they paid us...we have a lot of food and anyway, you need to take care of your horses and sheep."

At first, he seemed annoyed by her demand and refused categorically. However, she looked so disappointed that he finally changed his mind and consented. "Woman, you know what you're doing. I would not have accepted if they were men but obviously they are not. In fact, they will be more comfortable with you," and with a mocking smile on his face, he added, "They seemed to me that they don't trust men too much...but I must say that they have been good to us, so we will return the kindness."

They joined the two women in the barn. Lorenzo let them know that his wife would be pleased to be their guide. He assured them that she knew each site as well as he did."

Namui Mata interrupted him and said right away. "It's all right with me."

Kara nodded.

Without wasting time, Kara got out the maps and showed them to Sotoro. That one checked them reticently. She finally admitted she could not write or read, neither her husband. Kara pointed her finger on the map and named all the sites they wanted to visit— Sotoro nodded at each site. After looking at the equipment and food, she let them know, "You will need to bring more things if you want to visit all these sites."

Namui Mata took a pen and wrote down what Sotoro dictated. After reading the list of items for the whole excursion, Kara looked satisfied. In the background, Lorenzo just listened to his wife; he did not give a piece of advice. He was actually surprised of her confidence. He thought that he made the right decision. His male ego was satisfied and all was well.

Lorenzo drove them at the outskirts of the town. They walked the rest on foot. Namui Mata told Kara, "Sotoro has a very interesting tattoo."

"Do you think it could be related to what we are looking for?"

Namui Mata let her know what had happened in the field.

"Can we trust her?" Kara asked.

"Yes, we can. She's very reliable. Believe me."

The people they met in the street were graciously polite toward them. "The Rapanuis are the friendliest people I ever met," Kara said.

Amused, Namui Mata pointed out, "Well, I'm not surprised. The reason is they are supposed to be Polynesian descendants. Therefore like us, very...very nice. Okay! They are different and nicer...They had created their own unique style over the years—it differed greatly from other cultures. And you're right, these people are lovely."

Early in the morning, Sotoro was there waiting outside the residenciales for them to come out. As soon as they appeared, she informed them. "We will go buy everything we need," and then added, "My husband will pick up us to return home."

An hour later, Namui Mata and Kara got on the back of the old pickup with all the stuff. With the children, a lamb and four chickens in cage, they enjoyed the ride laughing heartily. Seizing the moment is the real happiness, Kara thought.

Lorenzo helped the women balance the load on each horse and then, told them, "Bringing another horse for the rest of the camping equipment will be better."

They all agreed. Each horse was already too loaded.

With a pat on the back, Kara said to Lorenzo with contentment, "The horses look a way healthier than the first day we saw them. You've done a great job Lorenzo."

He smiled. "You have helped us to make it happen," he said.

After mounting her horse, Kara said in half-English and half-French, "I'm amazed at how fast the horses came back to life. C'est presque un miracle! Do you have something to do with it, Namui Mata de la Papeete?

"Sorry to deceive you but I think Jesus was better at it than me..." She smiled. "Talking to them was not enough; the miracle happened when they had the right food and vet." She then mounted her horse.

Sotoro kissed her husband and children and got on her horse. Then Lorenzo said goodbye to the three spirited women. He kept looking at them riding away until he could not see them anymore.

They arrived to the site Ahu Vinapu. Once again, Namui Mata took a book and began reading aloud while walking around. She would stop to check things around and then continued. Sotoro and Kara were following her behind.

Slowly in Spanish, she read, "According to the experts, it's probably the most important site because it establishes the chronology of Easter Island—the Early Period from AD 400 to 1100, and the Middle Period from 1100 to 1680. The majority of Ahus and Moais were erected in those two periods. The Last Period dated from 1680 to 1868..."

After taking pictures of the site, Kara examined the ruins but did not seem too impressed. Seeing her disappointment, Sotoro told her, "I know that Ahu Vinapu is not as spectacular as some of the others but...but check closely the stonework here. There is something unique about that. Well...that's what the searchers once told my husband."

Namui Mata backed her up. "She's right Kara. Come here and have a look at the details of this stonework. They say that it could not be found at any other sites."

With the help of the pictures book, Kara scrutinized the stone. Then, she understood and lightened up. The work was unique and original. She made many shots of it. After all that, she felt that they should keep going and she let them know.

They continued their way and arrived at the site called Ahu Vaihu. To Sotoro, it was probably the most extraordinary sight along the stretch. Eight large statues wearing a kind of forlorn look had been pulled in a row from their Ahus. After exploring the site, Kara took pictures of each statue with Namui Mata and Sotoro beside them. Then, they went to the site of Ahu Akahanga. Kara observed again that the four statues had a similar humiliated look. She asked Sotoro what was the reason of it but that one simply answered that she had no idea whatsoever. And that was it. They decided not to stop and kept riding. They took a dirt road named the Road of the Moai, which brought them towards the huge volcanic crater. The view of fallen giants everywhere was breathtaking.

Sotoro saw that the two others preferred to ride slowly amongst the giants. "I will take some advance," she said. She pointed with her finger where she would be.

They nodded. And she rode away with the two horses. Kara and Namui Mata got off their horses and continued on foot. They really began feeling the surreal island.

"In absence of historical records, many contradictory versions had been written about this place," Namui Mata said.

While taking shots of the field, Kara agreed. "You're quite right. Confusion brought lots of distortions. I've read about the tribes and clans. A historian thinks the Long Ears carved the Moais and kept the Short Ears; the newcomers in an inferior class...To him, Short Ears did only the manual labour. Therefore, with the time they resented it, rebelled and slaughtered all the Long Ears...well, I think I have enough shots for today." She put back the camera in her big pocket. "Do you think one of these days we will know what really went on here?"

"As I said, so many different versions had been brought up about this island that we may never know for sure what really happened here. However, keeping an open mind is the only way to go while waiting for the science to give us more answers."

"I was expecting something else from you!" Kara exclaimed.

On a naughty tone, Namui Mata replied, "Sorry but it's not part of my mission to guess what went on here." She got on the horse and joined Sotoro.

#

It was getting hot; Sotoro told them that it was time to stop. Namui Mata gave some water to the horses and Kara made some sandwiches. After feeding the horses, Sotoro brought them behind two big statues where they could get some shade. She chose another statue for herself. Five minutes later, the others followed her there. While eating, Namui Mata reminded Kara that her dreams about flying over Easter Island were not so weird after all. "You know about the Birdman cult ritual. Don't you?"

With a sandwich in one hand and a map in the other, Kara said, "I know what you're talking about. This place is located south of the volcanic crater of Rano Koo. I heard about that bizarre birdman ritual."

Namui Mata asked Sotoro, "Do you know that place?"

Sotoro was tired; she just said, "Yes...but I'll talk about that later...for now, we'll give the horses a break and for us some rest." She went to another statue and lay down on the ground.

When they arrived on the spot, Kara exclaimed, "Wow! This site is really something! It is without a doubt the most spectacular place I have ever seen."

It was the turn of Namui Mata to play the historian. She started saying, "This site is a sacred place for the islanders. They had performed the last ritual around 1862. The ceremony was linked to the supreme deity Make Make who had created the earth, the moon and the stars. As any good God for believers, Make Make rewarded good and punished evil. For centuries, it has been the Spirit considered responsible for bringing visitors to the island from the outside world...The basis of the Birdman cult was finding the first egg of spring, laid by the sacred Manu Tara bird or tern—symbol of freedom for some because it could escape the island; and for others, it was a symbol of self-sufficiency. However, in order to retrieve the egg, each unfortunate servant of different important families had to spend about a month looking for the first egg in dangerous watery rocky places. While waiting for it, the rest of the islanders gathered on the Orongo cliff and made offerings and prayers to Make Make."

When Sotoro joined them, Namui Mata continued the story in Spanish. "As soon as the egg had been found, the tired but proud servant ran to present the prize to his successful master who then became the Birdman of the year. The important families bestowed on him many privileges. So his standing in the community increased..."

Sotoro added, "You see, the Birdman was seen as the representative on earth of the Creator Make Make. So everything he said or did in that year was highly respected. All the islanders followed it blindly...even if it was sometimes foolish..." She picked up her stuff. "Let's go to the top of the trail, the view is beautiful."

When Kara looked over the cliff, a strong sensation of vertigo invaded her body. Namui Mata put a hand on Kara's shoulder. "Can you feel what I feel?"

"I...I feel the...magical force of this place," Kara said.

Sotoro behind them, murmured, "We, islanders, called it Mana."

In complete silence, they contemplated the view for a long long time. They knew at that moment that a new era had just started for the world.

While coming down the trail, Kara in a better mood, cheerfully said, "Isn't that weird that they now called this place Easter Island?"

Namui Mata thought about it for a while and then laughed. "Okay; I got it. Easter Island, the Birdman and Easter egg!"

In French, Kara added, "Eh! Oui, mon petit coco de Pâques."

A little suspicious of their strange behaviour, Sotoro asked, "Can you tell me what is so funny about this place?"

Namui Mata translated the best she could the joke Kara and she had shared between them for years about

Easter Day and the egg. They would say to their baldy friends on Easter weekend, "Mais oui! Mon petit coco de Pâques." After picturing a bald head and an egg, Sotoro understood. She joined the hilarity of the moment.

#

While riding, they saw hundreds of Ahu stones and Moai platforms scattered all over the area. Some of the statues' faces were hidden in the ground. Sotoro told them, "In the past, my people used to bury bodies around the Ahus. I, sometimes, come here when I want to be alone. My ancestors are always available; they give me inspiration and encouragement..."

Then she suggested, "It would be a good idea to start looking for a place to spend the night."

They both agreed. Namui Mata specified. "I would rather trust your judgment for that one."

"Okay. The perfect spot would be Akana Beach," Sotoro said.

On the premises, they eased off the horses and prepared the camp.

They cooked their meal and ate slowly while watching the sun disappearing below the horizon. After it, they went sitting beside the Stones Sentinels with a thermos of coffee and there, simply enjoyed the view of sea and stars. Later on, Namui Mata and Sotoro went to feed the horses and gave them some water. For a while, Sotoro watched the French girl talking to them. The complicity she had with the animals made her smile. She then left her alone with them.

Before leaving, Namui Mata observed them grazing at whatever they found in the open field. She thought that it was a good thing that they brought some food for them too. Then she joined the others.

Kara asked Sotoro if it would be better to tie the horses before going to sleep. Sotoro shook her head. And Namui Mata added, "No need for that, they won't go away. I told them to stay close to us."

"Can you talk about your gift?" Sotoro asked. "How do you speak to animals?"

Namui Mata laughed. "I'm not quite sure how it works. You see, it's a gift; I got it when I was very young." She then told them about the first time she realized she had the ability to communicate with animals.

Still cautious, Kara suggested to Namui Mata in French, "Do you think it's safe to reveal this to her."

"Yes, it is. She already knows who we are," she answered in Spanish. "Isn't it Sotoro?"

Sotoro approached Kara. Under the moonlight, she showed her the tattoo. Then she said, "My people have lost their memory. Fortunately, this tattoo has helped me recover some pieces of the past. And it will help me enter the future." She smiled. "I knew you were coming...the secret force that inhabited this land revealed it to me years ago."

Kara wanted to know what the tattoo meant. Sotoro reached a flashlight and directed the light on it. "What do you see?" she asked Kara.

"Let me see...well...I see a bird's peak joined to two concentric rings with a row of dots that makes half the body form of a bird. However, I don't know what that means. Help me," Kara said.

"It means that Make Make is on my side," she replied. "You can now talk in Spanish because as Namui Mata said, I know who you are. Tomorrow, I'll take you to a special place and show you something very important."

Kara immediately asked, "What will it be?"

"I don't want to talk about that tonight. Tomorrow will be the day." She stopped talking and looked at the Sentinels with gravity.

Later in the evening, Kara lay down on the sand and gazed at the stars. Out of the blue, she asked Namui Mata, "Would you like to know one day who are your real parents?"

Namui Mata did not answer right away. She seemed to weigh her words before saying anything. She finally said, "I didn't want to tell you before but now it's the time. I know where I come from."

"What!" Kara riposted.

"All I can say about my biological parents is they are dead," she calmly said.

While looking at her shadow in the moonlight, Kara replied, "I guess there is still a lot of things I don't know about you. Yet, I'm surprised that you haven't said it to me before but..." She did not finish her sentence. Instead, she asked, "What now?"

"We will wait," she replied. "The Big Heads are going to let us know soon what we are supposed to do. So we'd better go sleep now. I think it will be a long night tonight."

"All right then," Kara said.

Namui Mata informed Sotoro. "We called the statues the Big Heads—no offense..."

Sotoro found it very funny. They got up and went to the tent.

The fresh air and tiredness helped them fall asleep quickly. In the middle of the night, Kara suddenly woke up. She checked her watch—it was three o'clock in the morning. She looked around. Sotoro seemed to sleep deeply but Namui Mata was not there. Rapidly, Kara picked up a flashlight and got out. First, she had a look at where the horses were. She thought that if the horses were still there, she may not be far away. She turned back and kept walking.

On the beach, she turned off the light. Her eyes got used to the dark and she could see farther. Then she saw Namui Mata sitting in a lotus position at the feet of one of the statue sentinels. As she was approaching her, Kara felt her knees knocking together. She stopped.

She could hear what the Big Head was saying to Namui Mata. "You will see..." It stopped talking. And then continued, "Ah! We have a guest. Welcome Kara; don't be afraid. We talked to you before. Remember! Come closer."

Kara walked slowly toward the statue.

"We thank you for fulfilling your engagement: finding Namui Mata and bringing her to us. The whole island is rejoicing since Namui Mata has touched the land. You have no idea how happy we are to meet the One! Tomorrow morning, Sotoro will show you the tablets, the special talking boards. I know that you have read that these tablets have been written by men and for men. Well, the writers were right and wrong. Although phallus and procreation seemed to be the favourite topics in most of them, many other tablets contained symbols including birth, animals, plants, celestial objects and geometric forms. These tablets gave lots of information concerning life in the universe and on earth. Many moons ago, there were writing tablets in every house. Unfortunately, lots of them had been destroyed, others hidden because some missionaries saw them as evil relics of pagan times. Therefore, the islanders have lost the meaning of these symbols with the time. All the experts, natural scientists, historians, epigraphs, anthropologists, linguists now conclude they cannot read the unreadable and...It is good news to us." The statue stopped for a few minutes. "Go back to sleep now. Come back tomorrow night and take Sotoro with you."

After a light breakfast, Sotoro got up. "Follow me," she said. She led them to a cave and entered it. Then she came back with some wooden tablets.

"In 1868, my grand-grandmother saved the rongorongo tablets from destruction by hiding them in this cave," she proudly declared. "These tablets have a distinct style from all the others. In fact, they are unique. You know that the other talking boards found on the lands are still a puzzle for researchers and my people. Fortunately, my grandmother explained to my mother how to read these ones."

She breathed deeply before saying, "When my mother showed me these wooden boards for the first time, she told me—the woman that made them could manipulate the mysterious force Mana. She carved every symbol by being inspired by the Mother of Stars. The lovely Mother told her that those tablets were destined for the One who would come here one day." She looked at Namui Mata and smiled. "That manipulator of Mana was my great great grandmother. She taught the story to her daughter and so on. I learned by heart all the symbols and their meanings. According to the wooden board, the story will end with me."

Sotoro placed the tablets on a flat stone. She turned each tablet around and around to find the beginning. "The direction of writing is unique starting from the left hand bottom corner. Then, you proceed from left to right and at the end of the lines you turn the tablets around before you start reading the next line..."

Namui Mata nodded, absorbing every word.

Sotoro said to her, "Do it now."

A few minutes later, Namui Mata touched Sotoro's tattoo with both hands. She then transferred the received energy on the boards. "That's right," she acknowledged. "It means that the orientation of the hieroglyphs is reversed every other line...by the way, I want you to know that your great great grandmother was a genius."

She showed to Kara the symbols with her finger. "Imagine a book in which every other line is printed back to front and upside down. That is how the tablets are written or sung if you like. The only problem is I cannot sing them in Rapanui but she knows. Go ahead Sotoro."

"Okay. However, just before doing it, I want you to know that the first tablet began with a lunar calendar, which consisted of twenty-eight nights representing the menstrual period and the moon cycle." Then, she began chanting its contents.

Kara and Namui Mata did not understand anything but the chant was so melodious that they became exulted just by the sound of it. When she stopped, she asked Kara to write down immediately the translation.

That night before going to sleep, Namui Mata let Sotoro know, "The statues will talk to us tonight. I will wake you up when it is time."

Sotoro seemed a little surprise but understood that she was then part of a starry tale.

They sat before the Big Heads and waited in silence. Namui Mata told them to relax. Shortly after, one of the statues sentinels said, "It is now time to deliver our message to you. According to the wooden boards, you know that the name Namui Mata means the Eye. Wherever she goes, she will be the Eye opener of the world. She has the ability to look at people and see right through them. They will be as transparent as the air to her. She will know their thoughts and feel their sorrow and joys. With the time, she will have a great understanding of the world." The statue paused.

The three women could hear the rest of Sentinels talking between them. Then the silence came back.

Another statue continued where the other had left, "Namui Mata, your mission is to set up a secret women network on this earth, which will be dedicated to help women and children in great distress. You will have to take great care about choosing the women who will be member of this secret society. One woman in every country will be representative of her own network. You will also form a kind of commando in a secret location—sorry, we don't have a better word for it— where special women will be trained to neutralize the enemy."

Then another statue continued, "Every two years, you will meet here with the representative of each country to talk about the progress you have made and what will be needed to be done next. Once this is established, the representative of each country will report to you where the emergencies are, and then the neutralizers will start operating. These ones will also serve as helpers for the abused women and children to flee the country. In order to help you make the first choices of these representatives, we have two names to give you but it is up to you Namui Mata. Through Kara's camera lens, we know that Elaine Duro would be the perfect candidate for neutralizing. As an actress, she can now play any roles and speak three other languages without accent. Therefore, she can enter any corrupted spheres or circles without being spotted. Another good choice for representing Canada would be Candice Brown—she had stayed for a year at Kara's apartment and picked up without being aware of it Kara's knowledge through Mitsou the cat. In addition, she has been working for the global women movement for a long time. To us, she is ready to undertake it."

The statue who talked first indicated to them, "At the beginning, the abusers will be very confused because women and their children will simply disappear under their very eyes—but it starts to be touchy here. Let me give you an example: after realizing what happened, the violent and angry man wherever he lives on the planet will try to find them. In some countries, where the perpetrator has one or more wives, he certainly will want revenge to save his so-called code of honour. However, the more he will be thirsty for revenge, the more it will work against him. And one morning, he will find himself in a fetal position—but before that happens—one of the commandos in charge will have to touch him in order to make it a reality. You, Namui Mata, will train the commando. We know—you have never thought of you as a fighter but indeed, you are. Don't worry. You won't be a murderer although you will sometimes need to use physical force for the tougher ones. But in general, you will teach these women how to neutralize the enemy instead of killing him. A warning here: if one of the members of the secret society ever tries to use the power for her own benefit, we are sorry for that person. Namui Mata, you are the Eye, and you will know what to do." The statue stopped.

Another one took over, "For setting up the operation, you need to find first ten women that will be able to speak different languages and briefed them on the recruitment of candidates. Now about the commando—Sotoro, don't take offense here but these commando women will have to be single and free in order to go anywhere they will be asked to go. Know that you will have a very important work to do on the island. Kara, you will buy a house located in the French countryside. The women will be trained and formed there. We are pleased to help you with that one. Life in its mysterious ways of working let us know that your sister-in law Michelle Dumont's parents are ready to sell their propriety. To us, France will be a perfect and permanent site. However Kara, you will continue renting places at different locations in the world—after a year on these premises, whoever is there, will have to leave rapidly. Kara, if you need to be seen as a couple when doing certain things, your friend Jason Moore will be the right man. We know his heart—he won't talk—he is a good man. He will help you a lot."

That was the turn of another Sentinel to talk. "As soon as the network will be well organized, neutralizers will be ready to go in the world. Sometimes, they will need to use force to stop the abuser, particularly the serial killer. We admit that it will be very dangerous to act sometimes but we promise you that you will be uplifted after accomplishing each task. Day after day, you will succeed to break up the narrow and senseless philosophy that still leads the world. Another warning: as you must know by now, there is a negative force that will try to stop you by any means. The more you will be powerful, the more you will be hated. Some of you will be persecuted, particularly in the countries where they bring down women. Take courage. And treat people fairly my loved ones—the bloody world is ready for a change in consciousness."

That time, a very firm voice took over, "Last thing Namui Mata, you are not on this earth to make a radical change. However, the transformations that you will bring will be the starting point of a new era. Kara will accompany you the first five years to support you.

Then the same voice added, "After that, my dear Kara, you will be free to do whatever you want to do with your life. Your job will end after these years. I can tell you that you will be happy to do so—after seeing young women relieving you, you will understand that the younger they are, the faster they will become powerful in making attitudes change once and for all. Their fathers, brothers, lovers and friends will understand that they will not get away anymore with trying to dominate others by using force, control and violence; it will simply not work anymore. You, women will make them understand that cooperation is the only way to go, and make sure this time they got it right by showing them how it works."

A thick silence planned over the beach. The three women stood up. One of the Big Heads asked, "Do you have any questions?"

"Who killed my parents?" Namui Mata asked.

"The man, who tried to kill you, knew about your coming to this world. He did kill your parents. The reason you were safe is your mother had been warned in her dream by the Tibetan nun. Now you know Namui Mata and Kara—everything makes sense in the long run. So Namui Mata, your mother saved your life by leaving you the day before at the hospital portal. That man belonged—we can say that now—he is useless—to one of many secret societies that try to impose their views over the world. Of course, women are the enemy number one. These men are actually so afraid to lose their power over you that they are ready to sabotage your efforts and destroy you at any cost. Namui Mata the Eye, we warn you one more time, they will come after you any chance they get. Therefore, after recognizing them, do whatever it takes to protect yourself. Just make sure to touch them before—your power is so strong that they will be instantaneously in a curly position. We call it the Blue Fetal Touch." He paused.

"Thank you Kara for showing the One how to do it. In your case, it takes longer to make it happen; between five hours or more. It will be the same for the other neutralizers. However, they will learn to cope with it. At the end, the Blue Fetal Touch will win and scare the bullies to death."

Then all the statues in unison said, "The keywords you will use all the time with the network and commando are Miti-Fetia-Po which means Sea, Stars and Night. These magic words vibe in the atmosphere and make the earth conscious of itself. You are living it right now on the beach. Isn't it wonderful?"

Flashes of lightning bombed the sky. Right after that, Namui Mata, Kara and Sotoro felt the earth shaking under their feet. They had the sensation that the earth's energy came up through their bodies. Though still trembling, the three women turned and looked at the sea and stars. All their body cells knew suddenly what to do and where to go without a doubt.

The Big Head spoke again. It said to Namui Mata, "After making the network operational, you will continue to be in charge of it for many years until it will be time for you to find the Peacemaker. You now understand that you are not here to bring peace yet—the world is not ready to receive it. However, you will be able to make radical changes for those who suffer the most on this earth. Your job ends there."

"Sotoro, you will organize the comings and goings on the island. We will help you do it without alarming the islanders and the government."

Finally, the Big Heads ended up by saying all together, "We let you go to your destiny. See you in two years, same time and same place. Love be with you."

EPILOGUE

Kara slowly came back to reality. Thanks to Namui Mata, the earth was a better place to be. She heard that the network was still performing very well. As the Big Head told her, she got her life back after those five years. Free to go or to stay, she chose to leave; the network needed new blood to keep the energy going and flowing.

Twenty years had passed fast in her world. She was then sixty–eight. She wondered what happened to Namui Mata. After leaving the network, she never got in touch with her for security reasons. As she was thinking about her, something got her attention. She saw far away a little form coming toward her. Then, she recognized it. It was Venusa the cat, her cosmic friend.

The cat sat on her behind before Kara. "I am here to let you know that Namui Mata has found the Peacemaker to replace her. And...She is no longer living on the planet. I would like to thank you on behalf of the Loving Energy and Namui Mata for following the plan and respecting the code of silence," Venusa said.

The cat rubbed her foot with her nose. She then slowly walked away.

Kara closed her eyes and just listened to the waves. Her body let her know that life was going to stop flowing soon.

She got up, grabbed the wine bottle and glass and walked back to her summerhouse.

In the living room, she picked up a blanket and went to the patio. She sat on a long chair and read the last chapter of the blue book.

After closing the book, she turned her eyes on the sunset. She murmured, "And so it is. I am ready to die."

Before giving up the last breath, she said to herself, "Well, I guess there must be a lot of suckers on this earth by now."

And with a big smile on her face, she closed her eyes for the last time.